We Owned the Night

M. VENN

Britain's Next BESTSELLER

First published in 2016 by:

Britain's Next Bestseller
An imprint of Live It Publishing
27 Old Gloucester Road
London, United Kingdom.
WC1N 3AX

www.britainsnextbestseller.co.uk

Copyright © 2016 by M. Venn

The moral right of M. Venn to be identified as the author
of this work has been asserted by her in accordance with the
Copyright, Designs and Patents Act 1988.

All rights reserved.

Except as permitted under current legislation, no part of this
work may be photocopied, stored in a retrieval system,
published, performed in public, adapted, broadcast, transmitted,
recorded or reproduced in any form or by any means, without
the prior permission of the copyright owners.

All enquiries should be addressed to Britain's Next Bestseller.

ISBN 978-1-910565-76-6 PBK
Printed in Poland

Supporter List

Juliana Uzaraga, Karen Reisler Eriksen, Sarah Workman, Charlotte Ellis, Adam Venn, AJ Broadway, Michelle Craig, Amanda Broadway, J Carter, Leanne Marie Martin, Sally Teall, Cindy Teall, Harriet Oliver, Karen Atkins, Emma Venn, Shelley Barnes, Michelle Young, Hayley Joyce, Dave Broadwat, Julia James, Zoë Best, Wendy Davis, Faye Gould, Nicola Maggs, Bev Barnes, Dean Broadway, Megan Harper, Sarah Sloane, Andrew Males, Laura Patterson, Liz Garrett, Harriet Wilkes, Matt Venn, Gilly Baker, Maria Best, Karrieanne Howard, Amy Brace, Alan Broadway, Helena Rees-Mogg, Natalie Coles, Emma Wollacott, Kayleigh Potter, Rachel Davidson, Rhiann Creed, Matt Venn, Rob Murat, Nicola, Stacey Watts, Nati Johnston, Dena Millwood, Jocelyn Kirby, Amy Young, Jodie Maggs, Abigail Coates, Megan Herrington, Dave Broadway, Nicola Griffiths, Karen Prater, Sarah Garden, Cassie Davis, Alexander Kettle, Hollie Lim, Charlotte Keevill, Kelsey Strass, Kirsty Bailey, Gemma Wherry, Karina Lamb, Sam Burton, Lisa Rogers, Amy Hands, Margaret Stewart, Emma Venn, Josie Trapnell, Sally Stanford.

Dedicated to

*Phoebe Isabelle, Olivia Sofia & Scarlett Esmé
In a world where you can be anything,
be yourself!*

Kenan
*You're the bravest person I know.
Never change.*

Millie's design sketch pad

Mils & Riri bffs!

A.Rose

Meeting with Mr S
4.40pm.

Mrs Dexter Rose!

Lace sample

Millie ♥ Dex 4eva

la douleur exquise
(n.) the heart-wrenching pain of wanting the affection of someone unattainable.

D.R.

Introduction

Firstly, the fact that you're reading this at all is amazing in itself. It means I actually saw it through and wrote an entire book without giving up! I'll be the first to admit I'm a self-confessed quitter. I get an idea in my head and run with it, full force for maybe a couple of weeks until the moment's passed and the next thing has taken over my mind. Pro or con, that's the way I like to live; no pressure, just enjoy the things I like while I like them. So, in saying that I'm not sure how we got here?!

The idea for this story actually came to me in a dream a few days after watching one of my favourite bands. I was woken early one morning by my baby daughter, having dreamt most of the story, I needed to know how it ended.

So I started writing!

14 months later, I finally found out how the story ends.

Enjoy.

Preface

Have you ever been in the front row of a concert?

Waiting for it to start you can't keep still, bouncing on flexed feet the excitement builds in the pit of your stomach as adrenaline courses through your veins in anticipation. You swallow hard, noticing your mouth has gone dry from your over-breathing, which borders on hyperventilation. You begin to hold your breath making your lungs hurt until you manage to relax your clenched muscles enough to exhale. Every minute seems to take forever to pass.

The venue is small, your knees touching the stage. You take a moment to glance around the room that's filled up behind you. The air around you is fully charged, you feel electricity run down your arms like a cold, sharp knife. You shiver, making all the hairs stand on end as you wait among people feeling much the same as you.

The moment comes when the lights change and the crowd falls silent in unison and you know. This is it.

Eyes focused on the stage you feel your heart rate increase, you try to breathe normally but your lungs involuntarily suck in a sharp breath making you feel like you're being crushed. It's a feeling you crave.

And then there he is. You've seen him on TV, you've heard him on the radio, you've seen photos of him standing there, microphone in hand so many times you've lost count! You've watched him perform before at a festival, a tiny figure you could just make out from the other end of the field bounding about the stage, but you've never been here. This close. You could reach out and touch him. The real him. You almost can't make your mind believe he's real. He's a hallucination. He'd never existed in the same world as you yet there he is in the flesh, stood just a foot away.

The band start and you feel more alive than you ever have before as the bass vibrates your rib cage, and once again you're shuddering in breaths of gasping completion. This is it. This is the moment you live for. As he sings his eyes scan the room, moving along the front row towards you. You're in a daze, eyes locked onto his face, determined not to look away for a second, knowing that it will come to an end. He looks up and his eyes meet yours and for a split second he smiles. You smile nervously back. Fighting to breathe through your gasps as your breathing quickens. You are connected, for a single second in time. You. Him. Two strangers, usually worlds apart, in the same room, in the same moment. And in that moment you're part of his life. And he part of yours. For a split second so short it's immeasurable.

And then gone.

I am not the only person to have ever lived that moment, many times. 'He' is not one person. And 'you' aren't either. He is every influential person that's ever been admired and 'you' is every fan-girl/guy to have been the admirer.

But what if that single moment doesn't end there? What if fate had plans for you. And him. What if you were meant to be stood there right at that moment…

CHAPTER 1

I really need blackout blinds! Millie thought to herself as the bright sunlight shone right into her tired hazel eyes through the tiny gap between her pink curtains. She loved the summer, but the light mornings drove her nuts. Her first thought each morning was often *Why couldn't the sun just stay in bed till 8?* She could only muster the energy to lift her head just enough to make out the time on her phone on the nightstand. 6.34am.

"You've got to be kidding me! It's my day off." Millie dropped her head back heavily into her pillow, her long chocolate-brown hair strewn over her face. She closed her eyes and rolled onto her side, hoping to fall back to sleep before thoughts began to fill her head keeping her awake. Snuggling into her thick duvet as if cuddling a person beside her she began to drift off, back into her own head again...

BEEEEEP! She jumped, eyes wide open as her phone vibrated loudly, dancing along the nightstand and onto her head.

"Ouch!" she groaned. Picking up the phone she squinted, trying to focus her eyes enough to read her message. She could just make it out through her blurred, sleepy vision.

Eeeeeek! See you later! xxx

Millie smiled, "Arrgh! It's today!" Millie was suddenly wide awake. It was from her best friend Cate. They had bought tickets to see Millie's favourite band months ago and the day of the gig had finally arrived. Millie was beyond excited, not just to see the band but she'd been working so hard lately she needed a good night out. She hadn't had a night out with Cate for ages and as she thought about being just feet away from Dex Rose in a few hours, she couldn't help but smile; a smile she knew nothing and no one could wipe off her face today. She had the biggest crush on him, even though she thought it was totally uncool to have a celebrity crush at 26!

Bounding out of bed like the spring chicken she usually wasn't, Millie flung open her wardrobe and sifted through tons of clothes looking for the perfect outfit for the gig.

"I've got nothing to wear!" Millie sulked, grabbing the tenth outfit from her huge collection and hanging it on her door to try on later. Playing her favourite song from her phone she danced around her room. Today was one of those days that made Millie appreciate how great her life was.

Later, as dusk began to fall, the huge black tour bus arrived at the venue. Zach peeked out of the curtain-covered window.

"Wow, this city is chill," he mumbled, barely heard over the noise from the other guys on the bus. The city was beautiful, alight with the glow of streetlights reflecting on the river that ran through the pretty southern English city centre.

Zach watched out of the window as the tour bus reversed in close to the side of the building and turned off the engine. Zach sighed. It was so nice to be there after 48 hours of being stuck on the road travelling. The band's security manager opened the doors and climbed down from the bus, disappearing inside the venue.

Leaving the bus doors open, Zach could smell the city. It smelled fresh, like summer rain. New York could be so hot and stuffy, so it was lovely to breathe in such clear, cool air. Zach took a deep breath; it felt good to fill up his lungs. He felt ready for this gig. He pulled back the corner of the curtain again. A queue had began to form at the entrance already, with doors not opening for another three hours. Zach thought it was crazy people were willing to wait that long to see him, Jesse and Dex, when just nine months ago he was as anonymous as everyone in that queue.

"Hey, Dex, look at your stalkers," Zach laughed, pointing out of the window at the growing queue of teenage girls. Dex rolled his eyes and threw Zach a sarcastic smile, barely looking up from sorting out his stuff on his bunk. Dex was the most popular in the band; he couldn't escape the hordes of screaming fans wherever he went. He seemed to be like some kind of god to them. He had girls fainting at his feet at their shows in the US. He didn't understand why. He was just a normal guy, he wasn't amazingly good looking, he didn't have the body of a Greek god, he stayed away from social media, and he rarely interacted with fans. He liked a quiet life of playing video games, writing songs and spending time with his family and friends. He just couldn't get his head around why there was so much fuss over him.

Ten minutes later their security manager emerged from the venue and cleared them to leave the bus. Behind large black hoarding they snuck in through the side door of the small venue, a nightclub. People were busy setting up the stage and rushing around getting everything ready. Jesse and Zach went straight over to set up their instruments, while Dex stood in the middle of the stage and looked around the empty room.

In just a few hours the emptiness would be replaced with hundreds of screaming fans all hanging off his every word, all hungry for so much as a touch of his hand. He still wasn't used to the fame, he still felt like a nobody.

He closed his eyes, took a deep breath and took a moment to take in normality. He suffered terribly with nerves but today he was even more nervous than he usually was. This was the band's first show outside of the US and he wanted it to be amazing. He knew that if it went well this could mean bigger and better things for 'Craze'.

"Oh, Jesus! Look at the size of that queue!" exclaimed Cate as she and Millie approached the venue. There must have been over 300 people queuing already.

"I bet we're right at the back," sighed Millie.

"That's because you tried on 300 outfits!" said Cate, laughing.

"I know," replied Millie, frowning and feeling slightly annoyed with herself that she took so long getting ready. She felt great, though. In skin-tight, black cigarette trousers and a white oversized t-shirt she looked effortlessly cool. Her denim jacket and favourite converse trainers finished off her look. It was worth being late for. She had to look her best just in case Dex caught a glimpse of her.

The queue began to move towards the doors, in what seemed like an inch at a time. Eventually they were in. Millie could feel the butterflies starting to flutter in her stomach. She grabbed Cate's hand so she didn't lose her in the crowds, dragging her along behind her.

"This way," she gestured. She led Cate through the double glass door and into the nightclub. Millie was surprised by how empty it was since they had been so far back in the queue.

"Everyone must have headed to the bar first," Cate shouted, trying to make herself heard.

"Not a bad idea!" replied Millie, but there was no way she was losing her spot at the front to go to the bar, they were just five feet from the stage.

"This is amazingly close, Mil," said Cate.

"I know," said Millie, smiling. She could feel the hairs on the back of her neck standing up. She was excited and nervous. She wondered what Dex would look like in the flesh. Would he be smaller, taller, would he be who she had imagined, who she had fantasised about, who she had married in her head 500 times? Or would seeing him in real life ruin the image she had built of her dream man in her mind? She felt a bit like this was their first date, except he didn't know about it!

There was a roar from the crowd as the show kicked off. Dex, Jesse and Zach sat backstage drinking shots of whisky with the rest of their entourage, while the warm-up band were doing their set. It had become a pre-gig ritual lately, it got the adrenaline pumping and took the edge off the nerves. Dex paced the room, whisky in hand, fidgeting and reciting lyrics to himself. His palms were sweating profusely. He could do this gig with his eyes shut, he knew it inside and out, but still he couldn't calm his nerves right before a show. Jesse swept his dark fringe from his eyes as he turned and looked over his shoulder at Dex.

"Hey, you okay, man?" he asked.

Dex didn't hear, he was somewhere else in his head. "DEXTER!" Yelled Jesse.

Startled, Dex stopped and looked up with a confused expression on his face.

"You okay?" Jesse repeated.

"Oh… yeah." Dex smiled. "I'm crazy nervous," he added.

"S'aight, man. It'll be fine, no different to every other show. Chill." Jesse tried to reassure him, but the truth was Jesse felt the nerves too and he only had to play his bass in the background; simple compared with what Dex had to contend with. He ran the show, he WAS the show, all the pressure was on him to deliver.

And he knew it.

The warm-up act came to an end and they were announced onto the stage, downing the last of the shots quickly they hurried to the side of the stage. Dex felt sick. He wanted to get out there, he knew the wait and anticipation was worse than the reality!

"Everyone please give it up... for CRAZE!" The lights went up and Dex's adrenaline kicked in as he burst onto the stage first with the enthusiasm of the Duracell Bunny, just like he did every single night. Dressed in a slim-fitting floral short-sleeved shirt and skinny jeans his clean-cut prep-school-mocking style made him stand out.

All that he could see was bright white lights. The crowd was invisible in the brightness, but a roar of cheering and ear-piercing screams made it evident that the place was packed. He began to relax; this was the bit he was actually good at!

The gig began like any other. As Zach and Jesse started to play, Dex took to the microphone. He cleared his throat, took a big deep breath and belted out his first line, which, as soon as he opened his mouth, was greeted with another eruption of screams and whistles. The lights were blinding. Dex couldn't see anyone in the crowd, just an array of bright coloured lights shining directly into his eyes, which he always liked. It was easier to not see anyone; it relaxed him into the set, but as the song slowed and the lights dimmed, Dex could finally see out over the crowd. The venue was heaving.

All he could see was a sea of heads. The place was so small and so intimate that the front row was less than two feet away from him. He was rarely that close to his fans; they all had their arms out trying to touch him, all shouting at him, waving banners and messages at him. *Wow,* he thought to himself. he still couldn't quite believe they were all there to see him. The other boys too but Dex was definitely the most popular and the most well-known.

Dex found it hard getting used to the sudden level of fame. They had all been at this for over ten years in previous bands but never, ever experienced fame like this and it was all so fast. Just a year ago they were playing to crowds of maybe 50 people; this year they were on a sell-out world tour playing to thousands most nights. They all found fame hard to deal with but for Dex it was the hardest. He had most of the attention and most of the headlines, he was swamped by girls wherever went, he was even getting marriage proposals on a daily basis.

He couldn't quite get his head around it. He had never been one of the popular guys at school, he never got the pretty girls and his quirky style meant he was always a bit of an outcast. He wasn't your obviously good-looking type, he didn't look like something out of a boy band and he was never going to be America's Next Top Model.

But there was something about him. He was alternative, he had his own sense of style, he rolled out of bed with perfect thick, dark, messy hair that fell in front of his face, he was constantly brushing it away from his mysterious, dark eyes and he had a smile worthy of a toothpaste ad.

But he didn't understand what all the fuss was about; he was quite shy, a little anti-social, awkward even. He wasn't overly confident in his looks but his vulnerability was what made him so attractive, almost sweet. The other guys embraced the attention but Dex shied away from it. He wanted a normal existence away from the stage.

It was a different story on stage, though. As soon as he opened his mouth to sing he was the only person in the room. He had the ability to switch off from everyone and everything. He was confident up there, and it was exactly where he belonged. He turned into a different person; he was a showman. He really knew how to work the crowd but he didn't need to, he could have stood on that stage and belted out the alphabet and nearly every girl in the room would be falling at his feet. He just had it.

As the next song started he took another deep breath and prepared himself for the first line of the song. He had calmed down a bit and sunk into it but he could still feel his heart beating in his mouth. He closed his eyes for a second and switched himself off from the craziness, in his head it was just him and his mic. As he opened his eyes again he took a moment to look around the room, just as he had done earlier when the place was empty. It was such a different view this time and he felt like someone else with hundreds and hundreds of gorgeous girls all screaming for him. Yet despite his huge popularity, he still felt a bit like most of those girls were waaaaay out of his league. In his head he was still the same person he was in school; the pretty, popular girls wouldn't have given him a second look.

The atmosphere in the venue was electric, and as he started to sing the crowds went wild, singing along, dancing, jumping around. His adrenaline was pumping and he could feel his heart racing even faster. He looked over at Zach playing guitar and Zach smiled back at him. Dex knew he was feeling the exact same rush, living their dream, yet still not quite believing it was happening.

As the sixth song came to an end it was time for the band to take a break. Dex wiped his hair from his sweaty forehead and took a gulp from his water bottle as he left the stage to rapturous cheers and applause from the crowd.

Millie was buzzing. "Oh my god, they're amazing!" she exclaimed. She felt almost sick with excitement and she felt strangely emotional; as Dex started each song her eyes welled up. She'd had a thing for Dex for so long, being there in front of him didn't seem like reality.

"I know, and we're so close!" said Cate. "You have to tweet a photo!" she added.

Millie nodded. she was glad to be reminded; she would want a reminder of this moment. The band was amazing live, Dex's voice sounded incredible and as usual he was putting on quite a show. He was a natural. Seeing him in the flesh Millie felt her crush intensify 1000% but at the same time felt a sinking feeling in the pit of her stomach. She was completely gutted that he was a just a dream and he was so unattainable. She'd never meet him, never talk to him, he would never even know she existed! She knew she was just one of a billion. She started to think maybe she would have been better off not seeing them tonight; it was easier to accept and forget that he would never ever be with her when he was only on the TV or the radio. *Stop talking to yourself!* she thought. She knew she was being utterly ridiculous and could feel herself getting annoyed. She wasn't a teenager, she was probably older than most of the girls in the room. She knew she was thinking like an obsessed teen and it wasn't healthy, she was a realist and hated that her fantasy was beginning to get the better of her.

It was taking over her rational mind.

Why can't I just enjoy the music like a normal 26-year-old woman? she thought, but she knew realistically no matter how hard she tried she still felt something for Dex… well, the image of Dex she had built in her mind. But so did every other girl in the room, right? Whether it was real or a fantasy it existed in her mind and there was no way she was going to be able to shake the feeling. Not today. Millie's head was filled with mixed emotions, but she knew that this was a once in a lifetime opportunity and she really needed to just let herself enjoy the moment.

As the second half of the show began, Dex led the band back onto the stage to the roar of screaming fans. He felt more relaxed now. As Jesse started to play his bass to begin the song Dex moved to the front of the stage ready to sing. He wiped his hair out of his eyes again and took a deep breath. His super confident alter-ego took over as he sang and danced across the stage. Millie took out her phone and snapped a close-up of him stood right in front of her, then posted it to her Twitter page:

@_MillieV: So close to Dex Rose I can almost smell him! #happydays #Craze

It came to a slow part of the song and Dex stopped to

catch his breath for a moment, exhausted, heart pounding out of his sweaty chest. He looked around the room and so many beautiful girls stared back at him, all fighting for as much as a smile from him. It had become commonplace in his life. As the tempo began to build and he prepared himself to belt out a big note, he turned towards the front left of the stage and stopped dead. something... someONE caught his eye.

"He's SOOOOO amazing!" Cate shouted in Millie's ear, trying to make herself heard over the music and fans screaming in her ears.

"I know!" squealed Millie. She sighed, feeling really deflated. He *was* amazing, as he stood on the stage right in front of her she felt the butterflies intensify. He was five feet away from her! In a daze, her eyes were locked onto his face, she was determined not to look away for a second, knowing that it *will* come to an end in no time and he would be gone again. Her palms were sweating and she could feel her legs shaking. *This is ridiculous*, she thought. *He's famous! Snap out of it and just enjoy the music!*

She looked at Dex stood there right in front of her. She looked right into his deep brown eyes and it was as if he was looking right into her. For a moment the room felt silent. She was alone with him, they were the only two people in the room. A bolt of electricity shot down through her, engulfing her entire body and rendering her breathless. It was the strangest feeling she had ever experienced. With her eyes still transfixed firmly on Dex she started to panic a little, she was sure she was about to faint. She knew he wasn't looking at her but she smiled... wondering what had caught his attention.

Dex looked right into the girl's eyes. He couldn't move, he felt sweating hot all of a sudden yet at the same time a shiver navigated his spine. He kept looking at her. Did he know her? She was strangely familiar; he was completely drawn to her.

It was as if he'd been paralysed on the spot. He felt dazed, confused, he shook his head, trying to shake the feeling off. He looked back at her and she smiled at him, his throat went dry and as he desperately tried to carry on with the show he stumbled over the words of the song. His mind had gone blank. All his mind could focus on was that girl!

Jesse looked up from his guitar for a second wondering what was wrong with Dex. Had the pressure of the first European show got to him? Had he forgotten the words? He had had several whisky shots before the show but he always did and could always deliver. He looked over at Zach, who looked slightly panicked; he was clearly thinking exactly the same thing. It was so unlike Dex. He had forgotten the words before but he would make a joke of it and carry on. This was different.

After a few seconds, which had felt like an age, Dex managed to snap out of it and remember the words to the next line. The others breathed a sigh of relief but as he sang and walked towards the other side of the stage he kept looking back at the girl. Jesse watched him, intrigued by his sudden odd behaviour. What was he doing? He seemed so distracted by something, Jesse began to worry that something was really wrong. Dex was just about managing to get through the song but his head was totally somewhere else. He'd seen thousands and thousands of pretty girls in crowds, so what was different about this one? She was beautiful, but so were so many others.

Dex had never felt so out of it on stage. He tried to finish the song as best he could but his concentration had gone and his entire body was trembling. He felt the same way he did after sex: hot, sweaty, shaky, exhausted, and yet euphoric at the same time, not a feeling he had ever experienced on stage before. She was all he could think about. His heart was beating in his mouth and he suddenly felt incredibly nervous, like it was only her watching him.

Millie was sure he was looking right at her. *He couldn't be... could he?* she thought. She turned and looked behind her. Who was Dex looking at? He was suddenly not the showman he was five minutes ago, belting out a song and bouncing around the stage with boundless energy. He seemed disconnected, something was up. Who did he keep looking at? Millie could tell that the girls around her seemed confused too, it wasn't just her that thought he was acting strange. She overheard the girl next to her talking to her friend.

"He's just on drugs, look how he keeps rubbing inside his arm, classic junkie!"

I hope that's not true, thought Millie. She despised drugs. There had to be a better reason.

With an instrumental section in the song, it gave Dex a break. He turned his back to the crowd and leaned over CJ's drum kit, he took a sip of water and composed himself. Caesar James, CJ, was their touring drummer and had been touring with Craze in the US for the past eight months. He had only known Dex for about a year but even he could tell he wasn't himself. Dex looked at CJ.

"Okay, man?" CJ mouthed. Dex nodded. CJ wasn't convinced but it was the best response he was likely to get mid-show. CJ gave Zach a quick *I have no idea* kind of glance.

Dex turned back to face the crowd. *Just get through the rest of this,* he told himself. He tried to switch off and just perform but every time he moved towards the left-hand side of the stage where she was he couldn't take his eyes off her. The stage lights lit her up like an angel and he could see into her seductive hazel brown eyes. Her long, dark hair framed her pretty olive-skinned face and her smile sent shivers down his spine.

It came to the end of their show. Dex had just managed to compose himself long enough to finish the last bit of their most well-known song. Everyone was singing and dancing along; it had been a great evening. Millie loved the song but she wasn't listening, she was completely wrapped up in her own head. She just stared at Dex, completely transfixed. She felt a little shaken.

The song came to an end and Dex and the other guys said their goodbyes and started to walk off the stage. Dex turned and looked right at Millie, he winked and smiled at her. Millie smiled back; she felt the hairs on the back of her neck stand up, she shivered as electricity ran down her arms like a cold, sharp knife . *What was that?* she thought to herself, confused. *I'm sure he just smiled at me*. She knew that she was clutching at straws, but anything to make her feel better about the fact that it was over. He was gone. She probably wouldn't see him again, not in the flesh. Millie felt her eyes well up a little. She tried not to make eye contact with Cate, she was completely aware of how pathetic she was being.

As she and Cate followed the crowd out of the venue, through her tears she couldn't help but smile. It was going to take some time to wipe that smile from her face! She'd had an incredible but strange night and she was 99% sure Dex had smiled at her. That was more than enough.

She dropped Cate off home and drove back to her apartment. All the way home all she could think about was him, her eyes welled up again. It was his eyes, she had looked right into his eyes and she felt something. She wondered if every girl there had felt like she did looking at him. *Was this normal?* She'd never been so obsessed over a celebrity before, she'd not even really felt like this about anyone she had dated in the past. How was she ever going to get over this crush? That was it now, gig over, she had to shake this feeling.

But instead Millie lay in bed going over and over the evening in her head. *He looked right at me, I'm sure he did.* She tried to convince herself he had felt what she did but she knew in reality it was only the truth in her head.

The band were ushered straight from the stage quickly back onto the bus before some of the more dedicated fans started to look for them outside. The curtains were closed and they settled down to chill while the venue emptied. Several security men from their entourage surrounded the bus. They had encountered some very crazy fans in the past, trying to smash windows to get to Dex, slashing the bus tyres to prevent the band from leaving, amongst other crazy stunts. They felt even more vulnerable being abroad in unfamiliar surroundings. Jesse slumped down onto the couch, hot, sweaty and exhausted. He wiped his long, dark hair off his wet forehead and pulled his phone from his pocket. Dex came and sat beside him, then tipped his head back and stared at the ceiling.

"Alright, man?" asked Jesse. Dex lifted his head.

"Uh, yeah, I think so," he replied, but he looked confused. Jesse could tell he was deep in thought about something but if he was going to spill it would be to Zach. Zach and Dex had known each other and been close since they were young. Dex was a private kind of guy so if anyone was going to get anything out of him it would be Zach.

"Hey, Dex, can you give me a hand a sec, dude?" asked Zach, walking towards their bunks in the back of the bus trying to find somewhere quieter to talk. Dex lifted his head from the back of the couch again.

"Sure," he replied, unenthusiastically dragging himself up off the couch. He followed Zach to the back of the bus. He found Zach laid on his bunk and he laid down next to him.

"'Sup?" asked Dex, sounding pretty moody, which wasn't unusual for Dex. He was often quiet, moody or distant, it was just his way of coping with the pressure and exhaustion of being on the road.

"Y'alright, dude?" asked Zach. "Did you forget the words?" he added, trying not to pry too much. Dex wasn't one to talk about feelings, emotions or anything deep.

"Nah… yeah… kind of," replied Dex. Zach could tell it wasn't just that. "I…" Dex continued, then stopped.

Zach turned to look at him. "Come on, man," Pushed Zach.

"Uh… there was just this girl. She caught my eye, looked weirdly familiar but I'm pretty sure I couldn't know anyone over here," he explained. "It just threw me off I guess," Dex finished.

Zach nodded. Dex was pleased that Zach seemed satisfied with his answer. He couldn't have said any more anyway, he had no idea what happened himself.

CHAPTER 2

"Morning, Mil!" chirped Sophie, the receptionist with a ridiculously big smile for that time of day.

"Morning," mumbled Millie, barely lifting her head to acknowledge Sophie as she walked through the door of the office building of the fashion labels headquarters where she worked.

Monday morning always came too soon! Millie was not a morning person. Not even a mid-morning person, barely even a lunchtime person. Especially on a Monday. She was anti-social at the best of times but on a dreary April morning Sophie's annoyingly cheerful face was more than she could deal with. As she breezed past Sophie's desk she made sure not to make eye contact or she would be certain to be forced into listening to a very long, detailed account of what wonderful, exciting, happy things Sophie had got up to at the weekend. Millie was pretty sure Sophie had to be related to Father Christmas or Mickey Mouse; there was no other rational explanation for someone to be so happy so early on a Monday morning... at work... on a miserable, rainy day! Millie did her best to avoid her each day. Her happy little round chubby face and neat strawberry blonde ponytail irritated Millie, she was just one of those people! Millie knew really she was harmless, most likely lacked friends and was just looking for a bit of attention. Millie often felt a bit sorry for Sophie and thought perhaps she should make a little more effort with her, she was only 19 and working in such a fast-paced office must be tough for her, but today of all days Millie just didn't have the patience for her.

Stepping out of the elevator on the second floor, Millie opened the door to her office. Instantly the phone rang and Millie jumped.

"MAN! That's loud today!" she groaned, rubbing her ears. She felt severely hungover, yet she'd not had a drink all weekend. She had definitely not woken up yet. Barely finding the energy to pick up the phone, she answered.

"Hiiii, Millie!" said an excited little voice on the other end.

"Yesssss, Sophie?" she sighed.

"Mr Salvatore is here to see your designs and he...."

"Fuuuuuck!" Millie interrupted. "He's early!" A feeling of panic came over her. Millie was a junior fashion designer and had been working in the design office of her favourite high street fashion retailer for the past five years; it was her first fashion job out of design college. The company was owned by world-famous Italian designer Franco Salvatore. After the gig Friday night and a busy weekend she totally forgot that she was supposed to be presenting her designs to Mr Salvatore this morning!

"FUCK, FUCK, FUCK!" she muttered to herself as she scrambled around on her desk trying to sift through a mountain of unorganised paperwork to find her portfolio for the meeting, forgetting Sophie was still on the other end of the phone.

"Millie, shall I show Mr Salvatore to the boardroom?" asked Sophie, trying to sound calm and professional in front of him and trying to drown out the sound of Millie's cursing in her ear in case he could hear.

"Uhhhhh yes, please," replied Millie, still frantically searching through papers. "BINGOOOO!" she shouted in Sophie's ear as she put the phone down and brushed piles of paper off her shiny black plastic folder.

She rushed towards the door, then stopped and looked in the mirrored door of the stationery cupboard to take a minute to compose herself and mentally prepare. Although she had taken big meetings like this many times, before every one of them, inside, she still turned into the shy little girl she was at school. If someone had told her when she was at school that she would be doing this in years to come, she'd never have believed it. She was the quiet one, she got nervous talking in front of her class, she got nervous if a boy spoke to her and here she was just a few years on, about to chair a meeting and share her own designs with the head of a major international fashion brand.

She stared at her own reflection in the mirrored door. A smile crept across her face. She stood confidently in her red, figure-hugging pencil dress and went over her opening line in her head. She was ready for this.

As she walked out of the design office a switch flicked in her. Quiet, shy, nice, Millie was turned off and replaced with confident, sexy, ambitious Millie who was determined to nail this meeting and get her designs on the high street. She'd worked hard since she was 16 and this was the closest she had ever got to a big break. Up until now all she had done was help other people with their designs, and now it was time for her to get her own out there. A busy weekend and a tired Monday morning weren't going to stand in her way. She walked along the corridor and paused for a second outside the boardroom door. She closed her eyes, took a deep breath in and pushed open the door. *Here we go.*

Dex sat staring out of the bus window watching the world go by. Despite playing two successful sell-out shows since, he was still thinking about Friday night. He still didn't really know what happened, maybe he had had too much whisky before the gig. He tried to rationalise it in his head but he knew what he had felt that night was very real.

"Zach, let me borrow ya phone, man," asked Dex. Zach was lying in his bunk opposite Dex. He took his phone out of his pocket and threw it over to Dex, who used it to look through Zach's Twitter. He didn't have any social media accounts himself, he thought it was all too much hassle. He had a browse through all the messages left after the gig, maybe someone would give him a clue as to what happened. He wondered if anyone had noticed that he fucked up. The other guys in the band hadn't brought it up again, after playing Saturday and Sunday nights in other UK cities without any disruptions they'd most likely forgotten about it.

"Ha! She's lucky she couldn't smell ya! Ya sweaty bastard!" laughed Jesse looking over Dex's shoulder, reading a tweet from a fan. Dex read the tweet:

So close to Dex Rose I can smell him!
#happydays #Craze

"It's true," he laughed. He was always dripping with sweat during a gig. His mind went back to thinking about the girl. He really wanted to say something to the other guys but no one had said a word about it. He didn't want to bring anything up, maybe he'd gotten away with it. If he mentioned the girl again he knew they'd think he was being ridiculous or just tell him to bed her and get it out his system! He was never going to get a sensible response from guys, certainly not those guys.

"This officially sucks!" groaned Jesse, as he climbed awkwardly over the top of Dex and laid down next to him on his bunk. After leaving England late Sunday night they'd been on the road for nearly 24 hours straight and were all becoming pretty fed up. Next stop was Hamburg, Germany and they wouldn't arrive until Tuesday afternoon.

"I'm so bored," moaned Jesse.

"Oh man! Tell me about it!" Dex replied. "I can't wait to get off this damn bus!" he added.

"Your 'rents coming over? asked Zach.

"Yeah," smiled Dex. "I'm stoked," he added. Dex's parents were flying over from New York to see him in Hamburg. He couldn't wait, he was really close to his parents and hadn't seen them since Christmas. They were going to travel on the bus with the band for the week through Germany to Italy then fly back home from Rome.

A message came through on Dex's phone and he jumped. Jesse laughed; Dex hit him with a cushion.

"Ah, that'll be Mom now with their flight details." He pulled his phone from his back pocket.

Hey cutie, missing you! Got a surprise for you. Luc <3 xxx

It was from his girlfriend, Lucie. She was a 20-year-old English pop star, currently also touring in Europe. They'd been dating for eight months now, they met at the Nouvelle Music awards back in September. Things were great at first. Lucie was fun, they had had crazy nights out together, they'd spontaneously get up one morning and decide to fly to Dubai, they'd stay up all night drinking and laughing. He felt happy for the first time in a long time. He could really see it going somewhere. She was in the same business so she understood him, she knew what his lifestyle was like and how busy his schedule was. By Christmas he had even considered proposing to her after just a few months of being together but the last couple of months he had started to feel different. Things had fizzled out a little, he'd been on the road for months now and had barely seen her, in fact he'd seen more of her in newspapers and magazines than he had in the flesh! Being on the road so much he had had a lot of time to think, a lot of time in his own head. He'd had time to take a step back and realise the age gap was becoming bigger and bigger. Lucie was still enjoying being young, she had her whole life ahead of her at 20 and the world already at her feet. He couldn't help feeling that he would hold her back. He had just turned 31 and needed to slow down a bit, soon he wasn't going to be able to do all the things she wanted to do and he knew at some point that was going to become an issue. Just not one he wanted to deal with right now.

Lying on his bunk, Dex just stared at Lucie's message on his phone. The radio and all the people on the tour bus were so loud he could barely hear himself think, let alone come up with what to reply. Nothing seemed like the right thing to say. Maybe things would be different when he saw her again and perhaps it was just the time and distance apart.

He pushed his phone back down into his tight back pocket, turned over onto his stomach and buried his head into his pillow. Dex was a happy depressed kind of person; it was how he wrote his best songs. He kind of liked feeling down.

"What time do they get in?" Zach shouted over the music. Dex didn't answer from under his pillow. Zach got up from his bunk and crept over to Dex, smacking him on the ass with CJ's drumstick. Dex jumped again.

"WHAT THE FUCK, MAN!" he yelled as he turned to see Zach kneeling behind him on his bunk. Dex smiled as he lunged forward and grabbed Zach round the neck, forcing him into a headlock. Not unusual behaviour on the bus. Dex loved it, it was so much fun to be living his dream with two amazing guys and the rest of the touring band, and play fighting was an added bonus.

"I heard ya! I don't know, text was from Luc." He smiled cheekily down at Zach, still pinning him down on his bunk.

"Ooooohhhh, boo-tay call!" Zach teased and laughed to himself, struggling to wriggle free from Dex's grip. He and Dex had just last night been talking about their 'dry spell'. Being away from their girlfriends for so long was tough going. Dex laughed and threw a pillow at Zach as he broke free and ran. He ducked and it narrowly missed their hairdresser Amy's head.

"Ha ha, ya need to take advantage of the situation, boy!" smiled Zach. Zach had had quite a few one night stands with fans, despite having a long term girlfriend back home in New York. He just couldn't resist the attention, he was of the understanding that what she didn't know couldn't hurt her. Dex on the other hand couldn't bring himself to do it, despite being very very tempted on a few occasions. Every time it came close his mother popped into his head. He was really close to his mom and he knew how disapproving she would be. His parents had been married and faithful to each other for over 25 years and that notion was engraved in his brain.

"I'm good, man," he smiled back at Zach.

As he laid back down on his bed he started to type a message back to Lucie. *Be nice*, he thought to himself, *don't write it off yet*.

Hey, miss you too, any clues for me? ;) D.x

He hesitated, hovering his finger over the send button for a few seconds before he pressed it, burying his head back into his pillow. In the back of his mind he knew it wasn't going to work. His heart just wasn't in it. He lay there just daydreaming, thinking about his life and his future. Despite having all his music dreams come true he felt somewhat empty, something was missing.

As dusk fell the guys settled down to a game of cards to try to pass the time.

"Blackjack?" asked Jesse, dealing the cards out on the table. Zach sat down to play. Dex was still lying on his bunk, reluctantly he dragged himself up. He wasn't in the mood but he needed something to take his mind off Lucie.

"'Sup with you, dude? Everything okay?" asked Jesse as Dex slumped into the chair.

"Nah, I'm alright, man," he mumbled. They both knew not to push him, if he wanted to talk he would. He was hard to read, he often seemed quiet and down even when he wasn't.

Usually it was because he was working through a new song in his head.

As she left the office Millie let out a little squeal of excitement. She'd had the best day! Her meeting had gone amazingly well, she had nailed her presentation and Mr Salvatore loved her designs for a new bag and purse range and had agreed to trial them in his stores nationwide. It was the best start to her fashion career she could have hoped for. No one was going to wipe the smile off her face. She'd totally forgotten about Dex, this was real life and he was a kind of fiction, he was never going to be part of her reality. She had spent all weekend on a huge comedown from the gig, this was just the news she needed to make her feel like herself again. She practically bounced to her car, desperate to get home and call her mum. As she drove home she had butterflies in her stomach – her bag designs were going to be in shops! She kept going over and over it in her head, it hadn't sunk in. As she pulled into her driveway, her roommate Amber was just arriving home too.

"Ambs! Ambs! Eeeeeeeeeeeeeeek my bags are going to be in all the Salvo stores in the country!" squealed Millie.

"Oh my god, Mils!" replied Amber excitedly. "That's amazing, babe!" smiled Amber as she threw her arms around Millie and gave her a squeeze.

"I know, I'm so excited, I can't wait!" replied Millie, still smiling.

"Well, there's only one thing we're doing tonight then! Partying!" exclaimed Amber.

Millie smiled, that was just what she needed. As

they went into their apartment Millie threw her work bags on the couch and made her way to the kitchen. She got out the champagne they had been saving for something special and popped the cork. Millie stopped for a moment and told herself to remember this moment; she was a happy, optimistic kind of girl but she hadn't felt his happy in a long time. She was proud of herself. She had worked so hard, she deserved this.

"TO MY GORGEOUS MILLIE VANILLY!" as Amber affectionately called her. She raised her glass to Millie's rather enthusiastically and as the glasses clinked they were splashed with champagne. Millie giggled, she could get used to the champagne lifestyle.

The girls spent the next hour getting ready and left for town to meet Cate and Holly. Going out on a school night wasn't something Millie made a habit of, but she let herself off this once. She was excited for a night out with her girls.

As they arrived at the bar Cate and their friend Holly were waiting outside with congratulations balloons and a huge bottle of wine.

"WHOOOOOOOOOOOOO! Hey there big fashionista!" shouted Cate; She was so pleased for her best friend. "I will be first in line to buy one of your bags as soon as they're in store," smiled Cate. "In fact, not one... ALL of your bags," she added.

Millie laughed. She couldn't imagine what it would be like to go into a store and buy one of her own bags, but she was excited to find out. They headed into the bar, which was jam-packed. "This is busy for a Monday night isn't it?" asked Millie.

"Clearly everyone's heard your news," joked Amber. Millie rolled her eyes. As she headed towards the bar she heard someone yell her name and she smiled, she knew that voice! As she turned around she saw Ricco, her best friend and her boss at Salvo's. Ricco was the son of Franco Salvatore, millionaire owner of the international chain of high-end fashion stores, Salvo's. Ricco was gorgeous, like a god! He was a dark-skinned Italian stallion. Millie always teased him that he was totally wasted being gay. He had a body to die for and Millie fancied the pants off him. He had the personality of Gok Wan but looked like Zac Efron's older brother, he was often mistaken for Zac when he visited the US on business. Unfortunately for Millie he was 100% into guys!

"Hey! Congratulations, baby girl," shouted Ricco as he put his arms around her and kissed her on the cheek.

"Thanks, Ri," she replied.

Ricco cuddled her for a minute while ordering his drink at the bar, and leaned across the bar still holding Millie in his arm. "Hey, Mojitos for my girls, please." The bar staff and most of the people in the bar knew who Ricco was; he was often on TV presenting the fashion section on morning TV shows amongst other things. He always got free drinks, which Millie thought was crazy as he was the richest person in the room!

Millie made the most of having his arms wrapped around her. It had been ages since a guy had held her and it didn't matter that he was gay; he cared about her, he was protective of her and being in his arms felt good. Dex popped into her head and she closed her eyes. She imagined she was in his arms and instantly felt an emptiness in the pit of her stomach. She longed for him, just the thought of him made her feel so down. He wasn't even real, well not really, not to her, so how did he manage to make her feel this way?

"We're hitting the dance floor," shouted Amber, above the loud music.

"Coming, you two?" asked Holly.

"I am!" said Cate. She turned to Millie. "Coming?" she asked.

"Nah, in a sec," she replied, still clutching on tightly to Ricco.

"'K," said Cate. She kissed Millie on the forehead and followed Amber and Holly to the dance floor. She knew there must be something Millie wanted to talk to Ricco about; she didn't usually miss any opportunity to dance.

Millie watched her friends as they headed off towards the

dance floor. As soon as they were out of sight she turned back to Ricco, and before she could say a word…

"What have you got to tell me?" he whispered in her ear. She just gave him a look. "Spill" he continued, flashing a gorgeous smile.

"Nothing! I'm alright," she lied. It was all in her eyes. He knew her better than anyone, he could tell instantly something was wrong.

"Yeah, yeah," he replied sarcastically. "You're out celebrating your success and you look as miserable as a hot polar bear!" he joked.

Millie giggled; burying her head into his chest to try to hide her smile and avoid answering. "God, I wish you were straight," she whispered as she rested her hand against his rock hard chest. She could smell his aftershave, he smelled amazing. *Awesome!* she thought. *First I am in love with a pop star, now I'm lusting after a gay guy! What is wrong with me?*

"Haha I heard that," he laughed. "Believe me babe, if I was straight you'd be first in my bed!" he teased. "So, missus! Tell me." He smiled a cheeky smile at her and she knew she would have to fess up. He was never going to let it lie. "You're not pregnant. Are you?! 'cuz if you are I'll hunt him down and kick his ass," he joked.

"That'd be a miracle!" Millie replied. She thought for a minute. *He's going to laugh in my face if I admit I'm in love with a man who lives in my imagination!* She had to lie. *Think of something quick*, she thought.

"I'm just worried that no one will like my bags… I guess I'm a bit overwhelmed." She couldn't look him in the eye, she hated lying to him.

"Oh, doll! Don't be silly," he replied, putting an arm around her shoulder and giving her a squeeze. "You're amazing and you'll be raking it in soon!" he tried to reassure her. "Now, let's own the night!" he laughed, That was a phrase Ricco used a lot but Millie was never really sure what it meant. Ricco knew that wasn't the whole truth but he wasn't going to push. He knew he would get it out of her. Just not tonight.

CHAPTER 3

The tour bus reversing alarm woke Jesse up; he tilted his phone towards him to see what the time was. 5am. He pulled back the curtain a tiny bit and peeked outside. Finally, after two long days on the road, the bus was reversing into the venue in Hamburg.

"Oh my fucking god," he exclaimed, which woke Dex and CJ. "There's a fucking queue of people already! It's 5am! We're not on till 8 tonight!" He couldn't believe it! He didn't know why would anyone wait out in the cold for that long just to see them, though it was becoming a familiar sight at each gig now.

"Fans are crazy here!" said Dex, squinting to see and rubbing his eyes, it was early and they weren't quite functioning yet.

"Dex, wasn't it a German fan who booked your wedding?" Zach asked, laughing to himself. A crazy German girl had written to Dex declaring her undying love for him and telling him she had booked for them to get married, even giving instructions for when and where he had to go! They had a lot of odd fan mail but that one took the crown.

"Ha ha, yeah," Dex replied, dragging himself out of bed. He was going to meet his parents at the airport that morning and he couldn't wait to see them. Being away from his family was hard and he was a self-confessed mommy's boy.

"Hey, Mac," he called to their tour manager. "Can you get me a cab to the airport, man?" he asked.

"Sure," he called back. Mac had been with them from the start and was more of a friend than a manager. His real name was Ray but they called him Mac as a bit of a joke amongst the band and tour crew. He was a big fella, an ex-bodyguard. He was a bit of a McDonald's addict and got one in every city they arrived in! So they'd affectionately nicknamed him Mac and it stuck.

As the cab arrived, Mac threw a black towel over Dex's head, he put a protective arm round him and quickly escorted him from the bus to the waiting cab. The second Dex emerged from the bus the crowds of people queuing outside of the venue went wild, screaming, shouting, fighting over each other to get to him, but in seconds he was in the cab and away. Mac went with him, he couldn't go anywhere alone these days, certainly not in an unfamiliar foreign country. Dex was cool with that though, he felt much better with Mac with him.

"Jesus Christ! Someone go tell that lot to shut the fuck up! It's not even 6am!" groaned Zach, putting his pillow over his head. Realistically he knew he was up for the day now. He wasn't a morning person and they had been up drinking and playing cards till 2am!

As the cab pulled up at the airport, Mac got out first and quickly ushered Dex inside. Dex felt so vulnerable out in the open, he didn't look up from the floor at all but out of the corner of his eye he could see people looking at him, whispering, pointing. It seemed absolutely mad to him that all these people in a foreign country knew who he was when less than a year ago most people in his home town didn't know who he was. Luckily it was still early and the airport was quiet. Taking a quick scan of the terminal he noticed that most of the people were of an older generation and wouldn't have known who he was, so he could relax a little. He walked over to the arrivals board with Mac closely in tow to see if Dex's parents' flight had landed from New York. It had. He could feel the excitement and anticipation building in his stomach; he was desperate to give his mom a hug! He might be a 31-year-old man, adored by the world, but he was still a mommy's boy at heart.

As Dex waited for his parents, a few fans spotted him and started to approach him for photos and autographs. He didn't really like doing either but he did it. As he signed a girl's ticket stub he looked up for a second and saw his mom and dad coming through the gate.

"I'm sorry," he said as he quickly gave the pen back to the girl. "Hey, Ma" he smiled as he threw his

arms around his mom and kissed her on the cheek. "Hey, Dad." He hugged his dad and took both their bags from them.

"Hey guys, good flight?" asked Mac.

"Yeah, not bad," Dex's dad replied, shaking Mac's hand. he appreciated the fact that Mac was looking after his son whilst he was away from home.

They walked together to the glass doors where their cab was waiting outside. As Dex went to open the door for his mom a girl's voice behind him shouted. "SURPRISE, DEX!" As he turned, confused, his heart sank. She ran towards him and threw her arms around his neck. Her long blonde hair whipped around his face, Dex had to spit out of his mouth to speak.

"Luc! Erm... what are you doing here?" he tried to sound pleased, but in reality he was gutted.

"I had a few days off and thought I'd surprise my baby" she replied, kissing him several times whilst he was trying to talk.

"Oh," he replied, with a total lack of enthusiasm. He hated

his private life being on public show but he looked into her piercing blue eyes he had forgotten how beautiful she was. Her skin was pale like a porcelain doll, she was flawless, but all he could think of looking at her was man, she looked so young. It reiterated in his mind everything he had been going over in his head lately, she was too young for him. She seemed younger than she had before, or maybe he was so wrapped up in her then that he didn't notice before. He felt embarrassed that she was kissing him in front of everyone, thinking people probably thought she was his daughter! All he knew was that he had been looking forward to spending some time with his parents, just the three of them for the first time in four months. He missed Lucie and he was kind of glad to see her, but he so badly didn't want to deal with her and their relationship right now, not while his mom and dad were there.

He felt totally deflated.

Outside as Dex helped his parents into the cab, Lucie felt uneasy as fans started to surround them, feeling slightly annoyed that Dex hadn't been protective over her like he'd been with his parents. She quickly got into the car to avoid the crowds of fans that had now gathered around the car, banging on the windows and asking for autographs. Lucie was nervous, she felt really alone without her security detail. Dex posed for a few photos and made his excuses, it was Lucie they wanted, she was a global superstar, much bigger in Europe than Craze was and everyone wanted a piece of her. It was getting scary with the amount of people that now surrounded them, they seem to all come from nowhere. One minute there was no one around then in the blink of an eye they were completely surrounded.

"Enough, man," said Mac, ushering the girls away from the car door so Dex could get into the back of the cab. As the door closed behind him he breathed a sigh of relief.

Lucie slid along the seat until she was so close to Dex she might as well have sat on his lap, she clutched tightly to his arm with both hands and nestled her head into his shoulder. He could feel himself getting annoyed that she was hanging all over him, but he kept quiet. Part of him felt sorry for what she had to deal with, she was so young, it had to be scary.

The cab ride seemed to take forever. Nobody spoke. Dex really wanted to talk to his parents but Lucie showing up had ruined his mood, there was an awkwardness. As they arrived back at the venue Dex felt a little bit relieved to have some space. Mac got out first and radioed for a few more security guys to help get them all inside, the queues had got even bigger and he knew as soon as Dex emerged from the cab they were going to go mad, especially with Lucie being there too.

Several big security men emerged from the venue all dressed in black. Mac took Dex's parents inside first, leaving Dex and Lucie alone in the car. As soon as the car door closed Lucie turned to him.

"What's wrong?" she asked, feeling utterly confused by his lack of enthusiasm.

"Huh?" he responded, playing down the question. He looked out of the window at the growing crowds of fans, to avoid eye contact.

"You don't seem very happy. I thought you'd be pleased to see me," she added. She tried to look him in the eye but he avoided it.

"Just tired," he casually replied. Lucie dropped it.

"Yeah," she mumbled sarcastically under her breath as Mac opened the car door. Lucie got out of the car and the crowds got a tiny glimpse of her, the eruption of screaming was intense! But it was wherever she went. As three of the security men surrounded her, Dex stayed in the car and watched her. She looked perfect in tiny denim shorts with the American flag printed on the back pockets and a black vest top that barely covered her stomach, her long blonde hair flowing down the back of her black leather jacket, occasionally blowing in the wind. She looked every inch the pop star but he could see the fear in her, she was just a little girl away from home on her own. For a moment he felt a bit sorry for her, like he should be the one to protect her. He didn't want to be.

Dex found the fame and the fans really tough to deal with and she was having to deal with it worse than him. She was only 20, just a baby really, and she'd been famous and dealing with all that comes with it for far longer than him. She was usually so bubbly, so confident and full of energy, it was the first time he had seen her vulnerable side and his protective male instincts kicked in. He knew Mac would go mad but he got out of the car. Mac gestured to him to get back in, they were still dealing with Lucie. Dex was a security team's nightmare, if he wanted to do something, he did it, he wasn't bothered about the risks.

"S'aight, Mac," said Dex. The crowds caught sight of him, they were already shouting for Lucie but as he came around to the other side of the cab where Lucie was the crowds of fans erupted into ear piercing screams. All shouting at him from every direction, trying to get his attention. Mac tried to put a black towel over Dex's head as he always did but Dex refused.

"It's okay, Mac," he said again as he put his arm around Lucie and walked her into the venue, both surrounded by bodyguards. Lucie felt relieved as she walked through the doors. She felt safe in his arms, she got the feeling he wasn't overly pleased to see her at the airport. She kissed him softly on the cheek.

"Thank you," she whispered, putting her hand up under his shirt. Her cold hand on his stomach made him flinch but it was nice to be touched, it had been nearly four months since anyone had touched him like that. He began to think perhaps he'd jumped the gun a bit wanting to end things, perhaps it was just the time apart and her showing up here was just what they needed.

Dex's parents looked on as he and the band performed their sound check. Lucie glanced over at Dex's mum, she was smiling from ear to ear. The love and admiration she had for son was evident in her eyes, she was so proud of her boy. Lucie felt her eyes well up a little, she'd lost her mum when she was a baby but she knew she'd have been just as proud if she'd got to see her perform. Lucie had never watched Dex perform live herself before, the only times she had been at one of his gigs was when they did a few festivals last summer but she was on the line up to perform too so she never got to watch. She was excited that was her man up there and she kind of understood how his mum felt. Plus he looked so sexy she thought, she couldn't wait for tonight when she would have him all to herself!

Dex took some slow deep breaths to wake his lungs up. He looked over at Lucie, his mom and his dad and yawned, just the thought of having to deal with all of them here at once made him feel even more tired than he already was that early in the morning! He pulled his sweater down over his hands, a habit he had picked up as a child, and put his hands around the microphone stand. He started his sound check, pleased that it gave him time to not have to talk to or deal with anyone. It was just him and his own voice for the next 30 minutes.

As Millie walked down to the canteen to grab a coffee her head was pounding, she could barely function. She still felt a little drunk as she staggered into the lift, but there was no way she was going to be able to navigate the stairs in her state – with heels on! *Whose silly idea was it to go out on a Monday night?* she thought. As the doors opened she looked up and was greeted by that little round, chubby face.

"MILLIE!" she jumped! Sophie's voice seemed to cut right through the air like a knife.

"Jesus fucking Christ, Sophie! You scared the hell out of

me!" said Millie as she walked right past her and went to get a coffee. Sophie followed quickly behind her talking at her constantly.

"Millie, you have a meeting at 3.30pm with Mr Salvatore and a telephone conference at 5.00pm with Mr…" Millie could feel herself reaching boiling point. Trying to stay calm she poured herself a coffee. It was just too early. Sophie continued to talk at her.

SOPHIE!" Millie snapped "I'm getting a coffee! E-mail it to me!"

Sophie stopped, shocked by Millie's outburst, her smiley annoying little face replaced with the face of a sulking five-year-old. "Umm. Okay," replied Sophie, turning to leave.

Millie sighed as she slumped down in the chair with her coffee. She felt bad for being mean to Sophie and knew she would have to go and apologise in a minute but she just didn't have the patience for her yapping in her ear today. She was massively hungover and not in the mood for chirpy Sophie. Her head needed a rest!

As she sat staring into her coffee her thoughts returned to Dex. She took her phone from her pocket and searched the internet for video interviews of him, she needed to hear his voice. It was something she did several times a day. Since seeing him live last week she had become obsessed with him, he was on her mind constantly. Her career was just starting to go somewhere and she knew it should be her main focus but it wasn't, her mind was elsewhere, she spent more of her time in her office Googling Dex than working! She wanted to know more and more about him, she wanted to hear his voice, see his face, it was the closest she could get to him.

She started to worry that her infatuation was beginning to affect her life and her work. She found herself in important meetings just wishing it would be over soon so she could get back to her phone to see if the band had posted any new pictures or videos on their Twitter or Facebook pages. She was exhausted every morning where she had been up late watching his music videos over and over again. She was completely losing touch with reality. She shook her head as if to shake her thoughts away. She opened her notepad on the canteen table in front of her, pulled the pencil from the spiral binding and started to sketch. She was meeting with Mr Salvatore this afternoon and needed six new bag designs to add to the six designs she already had for her debut collection and so far she had a grand total of... none! After a couple of quick sketches her mind was gone again and she began to scribble Dex's name on her page. Annoyed with herself she ripped the page from her pad, screwed it up and threw it across the room, missing the bin. She got up to pick it up; there was no way her OCD was going to leave the paper on the floor. She threw it in the bin and slouched back down in her chair. This was no good, she just wasn't with it today. She pulled out her mobile phone and dialled.

"Sophie, cancel all my appointments today please, I don't feel well," said Millie.

"Buuuuu!" Millie hung up before Sophie could say anything. She needed some time to get her act together.

She made her way back to her office and took a deep breath. *Right! Stop it, no more of this stupid shit!* she told herself. *Back to reality now.* She sat down at her desk, flopping her notebook down on the table with a loud *SLAP!* She began to sketch her ideas for her bags, feeling instantly better. She knew this was what she should be doing with her time, this was real life, this could make her happy. He couldn't.

An email came through on her computer screen:

Mr Salvatore re-arranged for 9am tomorrow morning, he's taking you to Italy on Thursday; He's showcasing your bags in our collection at Milan Fashion Week! Thought you would want to know that! - Call me. Soph x

Millie squealed with excitement! She read the email twice just to make sure it actually said what she thought it said. Picking up the phone she called Sophie right back.

"Hello," answered Sophie.

Millie had never been so happy to hear that ear splitting voice on the other end of the phone. "What?!" she said excitedly. "Your email! What?!" she repeated.

"Mr Salvatore wanted to meet with you today to tell you he wants to include your bags in our summer showcase on the catwalk at Milan Fashion Week. Your first five designs have gone into production today and are being shipped to Milan immediately."

"Eeeeeeeeeeeeeeeeeeeek!" Millie squealed. Sophie pulled the phone away from her ear, getting a taste of her own medicine. "Calm down, Mil, you need to meet with him in the morning and he will tell you himself. I just thought you might like to know in advance," explained Sophie.

"Thanks!" replied Millie, dancing around her office tangling herself in the telephone cable.

Mr Salvatore quite often took her abroad for a day or two for fashion shows, exhibitions, networking etc. *Brilliant* she thought, a little trip away was just what she needed, a distraction from her normal life. Her mood instantly lightened and her misery was replaced with excitement! Italy was one of the most exciting places for a young designer like her. It gave her some motivation. She knuckled down to her sketching.

You coming to Italy?! <3

She text Ricco, she hoped he was coming; a few days away with her best pal would sort her out. Seconds later her phone beeped with his reply:

Yeah babycakes! xxx

She smiled.

Millie arrived home bouncing down the path to her front door, she was beyond excited. With her arms full of bags and folders she struggled to open the door, dropping everything on the floor as she finally managed to push the handle down enough and the door flung open.

"AMBS!, AMBS!" she yelled up the stairs. "I'm going to Italy for a few days babe," she added whilst scuffling around on the floor trying to pick up all her papers that were strewn across the hallway carpet.

"What, hun?" replied Amber coming down the stairs as she wrapped a towel around her wet hair.

"I'm going to Italy with Ri for a few days," Millie repeated.

"Oh man! Best place work ever send me is the supermarket when we run out of milk!" said Amber. Millie laughed. "Bring me back an Italian," she joked.

"Will do," shouted Millie as she ran up the stairs. She threw her stuff down on her dresser and flopped onto her bed. Closing her eyes she began to daydream about Italy and about her designs. This could be such an exciting trip for her career, she had been to Italy and various other countries with work but only to assist Mr Salvatore, never to showcase her own work. She was taking her own bag designs to one of the fashion capitals of the world! This could be her big break, she thought to herself. Her mind began to wander, what if she did become a famous designer, what if one day everyone knew her name! What if… Dex knew her name… she stopped.

THAT'S IT! All she needed to do was become famous and then she'd have a shot with him. She was suddenly overcome with excitement. This was exactly the direction she needed her life to go in, this absolutely had to work out! Millie got her portfolio out from beneath the pile of stuff she had dumped on her dresser and looked through her designs. *They've got to be incredible,* she thought to herself. *This is your shot, don't blow it!* She settled herself on her bed with her work and began to draw.

She stayed up until the early hours re-sketching her designs. At 1.38am, her tired eyes gave in and she fell asleep on her paper.

"Geez, it's 2.40am!" exclaimed Dex as he looked at his watch. They quite often went out for a few drinks after each gig to see the city they were in and sample the local beers but they rarely stayed out late. But tonight the place was buzzing and the atmosphere was amazing, they'd completely lost track of time. No one seemed to recognise them in the bar so they could drink in peace. It was a long time since any of them had experienced a normal night out, Dex wanted to stay out and make the most of a bit of anonymity but after several beers and shots he was dying to take Lucie to bed! He couldn't keep his hands off her. Maybe he did want to make it work, perhaps it was just the stress of a long distance relationship that made him doubt her, but all he knew was that he couldn't wait to get her home tonight.

"Let's go, man," he said, gesturing to Zach and Jesse who were on the other side of the bar chatting to some very pretty girls. Girls loved them together, they were both funny guys and really bounced off each other. They always had crowds of girls around them, even in places where no one knew who they were. They were just genuinely funny, friendly guys who loved the attention. Dex on the other hand stayed out of it. He was quiet, anti-social and shied away from any kind of attention, he liked to just sit in the corner and drink. When he was off stage he wanted a quiet, anonymous life without people hassling him. Zach downed his pint and pulled Jesse away from the girls, spilling his drink all over the floor.

"Oops, sorry bro," he shouted to the guy behind the bar. Zach pulled him through the crowds of people in the bar with CJ following behind. Dex grabbed Lucie's hand as they made their way to the exit and opened the door for her. They came out onto the street expecting a quiet, dark, empty street at that time of night, instead they were greeted by dozens of flashes. As Dex's eyes readjusted he could see dozens of paparazzi, all shouting for Lucie. Someone had tipped them off that she was in town. Dex was annoyed, his relationship with her was not yet public... there were rumours but they'd managed to avoid being photographed together. Until now!

He hated his private life in the media. He took off his jacket and threw it over her head. Tightly clutching her hand he fought their way through the crowds. People were grabbing them, pulling them in every direction. He was irritated but he kept going, pulling Lucie through to the cab waiting for them across the street. He pushed her in first and got in himself, followed by the rest of the band. Jesse struggled to close the door with dozens of fans trying to pull it open, Zach leaned over and helped pull it shut and the cab sped away. Lucie turned and looked out of the rear window, they were still being chased down the street by paparazzi.

"Let's ditch 'em!" smiled Jesse. He knew the paparazzi would go straight to the tour bus, they would probably get there before them. "Let's sneak into a hotel and leave 'em waiting at the bus," he added.

"Yeah!" replied Dex, he looked at Lucie and threw her a cheeky smile.

She knew exactly what that smile meant. She could feel the excitement building in the pit of her stomach. Finally some alone time with him, instead of being crammed on the tour bus with several other people all night. She put her hand up his shirt and gently scratched his stomach suggestively.

He shivered, her touch made the hairs on the back of his neck stand up. The feeling sent his mind immediately back to Friday night. That girl! How could he have forgotten about her? He'd been so busy and preoccupied he hadn't given her a second thought. He could clearly see the image of her in his mind, as if he was back there in the moment. He could see her staring right at him with gorgeous big brown eyes, she was effortlessly beautiful. He rarely came across girls that stood out like her. He saw pretty girls on an hourly basis, they threw themselves at him everywhere he went but they were all the same, boring, unoriginal. He didn't know what made her so different. He suddenly felt a hot sweat come over him; he pushed Lucie's hand away from his stomach.

"What?" she exclaimed, confused.

"Nothing, I'm hot," he lied. He couldn't let her touch him now the girl was on his mind, he suddenly felt completely sober and now it felt wrong. As the cab pulled into the back entrance of the hotel, the coast was clear, the street was completely silent, ditching the paparazzi had worked.

Dex wished they'd gone back to the bus now so he didn't have to be alone with Lucie, he knew she would want to have sex and he just wasn't in the mood anymore. He was clear in his mind now, it was the drink that wanted Lucie, he didn't.

"Stay there, I'll go get some rooms," said Jesse, climbing out of the cab. He went in ahead with CJ and checked them all in, whilst Dex waited in the cab. He pulled his phone from his pocket and sent a text to Mac to let him know where they were staying so he could send cars and security for them in the morning. He knew Mac would be pretty pissed that they weren't coming back and had none of the security team with them but he didn't care, sometimes he just needed a bit of freedom like every normal person.

Jesse came back outside and gestured for them to come in. Inside, while they waited for the elevator Lucie leant her head against Dex's shoulder. He cringed at her touch and pulled away. *That's it*, he thought to himself. He knew that once he got to the stage of shuddering when she touched him that was game over! He'd been there before in the past and there was no recovery from that. Surprisingly he felt gutted, he may have known their relationship was never going to work out but man he had a crush on that girl! As she stepped into the elevator before him he couldn't help his eyes wandering to her bum, she looked so sexy in a tiny pair of denim shorts. As she turned around to lean against the back wall of the elevator his eyes wandered down her body, her tight t-shirt stopped short of her belly button showing her flat, toned stomach. She had the body of a dancer. She really was perfect, he wished he felt more for her but he knew he didn't. It was purely physical and that was never going to be enough for him. The girl from the gig had made him realise there needed to be more, just looking at her made him feel things he had never felt with Lucie and he didn't even know her name. As the elevator doors opened Lucie grabbed his hand.

"Night man, were down here," said Jesse, pointing down the hall and gesturing to Zach and CJ to follow.

"Night dude," replied Dex. He threw Zach an odd look. Zach was confused; it was as if he didn't want them to leave. Surely he wanted to be alone with his girlfriend. Zach shot back a look of confusion but Dex couldn't say anything. He turned, put his arm around Lucie and led her down the opposite corridor towards their room.

"Did you see that? asked Zach as he opened the door to their room.

"Yeah, what the hell was that?" replied Jesse.

"I get the feeling he didn't want to go with her, I don't know why, they've been apart ages! You'd think he'd be dying to spend the night with her," said Zach. "I'll have a chat with him tomorrow, see what's up."

"He's been acting kind of weird lately," added CJ, "Don't you think?" he asked as he turned to unlock the door to his room.

"Something's up, I'll find out tomorrow," said Zach.

"Yeah, anyway, night guys," said CJ as he disappeared into his room.

"Night, dude," replied Zach and Jesse as they closed the door to their room behind them.

Dex took his shirt off and got into bed. Lucie stood at the foot of the bed and undressed with her back to him as if she had no idea Dex was watching, but he knew she was fully aware. He knew he had to have sex with her and get it over and done with; the alternative was a night of arguing about why he didn't want to. He couldn't deal with that right now, he knew he could just switch off. It was far easier.

Lucie stood in her black lacy bra facing away from the bed, she unbuttoned her shorts and slid them down her slim tanned legs revealing her black lacy French knickers. She looked like she could have been an underwear model. She turned to face Dex, he had never seen anyone look so perfect but so young! It had never really been an issue but standing there in front of him she looked like a teenager. He felt uneasy, like he was doing something really wrong, he felt sleazy. *Every single red-blooded man in the world would kill to be me right now,* he thought. He knew how lucky he was to be in a hotel room with a perfect young pop star stood before him in her underwear wanting nothing more than to bed him, but somehow he just didn't want to be there, he'd have happily given up his place to any one of those guys.

She climbed onto the bottom of the bed and crawled her way up to him, she looked right into his eyes. Nothing. He was irritated, trying to fake some interest to get things over and done with. He looked back into hers but her eyes were empty, he felt absolutely nothing. She could have been anyone. She looked up at him with a sultry glance, sure she was hot, he could do this, and he had to do this. But he would be acting. His head was somewhere else. She straddled him, pushing her small perfectly round breasts into his face and circling her hips into his lap, he turned his head a little to breathe!

She could tell he wasn't into this; she slumped down into his lap and leaned back so she could see his face.

"Are you okay?" she asked, looking confused by his behaviour and general demeanour. She knew he was losing interest. She felt sick in the pit of her stomach, she loved this guy so much! She'd wanted him from afar for so long but never thought in a million years he would want to date her. She knew how lucky she was, he was so popular, there were a million other girls who would kill to spend a night with him. She couldn't lose him.

"Yeah," replied Dex, with a fake smile.

"You sure? Because we don't have to do this," she added.

"Nah, Luc. It's cool, I'm good," he lied. It was too late to back out; Dex knew he would have to take over now to make it believable. He took his mind off somewhere else. Lucie was still straddling him sat on the bed. He took a deep breath and put his arms around the bottom of her back, pulling her in closer to him. Lyrics began to fill his head, it was always situations like this that discovered the best new songs.

Man, it feels good to have his hands on me, thought Lucie. She could feel goose bumps all over her body with every touch of his hands. She closed her eyes and tipped her head back, pushing her breasts into his face again.

Dex was elsewhere in his head, he had the ability to escape his own body and get lost in his own mind when he didn't want to be somewhere. He was mechanical as he ran his hands up her back to her bra. He unhooked it and let it fall into his lap. Lucie put her finger under his chin and tilted his face up to kiss her. He tried hard to fake enthusiasm, he didn't want to hurt her or make her feel awkward.

This has to be over quick, he thought, lifting Lucie off his lap. He laid her down on the bed and knelt beside her and unbuttoned his jeans. He looked at her and he wished he hadn't. She looked so beautiful, so sexy, she had a look on her face that just a few months ago drove him wild. Back then he would look at her in bed and see everything he wanted. *How time changes things,* he thought. Tonight, instead all he saw was a stranger, just a vulnerable young girl. She looked younger than ever and he had never felt so old.

He climbed on top of her and nestled his head into her neck, her hair smelled so sweet. He couldn't look at her, he'd give the game away for sure. He kissed her neck as he felt her soft, warm hands slide up and down his bare back.

With every downward stroke she pushed his jeans down a little further, as she pushed her hips up into him she could feel him through his jeans.

He was getting uncomfortable. He knelt up and pulled down his jeans, Lucie watched with anticipation. It had been so long since she had seen his body, her eyes followed down as he slipped his jeans off. She felt a wave of excitement spread through her body, she grabbed him and pulled him back down on top of her. Her breathing was erratic, she tried to calm herself down but couldn't catch her breath, making her lungs hurt until she managed to relax her clenched muscles enough to exhale. All that was between her and her gorgeous rock star boyfriend was the thin material of their underwear, she could feel every inch of him… literally!

Every time Lucie had slept with Dex in the past all she could think of was the hundreds of girls who screamed for him at his shows, just longing for a smile from him or a touch of his hand. She was smug. He was hers, or at least he was for now. As he circled his hips down into her she could hear his heavy breathing right next to her ear. She put her hands round him and pushed herself up as she pulled him forcefully closer to her.

"I want you," she whispered in his ear as she tugged at his boxers to get him to take them off.

He lifted his head from her shoulder and smiled at her. Pushing himself up on one hand, he used the other to take off his boxers and relaxed back down on top of her. She felt his warm body against hers. *God, I've missed you! This!* she thought. Her mind wandered again back to the millions of girls that would kill to be underneath Dex Rose right now. She wanted this moment to last as long as it could.

Dex reached down and pulled down Lucie's knickers, trying to hurry things along and get it over with. He knew he would be quick, in a couple of minutes it would be over and he knew this was the very last time he was going to sleep with her. He was going to end it. Sure he was turned on, his heart was pumping, but not for her. He tried not to make eye contact with her, to avoid kissing her. He could fuck her, it was just an act, he could switch off his emotions from it, but kissing her was different, it was too personal. *Man up! Just do it,* he told himself. He pushed himself up with one hand and guided himself in. Lucie gasped.

CHAPTER 4

Thursday morning had taken forever to arrive! Millie turned over in bed.

"Arrgh! Fuck sake!" she exclaimed. The morning sunlight shone right into her eyes through the gap between the curtains as it did every morning. With her head buried in her pillow she felt around on her nightstand for her phone and pulled it under the duvet. *6 am! Yes! Another two hours in bed!* she thought. She was off to Milan today; Ricco was picking her up at 9am. She turned over, brushing her long dark hair off her face. As she thought ahead to her trip, she couldn't help but smile. It was her dream to be a successful fashion designer and with her dream so close to becoming reality her stomach tingled with butterflies.

She leaned over the side of her bed, almost falling out, and grabbed her sparkly pink portfolio folder from the floor beside her bed. Browsing through her designs she was confident, she knew they were good and if Mr Salvatore thought they were worthy of a trip to Milan, they had to be pretty special. She couldn't wait to see the prototypes when they arrived in Milan.

Millie was completely lost in thought thinking about her trip. Her phone beeped and she jumped, tipping all the pages from her portfolio onto the floor. Hanging on for dear life to the few pages she had managed to save, she glanced down at her phone beside her:

TWITTER: @_MillieV Milan baby! See you soon! Ri xxx #MilsandRiRiDoMilan!

Millie smiled; she could hear Ricco's excitable voice in her head as she read the tweet to herself.

9am arrived far too quickly after turning her bedroom upside down, packing and unpacking several times. She was just about ready as she heard Ricco pull up. He beeped. A lot! In a rather flamboyant tune. Millie giggled, rushing down the stairs.

"Come on, girl!" he yelled from his utterly gorgeous white Lamborghini Gallardo. The roof was down, his Louis Vuitton suitcases sticking up out of the seat. He looked every bit the millionaire!

"I'm coming, I'm coming," she yelled back struggling out the door with her arms full, dragging a dishevelled suitcase behind her.

"Bye, Ambs," she shouted as she pulled the door shut with her foot. Bags on both arms, keys hanging out her mouth, pulling her suitcase behind she hurried down the path trying not to fall over.

"Morning, gorgeous," said Ricco, blowing her a kiss as she approached the car.

"Hey," she smiled, playfully catching the kiss and planting it on her lips, dropping everything in her arms at the same time. Ricco laughed, she had to be the clumsiest person he had ever met!

"Oh FUCK," she exclaimed, as she bent down to pick up her bags.

"You need to wash your mouth out young lady… and then invest in a new suitcase, love!" he joked as she threw her old, tatty looking suitcase into the boot of his car. "A hot shot designer can't be seen with a scabby looking thing like that!" he added, giving her a cheeky wink. "Plus I don't want it in my car!" he joked.

Millie slapped him on the arm. "It's not scabby! It's... erm, well-travelled," she replied with a grin.

"So... excited then? Miss big fashion designer," he teased.

Millie rolled her eyes at him. "Shut up," she replied.

"Nah but seriously, Mil, they're going to love your designs, babe! I guarantee you'll have 'em on the shelves in Milan before the summer is out!" he exclaimed.

"I WISH!" Millie replied. She hadn't allowed herself to really think about it all. She was worried about being disappointed and having her bags on sale in shops around the world was a dream, it wasn't reality. It was never going to be real until she could see it for herself.

Ricco dropped Millie off at the terminal and went to park the car. As she approached the doors she saw Mr Salvatore.

"Hi, Mr Salvatore." Millie waved to him as she approached the terminal.

"Ah, Amelie," he smiled, throwing his arms out to hug her. He was the only person she could tolerate using proper name, she loved how it sounded in his Italian accent.

"Are you looking forward to this?" he asked, putting a friendly arm around her shoulder. The Italians were always so affectionate. Millie liked it, it made her feel like part of the family.

"Yeah, totally!" she replied as she turned to see Ricco coming up behind her.

"Hello, Son," said Mr Salvatore, leaning in to give Ricco a hug. "Right, let's go!" He gestured for them to follow him.

Inside, the terminal was heaving, it was the beginning of the Easter holidays and it seemed everyone and their dogs were flying today. Millie looked at her watch as they joined the back of a very long queue to check in. 10.07am.

She hated the long wait at the airport, she wasn't the most patient person but at least she had Ricco there. She was dying to tell him about Friday night and what happened at the gig but no matter how many times she ran it through her head she couldn't make it sound like anything other than she was a crazy, celebrity-obsessed groupie with a schoolgirl crush! *Best keep quiet,* she thought.

Eventually they were all checked in and went to get a coffee. As they sat down in the coffee shop Mr Salvatore's phone rang. He wandered off talking in an Italian accent, which gave Millie and Ricco a bit of time to gossip. Ricco came over with the coffees and sat down beside Millie on the sofa. She smiled as he slid her coffee in front of her.

"Thanks, baby," she said, rubbing his knee.

"Haven't even asked you about Craze yet!" said Ricco. "Were they as good live? More importantly, are they as hot live? You gave Jesse my number, right?" he joked and winked at Millie.

Millie smiled, though she wished he hadn't asked. Now she was going to have to lie, something she absolutely hated doing with Ricco. "Yeah, it was good," she replied, avoiding eye contact and taking a sip of her coffee, hoping he wouldn't ask anything else.

"Just good?" he asked, slightly confused by her lack of enthusiasm. He knew how much she was looking forward to it and how much she loved the band. He'd had to listen to her talk about Dex Rose a million times, though he didn't mind, honestly he'd have sold a kidney for a night with Dex himself!

"Umm… no it was amazing, we just weren't very close to the front so I was a bit disappointed," she lied. In reality she'd been so close she could have reached out and touched him!

"That sucks," he replied. Millie hoped that was it.

"So what is Mr Loverboy like in the flesh?" Ricco asked.

"Uhhhh…" she started, but was cut off by Mr Salvatore as he came to join them at the table.

"Sorry, work call," he said as he took a sip of his coffee. Millie breathed a sigh of relief as Mr Salvatore began to talk work with Ricco. She was off the hook. For now.

On the plane Millie was bored, both Ricco and Mr Salvatore were asleep. She switched her phone on to browse her Twitter feed. She did the same as she always did and read through Craze's latest tweets first,:

@CRAZETHEBAND on tour bus heading for Milan!

OMG! They're in Milan too! Just the thought of being in the same city was forcing her to over-breathe with excitement, bordering hyperventilation. She had to text Cate, she would be so jealous!

Cate! Guess who's in Milan too?....Dex! Eeeeeeeeeek! Mils xx

As she sent the text from the plane she secretly hoped that her text didn't bring the plane down! It was worth the risk. Sweeping her hair away from her face she put her phone in her lap and relaxed back into her chair. She closed her eyes for a minute and lost herself in thought, thoughts about Dex. She was more excited about being in the same city as him than she was about her bags being in Milan.

Suddenly she sat bolt upright in her seat. *Oh my god, if they're in Milan, that'll mean a show…. TICKETS!* she thought as she frantically grabbed for her phone to search the internet.

What?! Millie was trying to bring up a web page to search for tickets but the page wouldn't load. She had no internet signal on the plane. *FUCK!* She was getting frustrated, she knew she would have to wait until they arrived in Milan, but she had no patience. She tried to sit back in her chair and relax but she felt really agitated. The next hour was going to feel like forever!

After a long day of travelling the tour bus pulled into the underground car park at the five-star Milan Grande Hotel.

"Ah a night off feels good," said Zach, packing up his stuff for a rest in a nice hotel for a change. Most nights on tour were spent on the cramped tour bus so it was a real luxury to be staying in a hotel. They weren't playing Milan until tomorrow night so they had a rare day off. Mac had booked them all into a fancy hotel for Dex's parents' last night before they flew back home to the States.

Dex grabbed his parents' bags from them and carried them off the bus. The underground car park was quiet and no one was around. They followed him into the car park elevator.

"CJ, Jess, Zach, go with Dex and his parents, we will follow with Lucie in a minute," instructed Mac. He gestured for one of his security guys to accompany the band into the elevator, as he and three other security guys stayed behind to escort Lucie into the hotel. Mac hated that Lucie was with them, her fame was more than he and his small team of security could handle, with having to look after the guys at the same time.

The elevator opened into a busy mid-morning hotel reception. Zach stepped out of the elevator and he was immediately recognised, fans began to approach him asking for autographs and photos. Dex fought through the growing crowds and took his parents over to the reception desk whilst Jesse assisted Zach in distracting the fans with photos and autographs. With his parents safely with hotel staff at the desk, Dex knew Lucie was about to be mobbed. He moved away from the elevator across to the other side of reception and started to sign things and pose for photos, something he absolutely hated and rarely ever indulged in. He kept one eye on the elevator.

As the doors opened Mac snuck Lucie in and straight to the stairwell. Seeing that she was safely inside, Dex made his excuses.

"Sorry guys," he said, handing a pen back to a fan. He began to push his way through the crowds with Zach and Jesse, closely followed by three large men from their security team. His parents followed as they made their way to another elevator that led to the upstairs floors. The doors shut and he could finally relax for a minute. As the doors reopened on the 8th floor, Mac was there waiting.

"821 and 822," said Mac, handing Zach the keys to the rooms.

"803," said Mac, handing Dex his key.

"Thanks, man," he replied, sounding really tired. Mac could tell this was all really taking a toll on him. He was glad everyone was flying home in the morning, Dex just wasn't himself. "I'll show your parents to their room, go get some rest," said Mac.

Dex patted Mac on the shoulder appreciatively; he kissed his mother on the cheek. "See you guys later," he said as he turned away and walked down the corridor to his room. He felt a slight relief that Lucie was leaving tomorrow, but also gutted that his parents were too. He hadn't really spent any time with them and they were leaving again!

"Oh my goodness! This place is amazing!" Millie exclaimed, looking up at the front of the hotel. It was the poshest hotel she had ever seen! The shiny marble driveway circled a big water fountain with intermittent coloured lights in the water, the entire front of the building was glass and she could see through into the luxurious foyer, all decked out in gold furnishings with huge marble pillars.

As she followed Mr Salvatore and Ricco inside she was met with a stream of water that ran through reception, filled with tiny fish. Millie had never seen anything like it. She started to wish she had brought a nicer suitcase! She looked very out of place amongst the other guests waiting at reception all dressed smartly with designer luggage. Mr Salvatore was a regular, he didn't even need to check them in. Instead a member of staff came straight over to them, took their bags and showed them up to their suites. Mr Salvatore had his own, Millie and Ricco were sharing.

As they approached the door to their suite, Millie caught a glimpse of the dark-haired guy staying in the room next door as he turned to close his door. Probably a super-hot Italian, there were tons of them everywhere. She was in heaven!

"Here we go, babe, 804," said Ricco, holding the door open for her.

"Welcome to Ri Ri's boudoir," he joked in his sexy Italian accent, lifting his shirt to reveal his gorgeous tanned six-pack.

"Why did you have to be gay?" Millie replied, gently scratching her nails down his stomach as she dragged her suitcase past him into the room. She stopped, she could hear a couple arguing next door.

"Awesome," she sighed, just what she wanted to listen to all night!

"Urgh, they're English," she said, trying to listen in to their argument through the wall. "Thought I had me a nice Italian stallion next door," she joked.

"Lucky you got one in here then," teased Ricco, lying down and rubbing the bed suggestively. He laughed. She flopped down onto the super king size bed next to him. He put his arms around her and she nestled her head into his chest, his big arms felt so strong and protective.

"I'm nervous about tomorrow," she confessed.

"Nervous about what, babe?" Ricco pulled back from her so he could see her face. Her big brown Bambi eyes looked deep into his.

"What if they hate it all? Your dad will have wasted a trip, money, time on me," she explained quietly, biting her lip.

"Stop it! Enough woe is me! You have nothing to worry about." He gave her a reassuring squeeze.

There were moments like these every now and again when

he wished he wasn't gay too. He knew if he was straight he would have fallen in love with Millie a long time ago. She was absolutely everything to him, he loved her to bits, but he knew it wasn't in the right kind of way. He WAS gay and he knew 100% he couldn't give her what she needed. He knew he needed to get out of his thoughts; he'd been here many, many times before! He jumped up off the bed, before his thoughts led him somewhere he would regret, letting Millie fall into the huge fluffy pillows.

"Now come on, we've got the night to ourselves, let's get ready to party... Italian style!" said Ricco. He leaned over and kissed her on the forehead, then opened the wardrobe to unpack.

Millie turned onto her belly and wriggled into a comfy position hugging the pillow. She text her mum to let her know she had arrived and that the hotel was amazing. She opened her Twitter feed and as always checked out Craze's latest tweets. Jesse had tweeted a picture of himself with Dex and some fans. She stared at Dex in the photo for several minutes, wondering where he was right now. She didn't take her eyes off him for a second, only to realise that the background was the foyer of the hotel she was in!

Ricco pulled out a dress bag from his suitcase. "I've got a little something for you, princess!" he said, pulling Millie up off the bed. Standing behind her he unzipped the dress bag to reveal a very expensive looking red lace dress.

"Oh my god! That's gorgeous!" Millie touched the dress, it even felt expensive! "I can't wear that!" she sighed, turning to see Ricco's face. "I don't have the figure for it," she announced.

"Don't be ridiculous, you're wearing it!" Ricco stated. "I had Giorgio make it especially for you for your big break," he added.

"ARMANI!?" exclaimed Millie, turning around to face him in astonishment.

"No, Giorgio Jones! Of course Armani!" he said sarcastically.

"Oh my goodness, thank you so much!" she gushed, throwing her arms around his neck and planting a huge kiss on his lips.

"You're welcome," he smiled back at her.

As they were about to leave the room for dinner Millie stood in front of the full-length mirror on the back of the door and just looked at her reflection for a minute. For once there was no arguing, she looked absolutely beautiful. The dress looked amazing and hugged her curvaceous figure. She wasn't skinny, she had her mother's hips! But she didn't mind that. She embraced it; it was part of being a woman. It was rare she liked what she saw in the mirror but on this occasion she knew she looked good. Her skin was glowing and her dark smoky eye makeup made her hazel brown eyes a little more mysterious. She wished Dex could see her now.

Ricco came up behind her and put his arms around her waist. He rested his chin on her shoulder and looked in the mirror.

"You've never looked so beautiful," he whispered in her ear. A smile crept across her face, as cheesy as he was no one ever made her feel as good as he did.

"Can I marry you?" she moaned. He was so sweet; she knew he was right, she had never felt so good either.

Ricco linked arms with her . . .

"Let's own the night!" said Ricco as he escorted her down to dinner. Millie still didn't really know what that meant but she couldn't have been happier on the arm of her best friend, who happened to be a drop dead gorgeous Italian millionaire, and on top of that she was about to have dinner in the poshest hotel she'd even stayed in on the eve of the biggest day of her career so far. Dex was a million miles from her mind right now. She reached across and pinched Ricco.

"Ouch! What the…?" he yelped.

Millie smiled. "Just checking this is real," she replied. Ricco smiled and kissed her forehead.

CHAPTER 5

Dex and Lucie got out of the cab and hurried inside the Italian restaurant, followed by Ben, an ex-boxer and part of their security entourage. They were late! They'd spent most of the evening bickering about nothing of any importance. Dex was exhausted and couldn't be bothered with any of it. Lucie had ruined his last night with his parents. As he looked around the restaurant for everyone they were all already sat at the table, he hurried over with Lucie trailing behind. He didn't even give her a second thought, though he knew she was safe and that Ben was behind.

"So sorry guys... I fell asleep," he lied as he sat down next to his mum. She kissed him on his forehead.

"Don't worry love, you're here now," she smiled at him.

The band's bodyguards stood around the table to stop fans disturbing them and to give them a bit of peace and privacy.

"So, where are you off to next, sweetheart?" asked Dex's mom.

"Erm, Paris next then the UK, then I'm coming home for a few weeks, then back out here for four months," Dex explained.

"Oh fabulous love! I shall look forward to you coming

home," she said, stroking his forearm affectionately. She was incredibly proud but she missed her little boy.

Their meals arrived quickly, Lucie was glad. She hadn't said a word all evening, there was a horrible atmosphere between her and Dex and she felt really awkward. She couldn't wait to leave, but at the same time was dreading leaving as she could see dozens of paparazzi at the windows, she really wasn't in the mood for it.

Dex looked at her and noticed her staring at the window. He knew she would be nervous about leaving, she had some crazy fans that quite often scared her. She was only young, it was a lot to deal with. His anger towards her subsided a little, replaced with sympathy. He felt like it was his duty protect her, whether he wanted to or not. He could hear his mom in his head. She would have wanted him to be a gentleman and take care of her.

He put his hand on her knee under the table. It surprised her, she turned to him and smiled.

"I'm sorry," he silently mouthed to her and she squeezed his hand in acceptance. The air immediately felt better, Lucie relaxed into her chair.

Mac went through the next day's schedule whilst they were all together.

"Jess, you have a new guitar arriving from New York in the morning, so I need you at sound check early to make sure it's ready. 9am okay?" he asked.

"Uh huh," replied Jesse with a mouthful of food.

"The rest of you," Mac continued, "10am lobby call for sound check, Ben will let you know later who will be collecting each of you." The guys all nodded in agreement.

"Lucie." She looked up at Mac. "Your security team are flying in in the morning to escort you home, we just don't have the man power here to do it." Mac was massively relieved they were coming and that soon she would no longer be his problem!

"Oh. Okay," said Lucie. That was a pretty normal thing in her life.

They were coming to the end of their meal; Mac began to organise their exit. Several security men were sent outside to organise a clear route to the car. The entire restaurant were looking at them, they caused such a scene wherever they went. Nothing was ever low key! One of them radioed to Mac, the coast was clear. Jesse went out first with Ben holding onto the collar of his jacket, followed seconds later by Zach. Dex could hear the crowds scream as they emerged outside, it was deafening, it sounded as if there were hundreds out there, he knew most would have been there for Lucie! Lucie felt really nervous. Dex took off his denim jacket and put it over her head, he put his arm around her and walked over to the door. Mac went ahead with four bodyguards following behind Dex and Lucie. As Lucie stepped outside the crowds went crazy! For the band too but mostly for her, she was massive in Italy; she rushed to the car and got in quickly. Now Lucie was safely in the car Dex walked back over to join Jesse and Zach signing autographs, he didn't want to be alone with Lucie in the car, he knew it would result in him having to explain his hot and cold behaviour. He wasn't in the mood to talk.

"Another mojito, babe?" asked Ricco.

"Nah, I'll never get up in the morning!" replied Millie, leaning back on her chair. "I'm stuffed! This dress is never coming off!" she exclaimed, rubbing her stomach.

"Ha! We'll cut it off, don't worry!" he laughed.

"Not a chance you're taking a pair of scissors to my Armani, boy!" Millie replied.

"C'mon, it's midnight. Let's call it a night, babe, big day for you tomorrow," Ricco held out his hand to help her up. Pulling her chair out for her he led her out of the restaurant.

Walking across the foyer to the elevators there was suddenly a lot of commotion around the corner, it sounded like a big, loud group of people had just come into the hotel.

"They sound like they've had a good night out," smiled Ricco.

"Yeah," Millie quietly replied, feeling a little nervous and curious to see what was going on.

The elevator opened and she stepped in followed by Ricco. As the doors closed Millie caught a glimpse of the loud group of people. It wasn't quite what she expected. Instead of a group of drunken young people, she saw an older couple dressed smartly, arm in arm. As the doors closed completely she didn't manage to see the rest of the group.

Feeling tired, she leaned against Ricco and he kissed her forehead. She closed her eyes. She'd had a few drinks and could so easily take him to bed right now! And not in the 'best friend' way they were about to, sometimes sleeping next to him was torture! He was utterly perfect.

As the elevator opened onto their floor so did the elevator next to it. It was the noisy group from the foyer, there were loads of them spilling out of the lift.

"Trust the noisy ones to be on our floor!" Millie whispered. Ricco smiled. They stepped out of the elevator and turned to walk down the corridor to their room. Millie looked over her shoulder; the noisy group were saying their goodnights to each other.

In front of the elevators, a couple had broken

away from the group and were heading down the opposite corridor.

"Hopefully they're all down the other end," said Millie, turning back around as they approached their door.

Dex and Lucie said their goodnights to everyone and headed down the corridor, Dex was usually the loudest and stayed up the latest! But tonight he was thankful his room was the other end of the corridor, he felt physically and emotionally drained and was looking forward to a good night's sleep. As he turned to walk down the corridor he caught a glimpse of the couple going into the room next door. The girl looked stunning in a red lace dress, her long dark hair trailing softly down her back. Judging by the god-like guy she was with she was way out of Dex's league! They looked every bit the perfect couple.

Feeling a little inadequate Dex leaned over and kissed Lucie in an attempt to make his ego feel a little better.

Ricco held the door open for Millie. She took one last glance down the corridor and stopped for a second. *Was it?* She screwed her face up in an attempt to get a better focus, she'd had one too many! As Dex looked up from his kiss he caught a split second view of the girl's face as she stepped into her room. Ricco closed the door behind them.

Dex stopped dead in the corridor.

"Are you alright?" asked Lucie. Dex didn't say a word. He just stared blankly ahead. *Nah, it couldn't be, could it?*

After a few seconds he shook it off and walked to the door, opening it. He gestured for Lucie to go first and he had one last look out in the corridor, no one was there. He shut the door.

Millie kicked off her heels and opened up the glass doors to the balcony. She stepped outside and the cold, hard floor took her breath away, as did the view. Ricco followed behind carrying a huge bottle of champagne and two glasses. Millie leaned against the railing.

"Woah!" The view over Milan was absolutely stunning, she thought about how romantic it was but her attention was suddenly taken away by the sound of the doors opening onto the balcony next door. She listened. She heard a man and a woman talking quietly. *How nice it must be to be here as a couple,* thought Millie. They walked over to the railings and she caught a glimpse of them as they looked out at the city.

A young girl stood with her back to Millie, she couldn't really see the guy behind her. They were laughing and joking and seemed to be enjoying their night. Millie smiled to herself, how lovely. The blonde-haired girl moved out of sight revealing the man behind her. Millie looked straight at him for a split second and he looked right at her. Embarrassed, she quickly looked away; she didn't want to seem like a nosey neighbour.

It took a few moments to register in her head.

Then....

Her heart stopped!

She looked straight back.

"Oh my fucking god!" she muttered under her breath. She felt excitement like she'd never felt before, her body ached all over. Her mouth had gone dry and the lump that had formed in her throat made it hard to swallow. A hot sweat consumed her entire body. She was face to face with Dexter Rose! He was looking right back at her, what was only a couple of seconds seemed to last ages. Time stood still, the world fell away. His smile immediately disappeared and was replaced with a serious face.

It was her!

Millie was frozen to the spot. He recognised her, she knew he did. She felt exactly the same as she did back at the gig in her hometown. He did something to her.

The blonde girl came back and looked over at Millie, curious as to what Dex was looking at. *It was Lucie Goldham!.... But....What? He was with LUCIE GOLDHAM?!* Millie was confused, she suddenly snapped back into reality and her butterflies turned to a sick feeling. *He's dating her?!* Millie thought to herself. She felt utterly devastated. She assumed he was single, seeing him with a girl was heart wrenching. Especially a pop star.

Dex just stared. It was her! *Impossible,* he thought, but it WAS her, he was transported back to exactly how he felt at the gig.

The exact same feeling washed over his body; numb all over, his palms were sweaty. He wiped his hair from his wet forehead and licked his lips, his mouth was so dry and he could feel his heart beating in his throat. After a few seconds Lucie interrupted.

"Come on, babe!" she said, grabbing his hand and pulling him back inside. Reluctantly he followed, looking back the entire time. Millie heard the doors slam. He was gone.

Millie turned around to find Ricco stood right in front of her.

"What the hell was that?" he asked, looking confused as to what he just witnessed. "That was Dex Rose wasn't it?" he asked.

"I don't think so," she lied, trying to act casual and brush it off.

"It sure looked like him. Well, whoever it was I saw the way he looked at you! Think you're in there hot mama," he teased.

"Don't be ridiculous," she smiled, knowing he could always see through her lies. She was completely devastated; she was having such a good time with Ricco that she hadn't given it a second thought that Craze were even in Milan! How could she possibly sleep tonight knowing Dex was just the other side of the wall? With Lucie Goldham! She felt angry, angry with herself for feeling the way she did. She wished she didn't like him at all.

She grabbed the bottle of champagne off the table and downed it, slamming the bottle back down on the table.

"Woah girl, steady!" laughed Ricco.

Millie burst into tears. She always got emotional when she drank.

"Oh, Mils." Ricco was utterly confused but he stepped towards her and pulled her head into his chest. She sobbed her heart out into him, soaking through his shirt. He put his hands in her silky hair and rubbed the back of her head. He had no idea what had just gone on. He knew he had missed something. Somewhere.

"Baby, what's wrong?" he asked. He gently lifted her chin from his chest so he could see her face. He wiped the tears from her cheeks.

Millie looked into his eyes; she could see so much love in them. She was looking at him like she had done 1000 times but this time she felt different. She didn't know if it was just the alcohol or because she was emotional and jealous of Lucie. She pressed her body up against his and kissed him on the lips.

Ricco thought nothing of it. They were best friends, they kissed each other all the time, except this time Millie lingered on his bottom lip. She had shut her eyes. He had no idea what Millie wanted him to do, it was as if she was waiting for him to kiss back. They kissed a lot, but they never *'KISSED'*, not like that. They were best friends and he was gay!

Ricco didn't respond. Millie opened her eyes. She kissed him again, pushing herself closer into him. Ricco realised what she was doing.

"Millie," he whispered into her ear in a

disapproving tone. She slid her hand up under his shirt and ran it down his perfect, muscular chest, digging her nails in slightly. She stopped at the top of his trousers and attempted to undo the button. Ricco grabbed her hand

"Baby, what are you doing?" he whispered in her ear again. He was beginning to feel really turned on. She looked up into his eyes.

"I love you, Ri," she said, still sounding completely choked up. She had tears in her eyes.

"I love you too, babe, but this isn't right," he replied quietly.

With him still restraining her hand, she took her other

hand and pushed him up against the balcony wall. Dutch courage had most definitely kicked in. She was rarely the dominant one in the bedroom. It just wasn't her. She liked the power and strength of a man.

"MILLIE!" he said, his tone more firm this time, a final attempt to stop her. "Babes, come on. You know this won't end well." He grabbed both her wrists and pulled her arms up around his neck, attempting to defuse the situation.

"You've been with girls, I know you have," she replied, wriggling her arms free of his grip to start unbuttoning his shirt.

Ricco sighed. This was wrong, really wrong. Nothing good could come from this going any further but she was right, he had slept with girls in the past. He certainly knew what he was doing and he was beginning to find it hard to resist. She was absolutely stunning, he could feel himself getting hard. He knew it was too late to stop this. Passion took over, he took a deep breath and grabbed her, picking her up as she wrapped her legs around his waist. He was so strong and overpowering, exactly what Millie needed. He carried her inside, passionately kissing her all the way in. They had never been like this together before and they were both surprised by how right it felt. It was as if five years of sexual tension had finally been released. Holding her with one arm he turned down the lights a little and gently laid her down on the bed, he didn't stop kissing her even for a moment. He laid down on top of her, he was surprised by how intensely passionate it was. He had never felt that with a girl before, it was usually only men that made him feel that way.

He reached down and pulled Millie's dress up and off over her head.

All Millie could think about was Dex… probably doing the same thing with Lucie! She knew this was wrong, their friendship might never be the same, but right now she just wanted him to make her feel better.

As she lay there in front of him in her pretty pink underwear, he knelt up in front of her and just stared at her for a few seconds. His heart wanted to rip that underwear off her and make love to her, he wanted to give her every bit of him and he knew she wanted it but his head was telling him to stop here before it went too far. But by this time, it HAD gone too far, he had to have her now.

Ricco leaned down and put his hands under her, undoing her bra. Millie wasn't surprised by how confident he was, she knew he would be. She had often wondered what he would be like in bed, never thinking for a minute she would get to find out. He really knew what he was doing, more than any straight man she'd ever been with.

This was it; he was about to cross a line taking her bra off. He felt nervous, but was careful not to show it. Slowly he slid her bra down her stomach, he surprised himself as a wave of pleasure shot down through his body as he revealed her perfect breasts. He leaned down and kissed them, slowly kissing his way down her smooth stomach. His nerves were really kicking in now, it had been a long time since he had been with a woman. He knelt back up before her and looked her in the eyes as she took off her underwear, he kept his gaze fixed firmly on her face, it felt wrong to look anywhere else. He gave her a cheeky wink to acknowledge what she'd just done and she smiled. She had an amazing body but it felt strange to see her naked. She tugged at the waistband of his trousers for him to take them off. He got up off the bed, Millie couldn't take her eyes off him, every inch of his dark-skinned, perfectly formed torso rivalled that of one of those male models from a fragrance commercial. He could certainly give some of Giorgio's male models a run for their money, with his rock hard abs framed by his broad manly shoulders. Ricco was blessed with his body, he ate what he wanted, he was allergic to the gym, and the only weight he'd ever lifted was a bottle of champagne! He was one of those who was just born with good genes, something Millie thought the Italians were all blessed with.

She watched intently as Ricco unbuttoned his trousers and dropped them to the floor. He stood there, his black, designer boxer shorts evidently bulging! Millie had seen him in his boxers a million times but he looked different to her than he ever had before. She was about to see him naked, her body tingled all over with anticipation. Instead of taking off his boxers Ricco laid back down beside her, then propped himself up and looked down at her. He leaned in and kissed her neck and gently brushed her hair away from her face. He took a deep breath in an attempt to calm himself down.

"Mil, this is wrong, babe," he said softly.

Her smile quickly faded. She knew he was right but she wanted him so badly. She'd had a moment to calm down, he was right. She suddenly felt very aware that she was naked and very vulnerable. He pulled her in close and she nestled her head into his chest. She felt silly, her eyes welled up a little. Her head was a mess!

"You've got a big day tomorrow, you don't want this on your mind," Ricco added. He was right. He got up and turned the lights off and she heard him drop his boxers to the floor, she felt a bit gutted that it was too dark to see anything. He had never ever slept naked with her. He climbed into bed and pulled the covers up over them both. She knew he had taken his boxers off to put her at ease. He pulled Millie in close to him, snuggling into her naked body. She could feel him pressed hard up against her stomach, She smiled to herself. A naked cuddle would do. Exhausted, she fell asleep in his arms.

Ricco lay wide awake, it felt odd to feel Millie's naked body. He had crossed a line but it had taken every bit of his willpower not to go through with it and cross another line that could never be undone. He felt weird; his head was all over the place. The events of tonight were going over and over in his mind. He was gay, he'd known he was gay since he was 17! But he lay there wanting nothing more than to wake her up and resume what Millie had started. He still felt intensely turned on, he was still pulsating against her bare stomach and there was absolutely nothing he could do about it. He wondered what had gone on tonight, what had he missed out on the balcony. Was it Dex she had seen next door? And if it was, what had he said to her to spark this? What had gotten her so emotional and what had made her want to sleep with him? It just wasn't her. They had got drunk together a thousand times and slept in a bed together, but not once had Millie ever tried anything with him.

Dex had so many unanswered questions going around in his head. It was going to be a long night!

"What was that out there?" asked Lucie. "Why were you staring at that couple? Did you know them?"

"Oh, I, erm… thought I knew the dude, I've seen him somewhere before," lied Dex.

"Oh," replied Lucie. She seemed satisfied with his answer. She slipped out of her dress and walked over to the window in her underwear, looking out of the window at the city lights. She pulled out her hair grips and shook her head, letting her silky long blonde hair fall down onto her bare shoulders.

"I'm going to sleep, babe, early flight tomorrow," she said as she walked back over to the bed.

Ah good, thought Dex, she wasn't going to want sex. "Alright, darlin'" he replied. He kissed her on her forehead. He felt guilty for what just happened on the balcony. Whatever it was.

"I'm going to sit out on the balcony so I don't disturb you," he said, turning out the lights for her and opening the sliding doors. He stood at the railing and looked out over the city, it looked beautiful, the night was aglow with tiny twinkling lights. It was quiet.

"Ahhh," he sighed. The silence was bliss. He sat down on

a chair on the balcony and pulled his phone from his pocket. Lyrics to a song were starting to flow into his mind, he had to write it down. As he began to hum the melody in his head and write down lyrics he heard the sliding doors open on the balcony next door. The girl's room.

He stopped completely still and listened intently. Was he about to hear her voice for the first time? He sat silently for a minute, then heard a man's voice, he was on the phone. Dex listened and heard him speak with an Italian accent. Was this guy her boyfriend? HUSBAND?!

"Yes, 8am please, Ricco Salvatore." Dex overheard Ricco booking a cab. Dex stood up and pretended to be looking out at the city, he glanced over to their balcony and made eye contact with Ricco.

It WAS Dex Rose! Everything suddenly made a little more sense to Ricco. Not expecting to see anyone out on the balcony at 3am, it suddenly dawned on him that he was naked! He quickly went back inside.

Dex immediately Googled the name. He clicked on the first link, Wikipedia, and read the first few lines:

Ricco Michele Salvatore, born 18th August 1984. Italian fashion designer and son of millionaire design-house owner Franco Giuseppe Salvatore. Best known for high-profile relationship with England rugby star James Hart...

Ahhh, he's gay! thought Dex. He smiled to himself, he was relieved, but curious as to what was she doing here with him. He heard the sliding doors lock, then nothing.

Ricco crept back in, put his boxers on and slowly climbed back into bed, trying hard not to wake Millie.

"Ahhh," she sighed.

Ricco laughed. "Ya alright? I thought you were asleep?" he asked.

"Yeah, I was, but I'm glad I'm awake now, you're just so lovely to snuggle with," she replied, nestling into him a little more.

"Ha! You should be snuggling into fitty next door! So should I!" he joked.

"Yeah right! You saw him then?" she replied sheepishly, admitting defeat.

"Uh huh. I'm assuming tonight's little thang was inspired by our handsome lil' friend next door, right?"

Millie was silent.

"Maybe" she said quietly, feeling a little disappointed in herself by her own words. She felt guilty that she had used her best friend to try and make herself feel better.

"You'll be famous soon, babes, he'll be chasing you in no time!" Ricco assured her. He totally understood, he wasn't bothered at all, if he could have made her feel better he would have. "And I'll be fighting him off" he teased.

"Hardly! He's dating a pop star!" she announced.

He had a point. She laid silently thinking about it. In what seemed like a minute Ricco was snoring away. Millie carefully moved his arm and rolled onto her own side of the bed. There was no way she was going to be able to sleep tonight with Dex on the other side of the wall, no doubt having sex with Lucie! Plus she was nervous about the morning.

She picked up her phone from the nightstand and switched it on. The screen seemed so bright and she didn't want to wake Ricco so she got out of bed, grabbed Ricco's t-shirt from the floor and put it on. She snuck out onto the balcony. She leaned against the glass railing and looked out over the city.

"Wow," she whispered to herself, "how romantic!" The entire city was alight with hundreds of tiny twinkling lights. She took a photo with her phone and tweeted it. Moments like this needed to be documented.

@_MillieV: Crazy, odd night here in beautiful

Milan with Ri. Super nervous/excited for 2moro #fashionweek #dreams

Dex heard someone moving on the balcony next door, he sat silently listening for any clues as to who it was out there.

Nothing. He heard the sliding door open and close again. Whoever had been out there was gone.

He put his phone back in his pocket and put his feet up on the table. Looking out and listening to the sounds of the city by night was usually one his favourite things to do, it totally relaxed him and took away all of his stresses, but tonight he felt tense. The girl was a mystery, why was he so drawn to her? He didn't understand his feelings at all. His head was a mess. He'd never wanted to get involved with a fan, Zach and Jesse took random fans back to the tour bus and hotel rooms all the time but Dex just couldn't do it. Partly because of how he had been brought up and partly because he couldn't trust them. He had too much to lose, they all only wanted a night with a celebrity and to make money selling their story. They didn't want him, not really. And he wasn't going to give anyone the satisfaction of making money from him. He was a private person; he didn't want anyone to get close to him, to know him on a personal level and to be able to sell it to the world. It scared the hell out of him. He thought that fans should just appreciate the music; they didn't need to know him. Zach and Jesse didn't seem to mind though, they bedded girl after girl, making the most of their fame and the perks that came with it. Even CJ bedded his fair share and he wasn't even really part of the band, he just toured with them playing the drums for live shows since none of the guys could play drums. But despite the way he felt there was still something burning inside him to know this girl.

CHAPTER 6

As the cab pulled up Ricco held the big glass doors open for Millie.

"Thanks, babe," she smiled at him as she hurried past him, squeezing through the door with her bag on her shoulder and an armful of files and folders.

As usual she was running late. She struggled to navigate the steps in four-inch heels and a short dress with her arms full, concentrating so hard not to fall down. She didn't want her big day to start by falling down the steps in front of the cab driver and the general public! Chilled-out Ricco followed some way behind her.

She made it to the cab still in one piece, which was a triumph in itself for the clumsiest girl on the planet! Opening the door she threw all of her bags and files onto the back seat and turned to speak to Ricco but he was miles behind her.

"COME ON, RI!" she shouted. "You're going to make us late!" she added, getting more and more frustrated that he wasn't rushing. He laughed. He'd been awake all night and had been up ready for hours waiting for her. He casually strolled towards the cab sipping his coffee, his neatly pressed suit jacket draped over his other arm. His dark, tanned skin was glowing against his crisp white shirt which was only buttoned half way up revealing a tantalising bit of toned, tanned chest. He was such a show off!

Millie watched as he turned the heads of nearly every passing woman. He was every bit the Italian stallion.

"Take your fucking sunglasses off, can you see the sun? You look like a dick!" she teased, flashing him a cheeky smile. He laughed.

"Nice to see you're on form this early," he joked. Millie rolled her eyes as she climbed into the cab. Secretly she was pleased that the morning had been a big rush, it left no time for Ricco to bring up anything from the events of last night. Which after a heavy night of drinks she could barely remember!

Mr Salvatore emerged from the hotel with his PA and made his way down the steps to join them in the cab. He was immersed in telephone conversation as always, and the cab driver opened the door for him. He took the phone away from his ear, covering the mouthpiece with his hand.

"What do you call this? I expected a limousine!" he barked.

"Sorry, sir, this is what was booked," replied the cab driver. Mr Salvatore grumbled as he fell into the seat. Just what Millie wanted to deal with this morning, a grumpy Italian!

Mr Salvatore groaned as he struggled to turn around in the front seat to speak to Millie.

"Are you ready?" he asked her, straining his neck to see her.

"Yes, I think so," she replied nervously.

"Did you get a good night's sleep?" he asked.

"Err....yes," Millie replied sheepishly. *Apart from drinking excessively, crying my eyes out and trying to bed your son!* she thought to herself.

She had made herself feel really uncomfortable next to Ricco as she started to recall last night. As the cab pulled away she tried to take her mind off it by flicking through her portfolio. Ricco put his hand on hers to stop her turning the pages. With his other hand he shut the cover. She looked up at him.

"Relax. You're ready," he smiled.

She smiled back at him and put her files down on the seat beside her. She took a deep breath and tried to be calm. She was so nervous; her stomach was tangled in knots. Today was the biggest day of her career so far, this had to go well.

She looked out of the window, taking in the sights of the city as they made their way to the venue of Milan Fashion Week. *Don't let them ruin today,* she said to herself as thoughts of Dex and Lucie filled her head. They were living their glamorous life and today she was living hers, today was real life. Dex was a fantasy.

She could see the hotel in the distance where the event was being held. She was insanely nervous. It was nearly time! She pulled her bottle of water from her bag at her feet and took a sip, her mouth had gone completely dry and she started to feel dizzy.

As the cab approached the car park Millie saw how busy it was. Cars, limousines, coaches, filled the car park. It was bustling, people rushing around, carrying boxes and dress bags and piles of clothes.

"Oh my goodness, Ri, that's Leoni Mills, the supermodel!" said Millie, excitedly tugging on Ricco's sleeve. He laughed. Ricco had been to lots of these events where there were famous models and celebrities. This was Millie's first time at such a high-profile fashion event.

"Yes, babe, it is," he replied, rubbing her knee affectionately.

The car stopped outside of the main doors at the drop off point and Millie opened the car door, putting one foot down on the pavement and being careful not to flash her knickers to the paparazzi all situated in the doorway snapping people as they entered the hotel. Not an easy feat in a short black skater-style dress that flared from her waist, and killer red heels matching her bright red lips.

Ricco rushed around to her side of the car and held out his hand to help her out of the car. As she stepped out onto the pavement the wind blew her long dark hair up and she scrabbled to hold her dress down. It was a perfect Marilyn Monroe movie moment for the photographers.

Wow! thought Ricco, *she's stunning!* A small part of him wished he had gone through with it last night! He sometimes felt like he wanted to be more than friends, but he knew it would just complicate things if he acted on it, they had the perfect friendship. He hadn't been confused about his sexuality since he was a teenager but recently Millie had him questioning himself, she was really messing with his head. Millie usually shied away from attention but today she didn't mind the paparazzi taking photos. She felt confident, almost powerful. Not in her looks, no amount of compliments was ever going to take away her insecurities, but she was confident in what she was there to do. She was a *real* designer as of today and it gave her a new persona she didn't know she was capable of. She almost felt defiant towards Dex and Lucie. *If he wants Lucie, fine! It's his loss,* she told herself, not entirely believing it. In reality she was leagues above Lucie. Millie was a real woman, she was naturally beautiful, she would roll out of bed with no makeup on, hair a mess and still look beautiful. She was lucky. But she had no confidence in herself. She was quite shy, quiet and not overly social. She felt nervous being the centre of attention, but her recent successes at work and Ricco's constant support had given her a little more confidence to strive for what she wanted.

Mr Salvatore led the way with his PA, Ricco and Millie followed behind. Inside the hotel was just as manic, people rushing around everywhere, models half naked and staff with radios trying to organise the chaos. Each designer showing a collection had his or her own room to prepare in. A young girl showed them to Mr Salvatore's room where all his staff were already busy arranging the clothes and dressing the models. There was a big table in the middle with some of Millie's bags.

"Oh my god! RICCO, LOOK!" she grabbed him by the arm and pulled him over to the table, picking one of them up. "Eeeeeeeeeee," she squealed. It was the

first time she had seen her designs in the flesh, she'd only seen them on paper. And in her head. They had just come off the production line and were shipped straight to Milan for the show.

"They're gorgeous, babe" said Ricco, picking one up for a closer inspection. "They'll be flying off the shelves in no time," he added.

Her smile could not have been any bigger. It was hard to believe they were her own collection!

All of the models were being dressed to match her bags, she was so excited! She couldn't wait for the show to start. All her nerves suddenly fell away after seeing the bags, they were amazing.

Mr Salvatore, Ricco and Millie were led to their seats beside the runway for the start of the show.

Millie had never seen so many celebrities before, she felt so out of place amongst them. She couldn't sit still, wriggling around in her seat, nervous that they were all about to see what she had designed.

The show began and the 'Salvo', brand name was up first. The first model took to the stage, wearing black skinny jeans, a cream and black polka-dot blouse and carrying Millie's cream and black oversized bag, it was her favourite! She couldn't stop smiling. The feeling it gave her rivalled nothing! She couldn't have been more proud of herself. Her entire working life so far had led up to this point and it didn't disappoint. She could see all the celebrities sat on the opposite side of the runway whispering and pointing at the model. She wished she could hear what they were saying.

As the show continued she watched as the models carried each of her bags down the runway, she was dying to hear what Mr Salvatore thought but she had to wait an hour until all the designers had shown their collections.

The show came to a close and some smartly dressed men and women approached Mr Salvatore and he left the room with them, Millie wondered who they were. She and Ricco had a wander round the room where all the models were on display so people could get a better close-up look at the fashion.

Around ten minutes had passed when a lady tapped Millie on the shoulder.

"Ms Vine?" she asked.

"Yes" Millie replied, nervously.

"Come with me please," the lady asked.

Millie was nervous; it felt as though she had done something wrong and was going to be told off. She shot Ricco a terrified look.

"It's okay," he mouthed to her silently. She had no idea where she was being taken but she wished Ricco had come with her. She was led into a boardroom where the several smartly dressed men and women that had left with Mr Salvatore were sat around the table, with Mr Salvatore at the head of the table.

"Have a seat, Amelie," he said as Millie struggled to pull out a heavy leather chair perching on the edge, her throat so dry it was almost painful.

"Millie," Mr Salvatore began, "All of the fashion houses loved your handbags!" Millie was waiting for a but... "We've reached a deal here today and I'm pleased to tell you designers from Milan, Paris, New York, San Francisco, Tokyo and London have all signed contracts to sell your bags. They'll go into production this afternoon and will be available in stores in the UK and USA on Monday and the other countries in about two weeks' time," he explained. "And obviously they will be in all my

stores worldwide," he added. Millie gasped, she felt her heart skip a beat.

"Oh my goodness! That's amazing", Millie replied. She wiped her cheek with her hand as she felt a tear roll down her face. "Thank you, thank you so much, Mr Salvatore," she said, struggling to get her words out.

"No, thank *you* Amelie. You did a great job, I'm very impressed," said Mr Salvatore.

Millie was elated, the feeling nearly rivalled the way she felt about Dex. *Oh my goodness, DEX!* She thought, *maybe he will know who I am after all*. She couldn't wait to get out of there to tell Ricco and call her mum!

"Now listen, Millie," Mr Salvatore began, but she wasn't listening. She was too excited and dying to get out of that room! Mr Salvatore continued...

"It's Friday and with bags going to stores on Monday, I'll need you to work this weekend." She nodded enthusiastically, she'd have done anything he asked right now!

"I'm sending you straight to the airport, you'll meet with my branding agent Rachael this afternoon back in the office, Sophie is arranging things for you from there as we speak. You'll need to work with Rachael probably overnight to come up with a brand name for your collection, all your branding design, etc. So it's going to be a long night, but it all has to be done for Monday, okay?" he finished.

"Yes, of course!" Millie replied. She was so excited, her own brand name! She hadn't even considered anything beyond the bags themselves.

"Okay, go and find Ricco, he will organise everything and get you home" he said. Millie got up and turned to leave the room, she pushed the door open.

"Oh, and Millie…" said Mr Salvatore.

"Congratulations, my darling," he smiled at her.

"Thank you, sir" she smiled back. She couldn't get out the door quick enough! She ran across the hotel lobby and jumped on Ricco, wrapping her legs around his waist.

"OH MY GOD! Oh my god, Ri you'll never guess what… well Mr Salvatore, well your dad said that my bags are amazing and will be sold in…" she was so excited and talking so fast Ricco could barely follow what she was saying.

"Wow!" he interrupted her. "And… breathe!" he said. "Slow down, babe!"

She let go of him and stood up, pulling her dress back down and feeling slightly concerned that she had just flashed her bum to the entire room! She took a moment to catch her breath and started again.

"Your dad just called me into a meeting with a bunch of designers from all the major fashion labels and my bags are going to be sold in the UK, USA, France, Italy and Japan! On Monday!" she explained, still talking super-fast.

"Oh, Mils! I am so incredibly proud of you!" he replied, picking her up off the floor with a huge hug. "I knew you'd do it!" He added.

"Your dad said you have to take me home!" she smiled, sounding cute like a five-year-old. Ricco laughed.

"No problem, honey," he put his arm around her.

"Let's go!"

CHAPTER 7

"What's the time, Dad?" asked Dex, loading his parents' bags into the back of the cab. This was his second trip to Milan airport today after taking Lucie to catch her flight back home this morning. Now it was his parents' turn to go home.

"It's 3.15pm, Son," replied his dad, lifting his shirt sleeve to look at his super-expensive designer watch, a present from Dex when he got his first number one single.

"We'd better get going," Dex replied. He helped his mom into the back of the cab before getting in the front.

Mac was very nervous, he was letting Dex take them alone at his request. Not a request Mac would usually fulfil, but he got the feeling Dex was really struggling at the moment and could probably do with a bit of space. But still, he didn't feel comfortable with it. If anything happened to Dex he knew it was on him.

"I'll be back as quick as I can, man," Dex shouted to Mac.

"Yeah, call me if you need anything" Mac shouted back. Dex was on stage tonight in Milan and needed to be back for sound check at 4.30pm. He was feeling pretty down that his parents were leaving already, he'd barely spent any time with them, but he was desperate to find the girl as soon as they left. For the entire 20-minute journey to the airport Dex felt anxious. His mom could tell something wasn't quite right but she knew she couldn't ask, she knew she had raised a good man and that whatever it was he would find a way to figure it out. She gently rubbed his knee. He turned to her and smiled, he knew that was her way of saying; *It's okay Son, you'll be okay.* He might be 31 but god he loved his mom.

The cab pulled up outside the terminal and Dex handed some money over to the cab driver to help his parents out of the car and carry their bags in for them. Dex couldn't get out of the car, he had no security with him and would be mobbed. He knew he would end up stuck there for ages signing things and posing for photos when all he wanted to do was get back to the hotel so he could find her.

He turned around in his seat and gave him mom a kiss.

"Bye, Son, we'll see you when you come home. Take care of yourself," she said with a smile.

"Yeah, I'll miss you, Mom, but I'll be home soon," he smiled back and his eyes began to well up. She ran the back of her hand down his cheek and pinched his chin as if he was five years old again.

He leaned over the back of the seat and gave his dad a hug.

"Bye, Dad, safe flight."

"Goodbye, Son. Take care, see you soon," replied his dad.

The cab driver opened the door and gave his dad a hand out, then went around to help his mom. Dex felt bad he couldn't help but his parents understood, his mom worried about him so much and would have never let him get out anyway. Plus he wanted to say goodbye to them alone without a crowd of people surrounding them, pushing and shoving to get to him. He feared for his parents' safety, they were getting old and didn't need the drama that came with being Dex Rose!

He lifted his sunglasses for a second and watched as they

disappeared inside the terminal building. As soon as they were out of sight he slumped down in his seat. Wiping away tears he closed his eyes. Five minutes' rest was bliss whilst he was waiting for the cab driver to return. A cab pulled up behind his.

Ricco got out and opened the door, putting his hand out to help Millie out of the cab.

"Hang on a second," she said, swinging her legs out of the car door to change her heels for trainers. Leaving her to I, Ricco pulled their bags from the boot and carried them into the terminal building. Millie slammed the cab door shut and ran to catch him up. Dex jumped and opened his eyes.

"Jesus Christ! Can't even get 5 minutes' peace," he said to himself, looking in the wing mirror to see who'd disturbed him. *Hmmm, nice butt,* he thought, watching a girl in a little black dress and white trainers run into the terminal building. As she went into the revolving door his cab driver came out.

"Let's go!" Dex said to himself, anxious and excited to get back to the hotel before he had to go to sound check.

All the way back to the hotel Dex went over and over what he was going to say to her in his head. He couldn't just knock on her door! *Maybe I just put a note under the door,* he thought. *Or maybe I send Zach!*

He had no idea how he was going to get to talk to her, but all he knew was he had to do it. He kept replaying the moment he first saw her over and over in his head. What was it about her? Was it fate, destiny… love at first sight? He had no idea, he didn't really believe in any of that but something happened that night and he knew he couldn't make sense of it until he had met her. Properly.

Approaching the hotel he got some cash out of his wallet and gave it to the cabby, he didn't want anything slowing him down once they got to the hotel. It was already 4.03pm, he didn't have long. He knew the rest of the band and entourage would have already left for the gig venue.

The cab pulled up and he was gone, he ran up the steps into the hotel lobby and waited for the elevator.

"Come on!" he said to himself, it seemed to take ages. He was getting anxious, much longer and he would be recognised and mobbed!

The lift opened and he got in, pressing the 'close door' button frantically. As the doors closed he could finally breathe again. He stepped out on the 8th floor. He still had no idea what he was going to say as he ran down the corridor, adrenaline had taken over. He'd think of something.

As he approached her room the door was open. He looked in, housekeeping was cleaning the room.

"Have they checked out?" he asked the cleaning lady, and his heart sank as the words came out of his mouth. He already knew the answer.

"Yes, dear," she replied. *FUCK!* He couldn't believe he'd been so close and lost her again! He put his head against the wall and closed his eyes, screwing up his face. He took a deep breath and stood up straight again with his hands on his head. He felt empty.

Millie made her way down the aisle and found her seat. She hated flying. She sat down and buckled her seat belt.

"I don't think you need that on yet, love!" Ricco joked as he sat down next to her. "The engines aren't even on yet!" he added.

Millie ignored him, she was blocking out everything. she got her portfolio out of her bag. Take off was the worst part, it turned her into a blubbering three-year-old and she needed a distraction. She pulled out a pencil and started sketching.

"I need a name for my brand," she said, trying to fill her head with anything other than what was about to happen to avoid a panic attack.

"Okay, so what you thinking?" he asked.

"I want a rose in it," she replied with a sheepish smile.

She had to include Dex in there somewhere!

"Ohhhhh... I see!" he teased. "Come on, girl, that smile just told a thousand words! Spill! You're not telling me something!" said Ricco.

"What?" she replied, trying to act cool.

"Don't give me that! Spill!" he pushed.

"You stay in a hotel room with him the other side of a paper-thin wall and you have nothing to say about it? Did you sneak out on the balcony for wild, passionate sex with him while I was asleep? AHHHH YES! That's why you blew me off, isn't it!" he teased, laughing at his own joke. It was the first time either of them had mentioned last night.

Millie didn't say a word; instead she turned away to look out of the window, trying to hide the smile creeping across her face. Ricco put his hand under her chin and pulled her face back to him. He just looked at her.

"I…" she started, immediately stopping herself. "Actually, if you remember correctly, YOU blew ME off!" She smiled, feeling ever so slightly awkward talking about it. She was still a little embarrassed that she had tried to bed him, even more so that HE HAD NOW SEEN HER NAKED! She blushed, her cheeks were red hot.

"And you wish I hadn't, everyone wants a bit of Ri Ri love" he joked, trying to ease the awkward atmosphere.

"I did. I do. I dunno," Millie said, resting her head against his shoulder. Now felt like the time to be honest with him. "Last night wasn't just because of him Ri" she nervously admitted. Ricco was shocked to hear her say that, he felt nervous about what she was going to say next.

"I love you to death, I fancy the fucking Italian pants off of you," she laughed. Ricco smiled, waiting for the but. "But you've always known that and it doesn't matter, you're gay! You're my best friend and I never want that to change. I just. I…" Tears began to roll down her cheeks.

Ricco was beyond confused, he didn't understand where all these emotional outbursts were coming from lately. He felt uncomfortable, he had no idea what to do with her. He lifted her chin to look at her.

"Seriously, I'm missing something, right?" His face changed, she could sense he was trying to have a serious conversation with her.

"I don't know what to say. I..." Millie looked away, burying her head back into his shoulder. Once again he lifted her chin so she was looking at him.

"Why are you so emotional lately, baby? Have I upset you?" Ricco asked.

This was her chance and suddenly she just blurted it out and it was done! "I....think I'm in love with him." It was the only way she could describe it.

"What? With who?" Ricco was more confused than ever.

"Dexter Rose," she replied quietly, feeling like a silly schoolgirl with a lame crush.

"Love? Really?" he questioned, surprised by her admission but relieved to hear something he considered to be pretty trivial. It certainly didn't warrant the amount of tears she had shed as of late. "That's a strong word babe for someone you don't know," he said softly, trying to not make her feel worse.

"I know." Millie looked embarrassed, regretting saying a word. She felt pathetic. She was going to have to spill all now. "At that gig I told you about, he looked right at me and I felt....something weird! I didn't believe in love at first sight and all that bull but... it kind of happened.. I think!," she explained, feeling ever more stupid with every word she said.

"I totally believe in love at first sight, babe, but he's a famous rock star, I bet every girl thinks she feels the same when he looks at them," Ricco replied, throwing her a sympathetic look. Ricco was usually the one person she could rely on to understand her and make her feel better, but not this time.

"Yeah, you're right, it's silly," she agreed, as she picked up her pencil and began sketching again. She started to scribble out the rose she had sketched. Ricco grabbed her hand and stopped her.

"No, babe, it needs to be a rose." He smiled at her. He may not have really believed she had a chance with Dex, but he was her best friend and he needed to support her, whether he thought it was all in her head or not. He took the pencil and sketched the perfect rose logo for her.

Her face lit up! She stared at his creation on the page. "It's perfect! Thank you," she beamed, kissing him on the cheek. As the plane thundered down the runway she clung onto Ricco's arm. "I need a name too, babe," she whispered, trying to distract herself again.

"What about just Millie Rose?" he suggested. "Has a nice ring to it don't you think?" he smiled.

Millie playfully punched him in the arm. "No!" she replied, rolling her eyes. If Dex ever knew who she was he would think she was a crazy stalker using his name.

"What about just using your initials?" he suggested.

"Just M.V?" she asked.

"No, use your real initial, A. Rose," Ricco explained.

"Hmm, that's kind of cool!" Millie replied, thinking about it for a minute. "Yes, I like that! A. Rose." She kept

saying it over and over in her head, it was perfect! It sounded cool and it included her rose for Dex. Perfect.

CHAPTER 8

8pm arrived, Dex downed several shots of whisky in a row as he waited to go on stage

"Hey, slow down, man!" said Zach. "You'll forget the words!" he added.

"Or fall off the stage!" laughed Jesse. Dex had done that before...twice. "You alright man?" asked Jesse as Dex downed his seventh shot.

"Yeah," he replied, avoiding eye contact with Jesse. He didn't want to talk. Jesse and Zach looked at each other. Something was up again but now wasn't the time to get it out of him. His moods seemed to be getting worse and worse, did he not want to do this anymore? Was he on drugs? They knew he had dabbled a bit in the past but they were sure he had been clean for a few years now. All kinds of scenarios ran through the other guys' minds.

They were introduced to the stage and Dex flipped his showman switch, from depressed Dex drowning his sorrows in alcohol to clean-cut, full of energy, wholesome Dex Rose. The crowds went absolutely wild as Craze took to the stage. The song started and Dex began to sing, he looked around the crowd of the huge open air venue. There must have been over 50,000 people there, one of their biggest gigs yet. The atmosphere was amazing, it was just beginning to get dark and Dex could see the city lights beyond the crowd, it was a beautiful night. He looked back down at the front row at his feet, hundreds of gorgeous girls all shouting for him, all falling over each other to touch him, but all he could think of was that girl. Where was she? His mind was elsewhere tonight, but the crowd would never have known. He faked a good show, but Zach and Jesse knew something wasn't right.

The show continued as usual. Dex was amazing, he was born a showman and he had an incredible voice, probably one of the best male singers currently in the charts.

As he came off stage he knew he'd smashed it despite his mood. He was the kind of person who didn't let people down so no matter what was going on in his own life, no matter what his mood he was going to give 110% every single time he stepped out on stage. Something his mother had instilled in him. He walked down the steps off the back of the stage, a stagehand handed him a towel, and he wiped his sweaty hair from his face and made his way to the tour bus. He needed some space. Zach followed him.

"Hey, man," Zach said, poking his head around the tour bus door. Dex was lying on his bunk.

"Hey," he replied, not even looking up from his phone.

"Ya alright?" Zach didn't want to push too much, Dex wasn't the kind of guy to share his feelings. If he wanted to talk, he would. Zach wasn't going to ask questions but knew something was wrong and felt like perhaps if he stayed with him he might open up. He climbed up into the bus and laid down next to Dex, trying to think of something funny to say to ease the atmosphere.

"Got any whisky left?" asked Dex.

"Yeah," Zach replied as he got up to get the bottle.

Dex knew drinking wasn't going to fix anything but he needed to escape his own head for a while. He couldn't stop thinking about the girl but knew he wouldn't see her again. He had no way of finding her now. Fate had given him chances and he'd blown them all. He knew he had to finish things with Lucie but he had no idea how to go about that. He didn't know when he would see her again with her schedule being so hectic and he knew he couldn't do it over the phone.

Jesse climbed up onto the bus carrying a magazine. "Have you seen this, dude?" he asked Dex, handing him the magazine.

Dex looked at the cover. A huge photo of him and Lucie walking into the hotel in Germany graced the entire front cover, his arm was around her with the headline *Dexter Rose beds pop princess Lucie Goldham!* "Awesome," he said sarcastically, rolling his eyes.

Zach suddenly realised showing Dex something that was going to annoy him probably wasn't the best move with the mood he was already in!

Dex and Lucie had managed to keep their relationship secret up until now and now he was about to end it, it had been made public! He turned to the story inside the magazine; there were more pictures, one of him and Lucie on their Italian hotel balcony.

"I can't believe we were being watched, that's creepy," he said. He looked closer at the small picture. *Fuck! That's her!* he thought to himself. The photographer had snapped Millie and Ricco on their balcony next door in the picture. He couldn't help but smile; he finally had a picture of her!

"Do you know who this guy is?" he asked, pointing at Ricco in the photo, he couldn't remember his name.

"That's Ricco Salvatore. His dad is a millionaire, owns a fashion house, why?" asked Jesse.

Dex didn't answer, instead he got Google up on his phone and searched Ricco Salvatore as he had done before. There had to be some way of finding her through him. Ricco's Twitter page came up first in the search. Dex clicked on it and had a browse through his tweets, nothing stood out. He clicked on his photos, the first photo was Ricco and Millie at the Milan fashion show! Dex read the caption with the photo:

@MrRSalvatore: Me and my girl @_MillieV at Milan Fashion Week #Milsfashionshow #thatsmagirl #Beautiful #RiRiandMils

Jackpot! He'd found her! His smile couldn't have been any bigger! As much as he avoided social media, it had its uses.

"Someone's cheered you up," Zach teased, watching him on his phone.

Dex didn't answer. He didn't really even hear him; he was completely lost in his phone. He clicked through to her Twitter page:

@_MillieV - Amelie 'Millie' Vine, 26.

Fashion designer at Salvo's head design office.

He breathed a sigh of relief, it was as if a huge weight had lifted from his shoulders. He was finally starting to get closer to knowing who she was, he had a photo, her name, he was surprised she was only 26! But pleased that she was closer to his age than Lucie! He took a screen shot of her page and saved the photo of her and Ricco from his page.

His mood had flipped 180°, Zach and Jesse wondered what he was doing on his phone. His whole demeanour had changed in a matter of a few minutes. They assumed it was something to do with Lucie.

"If she's sending you naked pics, I want in!" joked Jesse. Dex smiled.

The rest of the band and entourage began to climb aboard the bus. They had to leave and be on the road by 11pm, they were due in Paris in the morning. Mac came and sat down with them in the bunks. He reached into a carrier bag he had and pulled out beers for everyone. Dex already felt a bit drunk, but one more beer wouldn't hurt! Dex, Jesse and Zach were messing about, laughing, joking, play-fighting. Mac smiled as he took a sip of his beer. It was good to see Dex back to himself again.

Five beers later and they were on the road, travelling from Milan to Paris. The bus was so loud, but that's how the guys liked it, all fellas having a few beers together, messing around, and playing video games. It really was the life.

Dex jumped on Zach, who was lying on his stomach in his bunk playing on his phone.

"Battleship?" he asked, lying on Zach's back, trying to nose at what Zach was typing.

"Uh huh," Zach replied, finishing up a message he was typing.

As the two guys laid playing Battleship between their phones Zach thought it was the best chance he'd get to talk. Jesse, CJ, Mac and the rest of their entourage were sat far enough away to not be able to hear them and they were noisy, drinking and playing cards anyway. He took his chance.

"Hey, what's been up with you lately, man?"

It seemed like the perfect time to ask, they were alone, Dex was happy and drunk!

"Ah nothing," he replied.

"Things okay between you and Luc?" Zach asked, trying not to pry too much.

"Nah, I'm done with that," Dex replied casually, not even looking up from his game of Battleship.

"Oh really, how come?" pushed Zach, cautiously, knowing Dex was going to get annoyed with the third degree soon.

Dex stopped, put his phone down and looked at Zach. *Here it comes,* thought Zach, *I've wound him up already!*

"I need to ask you something, dude," Dex said, looking serious.

"Uh... sure? Anything," Zach replied, confused yet intrigued.

"You sleep with a lot of fans, right?" Dex asked.

"Uh yeah, many, why?" Zach answered with a smile, somewhat proud of his conquests. "Have you slept with someone else?" asked Zach, surprised, but thinking that would make sense, though he never expected Dex to do that. He had always been so against it.

"Nah, I.... erm.... it doesn't matter," replied Dex. He wanted to tell Zach but he knew he couldn't explain it to sound anything but crazy.

"No, come on, man! Spill!" said Zach.

"Seriously, it's nothing, dude," Dex replied, resuming the game of Battleship. Zach knew better than to keep on. Dex was the kind of guy that kept himself to himself. He rarely talked about anything personal but Zach knew that when he was ready, he'd talk. They had been best buds for years; he knew Dex would tell him eventually, so he left it at that. Their Battleship game continued.

"I want to," Dex randomly blurted out.

"Sleep with someone?" Zach asked, slightly confused.

"Yeah... well, kinda," replied Dex.

Zach didn't know what to say. "If you're going to end things with Lucie anyway, then go for it, dude," said Zach.

Millie and Ricco arrived at Ricco's house. It was nearly midnight and they'd only just finished up at the office. They staggered up the driveway, arm in arm, both supporting each other's inability to walk in a straight line from sheer exhaustion! It had been a very long but amazing day. Millie was so excited, she had spent the evening with Mr Salvatore's branding director working on the name, logo and style of her brand. It was now designed and created and was all ready to go on Monday! Millie yawned as Ricco unlocked the door for her.

"I... yuuuuhh..." she tried to talk mid-yawn. She threw

her bags down on the floor and continued. "I love, love, love these!" she gushed, holding up a prototype tag for her bags.

"They're gorgeous, babe!" replied Ricco, taking it from her for another look.

"Hey listen… Ri, thank you so much. Without you this would have never happened!" she said, putting her arms around his waist and her head to his chest. She knew that her close relationship with Ricco had definitely made things far easier for her, she was sure he had some influence in Mr Salvatore's decision to let her design and launch her own collection. In career terms she had skipped a lot of steps to get to where she was, she knew she didn't do that on her own but Ricco would never admit to anything.

"This is all your doing, sweetie," he replied, kissing her on top of her head. "You're super talented and come Monday the whole world will see it," he added. "Plus I might have a little surprise for you, I just need to make a phone call," said Ricco as he left the room.

When Ricco came back into the bedroom he couldn't hide his smile.

"What?" asked Millie.

"Nothing, just my dad," he replied.

Millie wondered why he had to leave the room to speak with his dad but thought nothing of it; perhaps he had ordered her some flowers or something, which would be sweet, she thought.

"It's so late, can I stay over tonight?" asked Millie. She often stayed at Ricco's, though there was still a slight awkward air between them following last night and she felt a bit weird asking him. She hoped he didn't think she was going to hit on him again but she really wanted to stay. She loved being at Ricco's, he had his own place, a gorgeous expensive penthouse apartment in the heart of the city. With floor to ceiling glass in every room it had stunning views. They lived in one of the most beautiful southern English cities. Millie loved to sit out on the balcony at night and watch the hustle and bustle on the street below, it was buzzing, even at midnight. Nothing made Millie feel more alive than the crisp night air, the lights and the sounds of the city. It was almost magical.

"'Course," replied Ricco. "Now, do I need to padlock my boxers on or am I safe tonight?" he teased. Millie punched him playfully in the arm. "Ooh, I reckon I'm in for some rough loving tonight!" He laughed.

Millie felt a little awkward. She walked straight past him, completely ignoring him, trying to hide her smile, secretly she was glad he was just making a joke of it. Pulling out her hair band she let her gorgeous dark flowing hair fall effortlessly down her back. She collapsed onto his bed, she was exhausted. She turned onto her stomach and watched the people down on the street for a while. She liked to mentally pick out someone, she'd make up their life in her head. The lady walking past Marks and Spencer with the red umbrella, she's just finished work at the hospital, she's rushing to catch her train home to her boyfriend and her cat, Coco. The man stood outside the music shop on his phone, he's just received interest in his demo tape he sent to a record company earlier today, so he's meeting his friends here tonight to celebrate. It was a fun game she liked to play at Ricco's, usually in the mornings waiting for him to wake up!

Ricco took off his clothes and got into bed with his boxers on. "Mils, turn the light off when you're done creating the lives of strangers," he teased.

Getting up, she rolled her eyes, turned off the lights and slipped off her dress. She picked up Ricco's t-shirt off the floor and put it on to wear to bed, pulled the blinds down and climbed in next to him. As usual they both laid next to each other engrossed in their phones. Millie was online stalking Craze again, she wished so much that Dex had a

Twitter page; he was so mysterious, she knew nothing about him. She read through the band's tweets, Jesse's and then Zach's.

"OH MY GOD!" Her sudden outburst made Ricco jump a mile.

"Jesus fucking Christ, girl!" he exclaimed.

"Ri, look!" She shoved her phone in Ricco's face. He squinted, the screen was so bright in the darkness. "What am I looking at?" he asked, still struggling to focus.

"Zach's following me!" she exclaimed, still excitedly talking so fast he could only just make sense of it.

"Babe, you have issues!" he said, laughing at her. He turned his phone off and put it down on the nightstand. He snuggled into Millie, squinting as her phone shone in his eyes. "Get some sleep" he said. "You're going to have a manic few days! We've got to be in the office at 7am!" he continued.

"'K" she replied, putting her phone down. She snuggled down under the covers and Ricco put his arm around her. It was silent. She hated silence; it just made her feel really down thinking about Dex. She let out a little squeal of excitement and closed her eyes. Ricco laughed.

Five minutes of silence passed and Ricco began to drift off.

"Ri," Millie whispered.

"Yes, doll?" replied Ricco.

"Why can't I forget him?" she whispered, feeling annoyed with herself. Everything else in her life was great, he was the one thing holding her back.

"What?!" he mumbled, falling asleep.

"Dex. I know, I know! It's ridiculous!" She continued sarcastically, fully aware that Ricco thought it was just a silly celebrity crush.

"Colpo di fulmine," he muttered quietly, his eyes still shut; he was so tired he could barely find the energy to talk.

"Huh?" she replied. Was he so tired he forgot he was speaking in Italian again? Speaking two languages was often confusing and he would flit between English and Italian mid-conversation without even realising it.

"Colpo di fulmine, Google it," he mumbled, drifting off to sleep. Millie was beyond confused; she brought up Google on her phone, attempting to spell it!

She clicked on the first link:

Italian saying Colpo di fulmine: Love at first sight that hits you like a thunderbolt, rendering you paralysed on the spot. It's awkward and graceful at the same time; so intensely forceful it can't be denied.

Millie smiled. That was exactly it. He may not have believed in it but he understood. She closed her eyes. Despite her feelings for Dex she still felt unsure of her feelings for Ricco. That night in the hotel he had kissed her more passionately than anyone had ever kissed her. *Could he love a woman?* Millie had all kinds of questions floating round in her head. She loved Ricco as a best friend, but was she in love with him? She had never let herself think of him as anything other than a friend in the past. Why would she, he was gay. But now things were different, she'd seen a different side to him, and she liked it.

CHAPTER 9

After a hectic week of shows and non-stop travelling, as Monday morning arrived Dex was glad of a day off.

Though his mood had improved he felt physically and emotionally drained. Their European tour was coming to a break, just a few more TV appearances and a couple of festivals and it was back to the states for a few weeks.

Lying on his bunk he pulled back the curtain and peeked out. Paris was beautiful at dawn, the city looked empty; it was too early for the usual inner-city hustle and bustle. He'd never seen a city look so peaceful. He needed to be out there. He looked at his watch. 5.52am. He was wide awake. Everyone else was still asleep. He crept out of bed and pulled on his trousers and hoody, he grabbed his trainers and tiptoed to the door. Slowly pushing the door open it made a huge creaking noise!

He froze.

"SHIT!" he whispered to himself, listening for a second. No one seemed to be stirring. He crept down the steps and closed the door again, breathing a sigh of relief that he'd got out. Mac would freak if he knew he was out alone but he wasn't one for sticking to the rules. He put on a hat and sunglasses and went for a run.

It felt amazing to be out in the city at that time of day. The crisp morning air made just breathing feel amazing. He was cold, he hunched his shoulders up and pulled his hoody sleeves down over his hands, clenching his fists shut to hold them there. There were barely any cars on the roads and few people around; he could walk around freely without being hounded by fans or paparazzi. The sun was just beginning to peak over the horizon, it was so peaceful he could hear the sound of the river flowing. It was one of those times and places that made him forget everything and just be happy to be alive.

He walked down the side of the river, and as he did lyrics for a song came flooding into his mind. He got out his phone and sat on he edge of the river, typing the lyrics on his phone. Often the best songs were written when the lyrics came out of nowhere.

He finished writing what was in his head and turned on his camera to take a photo of the river. It was the most amazing view and he wanted to take a photo in every place he visited whilst he had the opportunity to see the world. He looked at his photo, and then flicked to the next. It was of Millie, the one he had saved from Ricco's Twitter. He stared at the photo, just seeing her face in a picture made him feel odd, almost nervous

"Who are you, Millie?" he asked himself. "Why do I feel like I need to know you?"

He looked up from his phone, the sun was just high enough to shine through the gaps in the Eiffel Tower, making it appear to glow.

"Wow," he whispered under his breath, lifting his phone to take a photo. *This place is magical! I need to bring her here*, he thought. Yet he couldn't quite understand why his mind was thinking like that. Of course he wouldn't bring her here. She was a fantasy in his head, a stranger.

He continued writing lyrics for a while longer, when he

finally looked up he hadn't even noticed that the city had started to get busy and fill with people on their way to work. All of a sudden the city had woken up, it was a different place, with a totally different atmosphere. He needed to get back to the bus before he started to get mobbed by fans!

He put his hood up over his hat and walked back through the city, it was so lovely to just be alone for a while. This tour was so crazy he never got time alone to just think and enjoy the cities they visited. As he walked alone his thoughts turned to Millie again. Would it be so bad to date a fan? Other people do it, she was obviously close to that Salvatore guy, he was well known and she'd not sold any stories on him. It was Dex's biggest fear. He needed his private life to be private; it was the only thing he had left to himself.

As he was walking he watched all the people coming and going, everywhere he looked were couples, walking hand in hand, arm in arm, talking, laughing, kissing. He suddenly felt quite lonely. It was the only thing missing from his life.

"DEX!" He heard someone shout his name. He jumped, looking around; a group of young girls dressed in school uniform were heading straight towards him, excitedly.

"Oh fuck!" he muttered under his breath. He'd been noticed! The girls hurried towards him, he stopped.

"Oh my god!" exclaimed one girl. "You Dexter Rose! From Craze!" He loved the way his name sounded in a French accent.

"I have picture?" another girl asked, already positioning herself next to him whilst handing her camera phone to another of the girls.

"AND ME!"

"And me!" came from two more of the group. Dex was nice and posed for photos despite feeling annoyed to have his peaceful morning shattered. He signed things for each of the girls as quickly as he could. By now passers-by were becoming curious about the crowds around him and were coming over to see who it was. The crowd was getting bigger and bigger and Dex was becoming nervous. He had none of his security with him, if he didn't get out now it would be impossible.

"I'm sorry, I gotta go," he said, trying to find a way out through the girls surrounding him, which by this time had grown to around 100 people. He walked quickly to the road with a trail of girls following him and hailed a cab,. He jumped in, breathing a sigh of relief. The cab pulled away with girls chasing it down the road.

"Wow, you popular," said the French driver.

"Where you go?" he added.

"Le Reservoir please," Dex replied.

"Okay. Celebrity?" asked the cab driver in his limited English.

"I'm a singer in an American band," he replied.

"We're touring Europe right now, we played Le Reservoir last night," he added. He wasn't sure if the driver understood a word he was saying!

"Ah," replied the cab driver. Dex looked out of the back window, they were gone. He was free. His phone beeped. Pulling it out of his pocket he had a text from Mac.

Where are you? Ya alright?

Yeah, back in 5

replied Dex. he knew Mac would be pissed that he'd left alone, mentally preparing himself for the third degree when he got back.

As the cab pulled up next to the venue, Mac was waiting for him, at only 8am crowds were already gathering outside the venue for so much as a glimpse of Craze before they left. Mac opened the cab driver's door and paid Dex's bill for him, then opening the back door he threw a black coat over Dex's head and helped him out of the car. As soon as he stood up the fans erupted into a deafening chorus of screams. Escorting him past the crowds of fans Mac whispered into his ear,

"You can't do this again, bro."

"Sorry, man!" replied Dex, he was a security nightmare, he knew he couldn't just go walking around in a foreign city on his own but he just felt like he needed it this morning and he was glad he did, he felt pretty good for the first time in a long time and he'd written nearly an entire new song. A pretty good one!

Dex climbed aboard the bus. Everyone was up now getting ready to head to the airport. They were flying to the UK for a few days for some TV appearances and promotional interviews, before doing a couple more festivals and then heading back to the US. As they left Paris for the airport Mac handed Dex a phone.

"It's Olivia from your management," he whispered, handing Dex the phone. *Great! a telling off from her now too* he thought, bracing himself.

"Dexter, we've had a private job request for you. They want you to launch a fashion line at a designer store."

"Nah," Dex said immediately, cutting her off mid-sentence.

"I know you don't do PAs and I wouldn't normally even bother to ask you, but they've put up £500k for you, so I thought it was worth pitching to you," exclaimed Olivia.

"What? Seriously?" he asked. "£500k for what?" he added.

"Just to be there," Olivia explained.

"That's crazy! But nah. I'm not doing a PA," said Dex. He was never going to be bought. It just wasn't his thing. He handed the phone back to Mac.

CHAPTER 10

Eeeeeeeek! It was finally here. Monday morning was usually greeted with miserable, tired, can't be assed Millie, but today was an exception. She woke up early, she had stayed at Ricco's all weekend preparing for her big day. Ricco was still asleep, mouth wide open!

"You're so attractive, babe," she whispered sarcastically. Getting out of bed she crept out of his room, quietly closing the door behind her. She tiptoed into the open plan kitchen/lounge and flicked on the kettle, she flinched at how loud the switch was, freezing for a second to see if she had woken Ricco. She couldn't hear any movement, being quiet or careful wasn't one of her fortes! She walked over to the window and looked out, like his bedroom the entire wall was floor to ceiling glass with a balcony off one side. She loved waking up in his apartment. She made a cup of tea and took it outside on the balcony. It was a gorgeous, warm spring morning. Still in Ricco's t-shirt the sun felt warm on her bare legs, she put them up on the chair next to her to get some sun for five minutes. She tied her long hair up on top her head and leaning back in her chair she closed her eyes and just listened to the busy city below. Her thoughts turned to her day ahead. She thought she would be really nervous but instead she was just excited. It was going to be a hectic day but with the sun already shining she felt confident today would be a good day.

Ricco opened the balcony door, Millie jumped a mile, spilling her tea on her bare legs! "Ouch!" she shouted, jumping out of the chair. "Jesus! You scared me!" she said.

Ricco stepped out onto the balcony; Millie couldn't help but look him up and down. *Man! What a body*! With messy bed hair he looked so sexy! A snug fitting bright white t-shirt clung to his abs showing the definition of his six pack, his tight black designer boxers shorts showed off his manly muscular thighs. His gorgeous after-shave fragrance surrounded Millie's senses.

"You're so wasted being gay," she joked. She felt like she told him that on a daily basis but it was true!

He smiled. "Cuppa tea on the table for you," she added.

"Ta, babe," he replied, lifting her legs as he slumped down in the chair next to her and putting them down on his lap. He rubbed his eyes, he hadn't quite woken up properly yet and it was already so bright out. He seemed quiet, almost irritated by something.

"You okay?" asked Millie.

"Yeeeeeeah," he replied, mid-yawn. "Just had a disappointing phone call, that's all. No biggy," he explained. Millie wondered what it was but knew better than to push a grumpy Italian!

"So, big day," he smiled, squinting to see her with the sun shining right in his eyes. She pulled her legs back onto her chair, putting her arms around them she pulled her knees into her chest, resting her chin on her knees. She breathed out heavily.

"You'll be fine," he said. "It'll be good," he added, rubbing her head as he got up. Millie followed him back inside. She picked up her schedule for the day off the breakfast bar and read through it.

"Wow," she said to herself, feeling slightly overwhelmed by her jam-packed schedule. Today wasn't quite going to be her normal 9-5! Butterflies were swirling around her stomach making her feel nauseous. She held the paper in front of her and stared blankly at the schedule for a minute, not taking it in at all. She shook her head as if to bring herself back to reality. Folding the paper she put it back on the counter and looked at her watch; 7.32am.

"Arrgh! I need to shower," she said, walking away down the hallway. In a sudden realisation of what was about to happen she turned back.

"Ri, you'll be with me all day won't you?" she asked. She knew she would feel so much more confident with him by her side.

"Yeah, 'course," he shouted back from the kitchen. His phone was ringing in the bedroom; Millie went in and picked it up.

"RI!" she shouted. "Your dad's on the phone." Ricco rushed down the hallway, took the phone from her and went in the spare bedroom, closing the door behind him. *That's odd,* thought Millie. *What's he up to?* The secrecy made her feel a bit uneasy.

"Hey, Dad," said Ricco picking up his phone.

"Olivia from their management just called back again, they've offered tickets to some TV show taping tonight instead. Which isn't going to be any good is it. What a jackass that Dix or Dax or whatever the daft-named fella is called. Turning down £500k to do nothing, more money than sense!" moaned Mr Salvatore.

Ricco laughed. "Ah no that's brilliant! We will make it. Say we'll have the tickets. Thanks, Dad," he replied. He hung up the phone. "Yesssssss!" he quietly said to himself. Ricco was gutted that Dex had turned down the £500k he offered him to come to Millie's bag launch. It would have made her day, her year, her life! But tickets would do, he knew Millie would be over the moon. Despite her long day!

Arriving at Salvo's store Millie already felt exhausted, with telephone interview after telephone interview she had never talked so much! Her nerves were building, she wasn't an 'in the spotlight' kind of person and was totally not cut out for it. She was a designer, she wasn't a talker. She hoped no one would ask her any questions; she just wanted to fade into the background.

As the fancy black Rolls Royce stopped outside there was a huge queue of press photographers waiting, roped off from entering the store. Two large men dressed in all black stood in the doorway. As Millie stepped out of the cab, the nerves hit her.

She turned around to Ricco as he got out of the car and grabbed his arm, nearly knocking him over! She didn't know what to expect, she just hoped the photographers would only want to take photos and not speak to her. She was really shy, she hated being put on the spot. She knew her nerves would get the better of her and she would end up sounding stupid or saying something she would regret!

Millie walked towards the door and photographers began snapping at her. *How do they even know who I am?* she thought. Puzzled, she continued. As she stepped away from the safety of the car, she felt very self-conscious, she really hoped she didn't look fat. White was so unforgiving! She wasn't skinny and at 5ft 4 inches she was never going to be a supermodel but her fitted white dress hugged her curvy figure. She hated her hips but in reality she had a pretty perfect womanly shape. Her hot pink shoes gave her a little extra confidence; she carried a pink bag from her collection on her shoulder which she clutched onto with one hand, hanging onto Ricco for dear life with the other. This was quite possibly the worst time in her entire life to fall over! She was naturally clumsy, but when she was nervous her clumsiness reached a whole new level! She walked slowly, taking care with every step. She wasn't going to fall over in front of the world's press, she was not going to be *THAT* girl!

Millie tried to walk confidently, her hair blowing behind her in the warm spring breeze, like something out of a shampoo advert. She felt a huge sense of relief as she walked through the door, there were no cameras inside yet so at least she could relax, if only for five minutes. She saw her display for the first time. It looked incredible, a huge white shabby chic circular tiered stand stood in the centre of the store, like a huge round dressing table with a mirror running around the centre, scattered with real pink roses and petals. Each of her 12 bags sat neatly in its place, she couldn't believe she had only sketched the designs for some of the bags last week and already she was looking at them in the flesh! Her branding and artwork looked incredible, it was girly, romantic with a vintage feel. It was exactly the vision she had in her head. It was her!

She couldn't help but smile. She rushed over to take a closer look holding Ricco's hand, dragging him behind her. As she approached the display it looked even more amazing, she could see her branded tags attached to each bag. She picked a small bag up and turned to Ricco.

"THIS.......IS......AAAAH-MAZING!" she said, having a closer look at HER tags. "I can't believe this is all mine, it's perfect!" she gushed, smiling from ear to ear. It was an absolute dream come true and it had all happened so fast it had barely had time to sink in!

"It looks incredible, babe!" smiled Ricco, putting his arm around her. "I'm so proud of you."

"Thanks, Ri," she replied. She couldn't thank him enough, she knew he had a big hand in making this happen. She picked up a cardboard stand; it had a big photo of her on.

"This is so cool!" said Millie, showing it to Ricco.

"I know, I'm taking it home with me," he joked. She rolled her eyes at him. "Not the cardboard cut-out! This! Just all of this!" she replied, looking around the room. She glanced over at the door as Mr Salvatore, his PA and two other smartly dressed women walked in. The security guards closed the doors behind them.

"Good morning, Amelie," he said in his deep Italian accent as he approached her.

"Good morning," she replied cheerily.

"Hello, Son," he said, putting out an arm to hug Ricco.

"Hey, Dad," he replied. Mr Salvatore handed Ricco an envelope that he quickly folded and put in his back pocket. Millie wondered what it was.

"So what do you think, Millie?" asked Mr Salvatore.

"Oh I love it! It's perfect!" she replied, picking up another bag from the stand. She almost wanted to cuddle it! It seemed completely surreal that all this was for her. "Thank you so much!" she added.

"Your talent earned you this, young lady!" he replied with a smile. "Are you ready for the press?" asked

Mr Salvatore.

Millie's stomach was doing flips; she had butterflies on top of butterflies and could feel her legs shaking. "Erm… I guess so," she answered nervously, wishing so hard that she could skip this bit!

"You'll be fine, kid," said Mr Salvatore,

reassuringly patting her on the shoulder as he walked away. He gave the nod to the doormen to let the press in for their preview. As the doors opened a huge surge of people crammed through the doors and began to fill the room. Millie stood back a little from the display, cameras began to flash as photographers, reporters, stylists and journalists began to look through her bags on display. Ricco walked off to talk to people, she was on her own! Standing awkwardly to one side someone tapped her on the shoulder.

"MUM!" she shouted, throwing her arms around her

mother's neck. She gave her a squeeze; she was close to her family and missed them with working so much. "Dad, hi." She leaned past her mum to hug her dad.

"Hello, darling," smiled her dad. "This is cool," he added, trying to sound like he knew what he was talking about. Millie smiled.

"This is way cool!" she replied, mocking her dad, A huge smile across her face. It was great to have her family there for a bit of extra support, just some familiar faces in the crowds was comforting to her. Even though Millie was out there on her own, building her career, she still often felt like a little girl who needed her parents by her side.

"Woah! This is brill!" said a voice she recognised, peeking over her dad's shoulder.

"ARIA!...LEX!... What are you doing here? I thought you had to work?" asked Millie; surprised to see her sisters had come.

"As if we'd miss it!" replied Aria, leaning in for a cuddle with her little sister. Millie didn't get to see her sisters very often. Her big sister Aria was two years older. They used to be really close but Aria had moved to London a year ago to pursue a career in makeup artistry but never really got anywhere, taking a job as a beauty therapist in a small spa. Her little sister Alexia had just turned 18 and recently moved away to university to study creative arts in Cardiff. She saw her during holidays but that wasn't often. Millie wrapped her arms around her sisters. With all her family together she didn't think this day could get any better!

"I'm going for a nosey," said Alexia, pulling Aria with her.

"Me too," added her mum. "I'm buying the first one!" she added.

Millie stood at the edge of the room with her dad, watching the circus of people all pushing and shoving to get a good photo of her bags. She felt as if she was on the outside of a bubble looking in. Her dad put his arm around her shoulder and pulled her in to him. He wasn't one for words but she knew it was his way of saying he was proud of her.

A journalist approached her, sticking a dictaphone in her face.

"Millie, right?" asked the journalist.

"Yes," she replied quietly, annoyed that she had interrupted a rare moment alone with her dad.

"It's okay, love," said her dad, sympathetically patting her on the back. "I'll see you in a minute." He wandered off through the crowd.

The journalist continued. "Millie, what gave you the inspiration for your collection?" she asked.

Millie could feel herself getting hot, it was an easy question, one she had prepared for, but her mind was blank. "Erm." *Think, Millie, think!* "Uh, my parents actually, old-fashioned romance, when men were gentlemen. Romantic cities mixed in with a little bit of vintage. I love the vintage style," she replied. *Ah thank god, good answer,* she thought to herself.

"So, this is your debut collection, right?" asked the journalist.

"Yes, it is," replied Millie with a smile. "I'm really excited about it," she added. "It all looks fabulous! Thank you, Millie, good luck with the launch," said the journalist, turning to walk away.

Oh, that's it. That was easy, Millie thought. She relaxed slightly; if they were all that brief she'd cope! She began to walk around a little and chat with other journalists and various stylists that had come for a look. She had loosened up and was getting the hang of it all. Catching Ricco's eyes across the room, he smiled. At that moment Millie couldn't have asked for any more.

CHAPTER 11

"Wheels down," said Zach as the plane hit the runway with a thud. "Thank fuck!" he added. Zach hated flying. Dex looked out of the window as the plane thundered down the runway, it was a gorgeous day and he was happy to be back in the UK. There was nowhere like home, New York would always be where he belonged but if he was going to be anywhere else then the UK was the only other place where he felt somewhat at home. He'd spent a lot of time there and the culture was most like home. Plus, he knew Millie was English so he felt closer to her being on the same soil.

Approaching 4pm he felt tired, he needed to perk up before they had to perform at a nightclub at 10pm. Dex liked late shows, it meant he could drink all evening and chill out, which always made him feel more relaxed on stage.

"Let's hit the bar," said Dex, leaning over the seats in front where Zach, Jesse and CJ were collecting all their stuff up ready to disembark the plane.

"Go steady today!" Said Mac, sitting beside Dex.

"I know you've had a tough few weeks but don't go crazy," he added.

"I won't," Dex replied with a cheeky, defiant smile. He wasn't going to be silly. He had a massive amount of respect for Mac, he was like a dad to him and he felt bad that he'd been such a headache to him on the tour so far.

The plane began to empty and passengers made their way down the aisle. Dex grabbed his bag and pulled his cap firmly down low over his eyes to try to get through the airport without being recognised. It was impossible to blend in with how loud Zach and Jesse were. As they walked through the airport laughing, joking and singing they couldn't have drawn more attention to themselves if they tried, the trail of fans following them seemed to get longer and longer. Dex hung back with Mac and the rest of their entourage, he kept his head down. He wanted to be left alone but in reality, he was the most popular and the one that all the fans were waiting for. It wasn't long before he was forced into signing autographs and posing for photos. It was the worst part of his job. He hated the attention. It seemed to take forever to reach the exit. Dex was glad to finally get outside, he felt suffocated. He saw their bus parked across the car park and he picked up his pace to avoid having to stop for any more fans.

He stepped up onto the bus, relieved to have regained a little bit of privacy with the bus' blacked out windows from the hordes of fans that surrounded it. The bus pulled out of the car park with a crowd of girls chasing it down the street.

"DRINK!" exclaimed Dex, feeling very wound up. CJ opened the fridge and grabbed a six-pack of beers, breaking them out of the pack he passed them around. Dex sighed as he took a sip and relaxed back into the couch.

Zach was pleased that Dex was starting to seem a little more like himself, airport chaos aside. Maybe it was just the stress of having Lucie and his parents with them but whatever it was he definitely seemed to be more chilled out than he had been for the past week or so.

Dex looked around the bus, his best friends and their brilliant crew drinking, laughing, joking and messing around.

It was nice to be back to just the band and crew, as much as he loved seeing his parents he couldn't truly relax with them there. He laughed as he watched Zach twerking up against the oldest member of their crew, 59-year-old Caroline, the band's press officer. She didn't look overly enthused but Zach was sure she was enjoying his grinding!

"Hey, Zach!" shouted Dex, trying to be heard over the top of the music. "When you said you scored last night I didn't realise you were talking about Car!" he teased.

"Oh yeaaaaaah," said Zach who had turned around and was now nestling his face between her breasts. They loved to wind Caroline up, she was so prim and proper and... boring! They were pretty sure she was loving it, whether her face said so or not. Even if she wasn't, Zach enjoyed it! Dex could barely breathe through laughing, Zach was one of those people who could find fun in anything, and he was always entertaining the group with his risky and controversial endeavours. Dex was pretty sure someone was going to slap him at some point.

Zach gave up and fell into the couch next to Dex, exhausted; as he tried to catch his breath he shouted to Caroline as she walked away down the bus. "Same time tomorrow, Car!" he teased, nursing a stitch in his side.

"Fun's over, fellas, we're here," said Mac, slapping them all over the head with a rolled-up tour schedule as a feeble punishment for what they were doing to Caroline.

"Ouch, man!" said Zach, as he tried to punch Mac back, but instead fell off the arm of the couch.

"No more drinks for Mr Slater," said Mac, taking the beer from Zach's hand. "Come on," said Mac, trying to move three drunken fellas to get motivated and get off the bus, something he was used to doing on a regular basis!

As they stumbled down the steps, the bus had parked up against the side of the building, they could walk straight into the side door of the nightclub without being seen by fans waiting outside. Tonight they were recording a nightclub performance for a TV show. Mac knew he had to sober them up or the TV producers were not going to be happy. As Mac followed them into the venue he met with the TV executives inside.

"I need food for the guys please," said Mac, "and no one let them have alcohol!" he demanded. They sat down in a booth watching as the TV production crew set up the stage for them. With sound check in 15 minutes Mac knew this wasn't going to go well. He was stressed!

"Ah finally, HOME TIME!" Millie sighed, slumping into the back seat of the car. She was looking forward to just relaxing for two hours on the drive home. "What a crazy, hectic day!" she added, tipping her head back against the seat.

Ricco looked at her and smiled, but her eyes were closed. "It's erm... not quite home time," he said

reluctantly, worrying that Millie was going to turn him down and he wouldn't be able to get her there.

"What?" she said, opening her eyes and pushing herself up straight in the seat. All she wanted was to go home and go to bed! She hadn't felt so knackered in a long time.

He wasn't going to be able to get her there if he kept it a surprise. He reached into his back pocket and pulled out the envelope his dad had given him earlier. Millie was intrigued. He handed her the envelope and she pulled out the paper inside. She began to read:

VIP GUEST LIST - CRAZE

Ricco Salvatore, Amelie Vine

Oracle music taping

Monday 29th April - 10.00pm

"What? Craze? They're here? Really?" she asked excitedly.

"Uh huh," he replied with a smile.

"Oh my fucking god, I fucking, FUCKING love you!" she gushed, throwing her arms around him and kissing him all over his face. He laughed. "Eeeeeeeeeee," Millie squealed as Ricco gave directions to the driver and the car pulled away. She squeezed his hand, silently showing him her appreciation. He phoned a hotel and booked a room for the night. Millie suddenly perked up, all the excitement had taken over from her tiredness and she had a complete new lease of life in her.

They arrived at the venue a bit late, Ricco worried they wouldn't be allowed in late since it was a taping for TV. Luckily the man on the door knew who Ricco was and let them in a side entrance. The place was jam-packed. Craze were already on stage and Dex was already in full swing. They were squashed right at the back but Millie didn't care. She had come to life, forgetting completely about how exhausted she was.

"Ri, put me on your shoulders, babe, I

can't see!" she groaned. She pulled her dress up to just under her butt and Ricco lifted her up onto his shoulders. "Thanks!" she yelled, rubbing the top of his head.

He smiled. This band turned her into a kid in a sweet shop! Ricco thought it was sweet but he felt very protective of her, she was his girl and he was surprised to feel slightly threatened by Dex. Especially lately, his feelings had changed for her in some way. Since their night in Milan he had started to look at her differently. He knew nothing would ever come of it but at the same time he kind of wondered if it would.

Millie's entire body was tingling with excitement as she watched Dex just a matter of feet away from her. Being this close to him made every inch of her body ache. The second song came to end and they said their goodbyes. Millie was disappointed that it had ended so soon. That was it, he was gone again. Ricco lifted her down from his shoulders; he could see the disappointment on her face. He felt bad.

"Sorry it wasn't longer, babe" he said,

sympathetically putting a comforting arm around her.

"Don't be silly, it was amazing," she replied with an appreciative smile. She was really grateful to Ricco that he'd got them in and didn't want to seem ungrateful, but in reality she felt worse every time she saw Dex and then he left. Not seeing him at all was far easier.

Hand in hand they followed the crowds outside, approaching the doors Ricco stopped. "Babes, wait there a minute, I need to do something," he said.

Millie watched as Ricco pushed his way back through the crowd and into the nightclub. She was curious at to what he could possibly be going back for.

Approaching the stage, Ricco spotted a steward through the crowds of people still pushing their way out of the nightclub. "Hi, can I have a quick word with one of

their security people?" The steward looked really put out by Ricco's request, Ricco was sure he was about to say no. To his surprise the steward turned and went to find someone.

Minutes later he re-emerged from backstage with Mac following him. Mac was annoyed that someone had dragged him away from the band.

"Mac, head of security," he said holding

out a hand to Ricco. Ricco stepped forward and shook his hand. "Ricco Salvatore," he replied. Mac knew he knew the name but couldn't think who he was.

"Could you please see that Mr Rose

gets this?" Ricco asked, holding out one of his business cards. Mac took a quick glance.

Ricco Michele Salvatore

CEO Salvo's Fashion House

London, England/ Roma, Italia

"Uh.. I'll try," he replied, shoving it in his

pocket and leaving immediately, even more annoyed that he'd had to go out there for something so unimportant! Ricco hoped that it would find its way to Dex.

Mac followed the band back onto the bus, forgetting about the business card.

Ricco rushed back to find Millie, knowing she would hate being left on her own in a crowd. Stuck behind a sea of heads Ricco could see her in the distance waiting for him. He made his way towards her.

"Hey, everything okay?" asked Millie as Ricco got closer.

"Yup," he replied. Millie was curious as

to where he went, but knew if he wanted to tell her he would.

Outside, the crowds began to disperse as the venue emptied. Millie and Ricco walked arm in arm along the side of the river towards the hotel. London looked so gorgeous at night, so quiet and twinkly thought Millie, as she watched the reflection of the flickering street lights on the water. It was such a contrast to the busy hustle and bustle of London by day, which Millie really didn't like. She felt uneasy in London, it was such a big place with so much going on, she was a home bird and never felt as truly happy as she did when she was in her own, much smaller, familiar, city. But as she walked along the riverbank she thought to herself that these were

the kind of places that she was going to have to get used to now. If she wanted to be a big-time designer she was going to have to spend a lot more time in London, Paris, Milan, possibly even New York and Tokyo, and Ricco wasn't always going to be there to hold her hand. He had his own life, his own work and whilst the thought of it totally freaked her out at the same time she felt a little excited. She was no longer going to be a small-time girl living in mummy and daddy's pockets. She was going to be out there on her own, making something of her life and fulfilling her dreams, and though she felt slightly terrified by it, she knew it was exactly what she wanted. Her life was going to change dramatically, for the better. A smile crept across her face and she snuggled into Ricco's arm.

His phone rang and vibrated against her head. She jumped. "Sorry, babe," he said, pulling it from his jacket breast pocket. "Good evening, Ricco Salvatore," he said.

Millie giggled. Italians were so formal.

"Yeah, okay, fabulous." Millie could just make out that the voice on he other end was his dad. "I will do, thanks Dad, see you Friday," said Ricco, hanging up the phone.

"Friday?" asked Millie. "Is he going somewhere?" she added.

"No, he's not going somewhere, we are!" said Ricco with a smile.

Millie was confused. "We are? Where?"

"Wherever you want!" he replied.

Millie looked at him, puzzled "Huh?" she replied.

"After working the weekend Dad's given us the rest of the week off! He's giving you a bonus in the form of a three-night break anywhere you want as a little congratulations on your launch. And a little rest!" he explained.

"Eeeeeeeeeeeeeeeee," squealed Millie, more high-pitched than usual! She assumed she would go back home in the morning and be back in the office by lunchtime. It was her turn for 'you choose Tuesday' in her office, where she got to choose what they got for lunch, and she was slightly ashamed to be pretty excited about that! But this was better. "Oh, yay!" she said, bouncing down the street.

"Where are we going?" asked Ricco.

"Er, I don't know?" she replied. "You choose!" she added.

"I'm not choosing, it's your bonus trip," replied Ricco.

"Oh man!" Millie wasn't good with decisions. As they approached the doors of their hotel she stopped and let go of Ricco's arm.

"DUBLIN!" she shouted, over excitedly.

"Dublin?" Ricco questioned her choice. "You can go anywhere in the world and you want to go to Dublin?" he asked, laughing to himself.

"Yes! There's this little place in Dublin, well not in Dublin but just outside Dublin buuuu…"

"MIL! Slow down!" said Ricco, who couldn't understand a word of her over excited, super-fast rant!

"Ha! Sorry," giggled Millie, taking in some deep breaths in an attempt to calm herself down.

"There's this little designer boutique shop, just outside Dublin, that I've always wanted to visit," she explained, slower this time! "Plus, there's no point going anywhere exotic for three days!" she added. In reality she was scared of flying and didn't want to go any further.

"That's true, Dublin it is then," said Ricco, holding up a hand for a high-five and opening the hotel door for Millie with the other.

Millie stopped. "But wait! We have no clothes here!" she exclaimed.

"Don't worry, we'll shop when we get there" said Ricco. Millie was excited! She loved an impromptu shopping trip!

Dex looked out of the blacked-out bus window that ran along the side of his bunk. Inside the bus was so quiet for once that he could hear girls screaming as it pulled out onto the road from behind the venue. All of the band were already in their bunks and he could hear the crew members sat talking quietly in the seating area at the other end of the bus. He laid transfixed on the streets outside, watching the fans all walking away to wherever they were going for the night, laughing, talking, having fun. *It must be nice to be a normal person and just go watch a band with friends,* he thought. It wasn't something he could ever do now and as much as he was loving living out his lifelong dreams, part of him ached for a bit of normality, normal friends, a normal girlfriend. He shrugged it off; part of him knew none of that would top his life right now. He was very aware of how lucky he

was but he still felt jealous watching a couple walk along the side of the river, arm in arm, stopping to kiss from time to time. The street lights lit up the river, it looked almost magical. *What a nice place to be with someone,* he thought as he watched a dark-haired girl high-five her tall handsome boyfriend, both smiling. They looked like they were enjoying the night as he opened a door for her to go into a hotel. Dex smiled. They looked so happy.

The bus headed out of the city and the river was no longer in sight. Dex closed the curtain and laid back on his pillow. He was shattered. He was looking forward to a couple of days off, only a few more days to go and he'd be able to take a break and go see his mom and dad. "Hey, man, some dude gave me this," said Mac, handing a crumpled business card down to Dex on his bunk.

"What the fuck?" said Dex. "R. M Salvatore?" He was confused. "Who the fuck is that?" asked Dex.

"I don't know, but he was a handsome fella! I'd call him," joked Mac, walking away.

"He's a millionaire fashion designer's son," shouted Zach from the next bunk. "I Googled!" he added.

Dex was more confused than ever. "Why has he given me his card?" he wondered. Dex knew the name sounded familiar but he couldn't think where he had heard it before.

"Maybe it's just the offer of free clothes," added Zach.

"Yeah, maybe," agreed Dex, tossing the card down on the bed beside him. They often had designers and brands wanting them to wear their clothes, it was probably just that. Dex thought nothing more of it.

He pulled out his phone and began to type lyrics that he'd had in his head all day. All he could write about was 'her'.

It felt strange to him to be writing about someone he didn't know but for some reason she inspired his creative mind and lyrics had been floating around his head for days.

CHAPTER 12

Tuesday morning arrived with a bang. Literally!

"What the hell was that?!" said Jesse as the bus came to a sudden halt, sending him off his bunk and leaving him in a duvet-wrapped heap on the floor. "Sorry!" shouted the driver, rubbing his eyes. Mac got out of his bunk and went up to see what had happened.

"I'm sorry," said the driver. "Damn girl just threw herself in front of the bus so I had to jam the brakes on!" he explained.

"Oh shit! Is she okay? Where is she now?" asked Mac, feeling very shaken all of a sudden. Today was going to be one of those days!

"Yeah, fine. I stopped short of her, her friends dragged her over into that toilet block," explained the driver.

"Okay, I'll go and see if she's alright. Damn teenagers!" he replied, putting his t-shirt on. Mac opened up the doors to the bus. Outside was so bright, he squinted to try to see properly as he tried to navigate his way down the steps with only partial sight cooperating this early – and Scotland was freezing cold at 6am! They had travelled through the night from London to Scotland ahead of a festival tomorrow. He crossed an empty road and stood outside the toilet block, shivering.

"Hey?" he called, hoping to get a response from the group of teenage girls inside. "Hey, is there anyone in there?" He asked again but got no response. "I work for Craze. They sent me to…"

"Craze?" came a voice from inside the girls' toilet.

"Yes, I'm tour security manager for Craze," explained Mac. "Is everyone okay in there? Can I speak with the girl who ran out in front the bus, please?" Mac asked. "You're not in any kind of trouble," he added.

Three young girls emerged slowly from the dark toilet block, one dabbing wet tissue to a bleeding wound on her elbow.

"Hey, are you okay?" Mac asked. The girl nodded. He was concerned as to why they were out alone this early in the morning, they looked no older than 12 or 13.

"Come up on the bus and let my medic check you over" he said.

"Come aboard the bus with Craze on?" asked one of the other girls excitedly.

"Yes," replied Mac. Ordinarily fans on the bus was an absolute no go but Mac thought given the circumstances it was probably better than the headlines that may follow if he did nothing. The teenagers followed him across the street to where the bus had stopped. "Where are you heading?" asked Mac. "School?" he added.

"Yeah, we just wanted to see if we could see the band first, someone told us they would be here early this morning" said the injured girl.

"Pretty silly jumping in front the bus," said Mac, trying to engage in a conversation to find out why she had done it. "Yeah" said the girl quietly, looking embarrassed.

"What are your names?" asked Mac, as he opened the door to the bus and held it for the girls to climb aboard.

"Lilly," said the injured girl quietly. "And these are my best friends, Alice and Rachel," she added. Mac shut the door behind them. The girls hunched together nervously by the door. No one was up yet, the bus was silent.

"Take a seat on the couch," said Mac. The girls shuffled nervously towards the couch and all sat huddled together at one end. "They're fine," said Mac, poking his

head around into the cab to reassure the driver who was pretty shaken after the incident. Caroline came through to the seating area in her dressing gown.

"This is Lilly, Alice and Rachel," said Mac, introducing them to Caroline and hoping she knew what to do with teenage girls more so than he did! "Lilly had a little run in with the bus," said Mac.

Caroline spotted her bloody arm. "Oh goodness, are you okay, sweetheart?" asked Caroline. "Let me clean that up for you," she added, flicking the kettle on and reaching on top of the kitchen cabinet for the First Aid box. She dampened a cloth with warm water and sat down beside Lilly to clean her cut. "How did this happen?" Caroline asked.

"I....errr..." Lilly felt embarrassed, she knew she had done something pretty stupid. "I ran in front of the bus," she explained sheepishly.

"Why on earth would you do that?" asked Caroline. Teenagers scared her, they had no fear nowadays. They were worlds away from how teenagers were when she was young. She couldn't understand them at all.

"I don't know, I wanted to see the band," replied Lilly.

"You could have been dead instead," said Caroline sympathetically, her mothering hat was well and truly on.

"I know," said the girl quietly. Just then the girls looked up as Dex emerged from behind the curtain to the sleeping area. One of the girls let out an 'eeeeeeeeeeee' sound. Another gasped. It was Dex Rose, stood before them in just a pair of shorts, his perfectly messy bed hair flopped in front of his gorgeously sleepy face. He put his arms above his head and stretched as he yawned. A small smile crept across his face as he noticed the girls on the couch.

"Err... hi," he said. he had slept through all the commotion.

"Hi."

"Hi."

"Hi," said the girls through nervous giggling.

Dex noticed that Caroline was cleaning up a bloody elbow.

"What happened?" he asked.

"Lilly's been a very silly girl! She thought a good way to meet you would be to throw herself in front of the bus!" explained Caroline, rolling her eyes.

"Woah, that's not good," replied Dex looking concerned. Lilly shivered as he spoke in his gorgeous American accent.

"Are you okay? My sister's called Lilly," he added with a smile. Lilly knew that. She smiled. The kettle was just done boiling, Dex got out some cups and poured tea for everyone, handing cups to the girls as he sat down on the couch opposite them. All three of them just sat completely still staring at him. He felt uneasy. The curtain was pulled back and Zach emerged to the same nervous giggles and gasps from the girls. Dex was relieved that he had taken the attention off him for a second. As Zach asked them about what had happened, it gave Dex the chance to slip away for a minute. Joining Mac and the driver in the cab he handed them both cups of tea.

"Thanks man," said Mac.

"Yeah thanks a lot," said Frank, their driver.

"Teens are crazy, right?" Said Dex.

Both Mac and Frank agreed. Mac got fed up of dealing with silly teenage girls all the time; he was too old for all the drama!

"What you going to do with them?" asked Dex.

"I've called them a cab to take them to school, just go sign something for them would ya? So they don't sue my ass!" groaned Mac.

"Sure," laughed Dex. He went to find something he could give them as a plea bargain. He found an old band t-shirt in his bunk. "That'll do," he said looking for a pen. He grabbed one and tried to sign the t-shirt but the pen didn't work, he picked up a little scrap of paper from the floor next to his bunk and began to scribble on it to get the pen working. He stopped for a second, reading something scribbled on the back:

Millie Vine

07885550987

It took a second before he twigged. "Oh fuck! Of course! Ricco Salvatore! That's the dude!" he said aloud.

"What?" asked Jesse, just stirring in the opposite bunk.

"Oh, nothing," replied Dex. His heart began to race as excitement engulfed him. Why hadn't he just turned the card over and seen that last night? He quickly signed the t-shirt and threw it over to Jesse in his bed. "Sign this and give it to Zach please," said Dex. He laid down on his bunk and closed his curtain. Lying on his back he just stared at the card, running his finger over her name. He had her number!

He grabbed his phone, staring back and forth between the blank screen of his phone and the number on the card. What was he going to write? Was he going to text the number at all? What could he possibly say?

He listened as the cab arrived and the three teens were taken off the bus, he could relax now. He hated having fans on the bus. Zach often brought girls back on the bus and it made Dex feel uneasy, he couldn't relax. He couldn't trust any of them. Whilst touring his entire life was in that bus and everything he owned, he couldn't bear anyone making money from him or his stuff. Even just a photo of him on there would be a worldwide sought-after thing and he hated that, he needed his privacy.

Why did that guy give me her number? he thought, *had she asked him to? Who was he to her? Did she want him to have her number?* So many questions were going round in his head. *Was it even really her number?* He knew he had to at least send a text. Play ignorant, he thought. He wrote out a message several times but deleted it each time. Nothing sounded quite right.

Hey, who is this?

He pressed the button. Sent. *That will do for now,* he thought. He waited for a few minutes excited to see what reply he would get. After ten minutes with no reply, disappointment set in.

The airport was busy for 7am, Millie thought as they got out of the cab. Usually early morning flights were lovely and quiet but this morning the airport was buzzing with people and she hadn't even got inside yet. She wasn't a fan of airports and flying, the crowds of people made her feel even worse but she wasn't going to let her fears get the better of her anymore, she was really looking forward to her trip and the flight was going to have to be endured.

Ricco held the door open for her and laughed as she passed by him still dragging her old, dishevelled suitcase. "Good god, girl, PLEASE get a new suitcase,"

joked Ricco. "I'm getting embarrassed to travel with

you," he added, laughing.

Millie looked back at him and stuck her tongue out, she attempted to slap him but with her arms full of bags she couldn't move! She was relieved that she had been forced to bring her suitcase with her to her bag launch, she couldn't fit all of the stuff she needed for the day into any of her handbags! Millie's fear of flying meant she was the kind of person that liked to do exactly the same thing with each safe and successful flight she took, changing her old faithful suitcase would almost definitely mean sudden death in an air crash!

Inside, the airport was heaving. Millie followed Ricco to the end of a very long line, putting down her bags on the floor she sighed. "Ahhhh, this is going to take ages," she moaned. She pulled out her phone to entertain herself for a while. She had a text:

Hey, who is this?

Hmm, I wonder who that is, she thought, she didn't recognise the number. Ignoring the message she opened her Twitter app and went straight to Craze's Twitter page.

@CRAZETHEBAND

En route to sunny Scoot-land, second to last UK show before we take a little break.

Who's coming tonight? Zach. x

Wish I was! thought Millie. She didn't really feel like she had been there with them last night, it was over so quickly she barely had the chance to experience it. Still, being in the same room with Dex was still incredible, if only for a minute. As the queue started to go down and they edged towards the check-in desk Millie's thoughts changed to her trip.

"I am so looking forward to this, babe!" she said, putting her head into Ricco's chest for a cuddle.

He put his arm around her. "Me too," he replied.

"I could really do with some time to unwind with work being so crazy lately," Millie added.

"And unwind we shall!" joked Ricco, moving forward in the line.

After checking in they made their way straight to the bar. Millie went up to get them some drinks, leaving her phone on the table; Ricco peered over to see if she had any messages. Nothing. Feeling slightly disappointed, he hoped that Dex had got her number. He knew he hadn't text yet, he was sure

Millie would have mentioned it if he had.

Millie came back carrying two huge cocktails with several straws, an umbrella and a huge piece of pineapple sticking out the top.

"Woah," exclaimed Ricco as she put them down in front of him.

"I've got to get on a plane in a minute! Plus we might as well start as we mean to go on," Millie smiled, poking herself in the eye with the umbrella as she took a sip from her bright green cocktail. "Ouch!" Ricco laughed. 9am came round too quickly and the plane started to board. Millie was feeling merry after she had downed her third cocktail and hurried to pick up all of her bags. They rushed to join the end of the queue. Despite a few drinks and a little talking to herself Millie could feel the nerves building. This was the worst bit, right before the flight, the anticipation and the waiting drove her nuts. This time she also had an added feeling of dread at the fact that Dex was in the UK, closer to her than he usually ever was and she was leaving the country and flying further away from him, it didn't feel right. Almost like she was leaving a piece of herself behind.

She followed Ricco up the steps to the plane, holding onto the back of his shirt like a little girl not wanting to get lost. He led her to their seats and she flopped into the window seat. Ricco put the bags in the overhead locker and sat down beside her. He squeezed her hand.

"You'll be fine, bab," he tried to reassure

her. Millie giggled at him calling her bab, her Southern vocabulary didn't sound right coming from an Italian! But nothing was going make her feel any better, she hated this and no one was ever going to make her feel any differently about flying. She sat quietly, lost in her own thoughts and fears, clutching into the armrests. She didn't say a word to Ricco as the plane thundered down the runway and soared into the air. She barely moved an inch, it was as if she was flying the plane with her statue-like stance, if she moved it almost certainly would result in the plane hurtling back down to the ground. No one understood.

Once the plane was up she very slowly turned her head to see what Ricco was doing. He was riffling through his bag looking for something, wiggling around in his seat, it worried Millie.

"What the hell are you doing?" she snapped. "Sit still!" she added.

"Why?" asked Ricco, slightly puzzled. "Because... uhh... oh, nothing," she replied, he would only laugh.

As the plane flew smoothly Millie began to relax a little and could feel her limbs loosening up. She readjusted herself in her seat and pulled out her phone from the pocket of her bag, very slowly so as not to cause the pilot any confusion or distraction that resulted in certain death! She had completely forgotten about the text she had had earlier. She opened Twitter and did her usual band stalking routine. Nothing new.

"So, tell me about this place you want to see, babe," asked Ricco.

"Huh?" replied Millie, taking a second to look up from her Twitter feed.

"This store you want to see, tell me about it," he asked.

"It's a New York designer I like, she has one of her stores in Dublin. There are only four in the world: New York, Paris, California and Dublin, so this is the closest," she explained.

"Charlotte Hart?" asked Ricco.

"YES!" replied Millie. "How on earth did you know that?" she asked.

"Haha, well, one: You forget how well I know you, and two: You forget I've been a fashion designer a lot longer than you! I know where all the good designers' shops are!" he explained.

It was true, he did know her better than anyone else and

he was an amazing designer, he designed most of what his dad's stores sold and he also had his own collections in really prestigious stores, Harrods, Saks and many more all across the world. But to her he wasn't some big shot, millionaire designer, he was just Ri, her best friend.

"What? That was quick," exclaimed Millie, hoping that the lights were on for landing and not because of imminent turbulence!

"Yup, that's it, babe, it's only a 50-minute flight," replied Ricco, knowing Millie would be super happy that it had gone so quickly and she would be getting off the plane shortly.

Millie smiled; she could finally get excited now the worst part was over. A few days off work with Ricco was going to be fab! She was glad that their night in Milan hadn't created awkwardness between them, they had spent the night in a hotel together last night and it was as if nothing had ever happened. Millie was glad nothing had changed and that she could still spend nights with him. He was the most fun of all her friends, she knew it would be a great trip.

CHAPTER 13

"Dex!... Dex!... DEXTER!" yelled Mac, stood on the stage getting frustrated waiting for him.

"Oh, shit!" said Dex, putting his phone back in his pocket as he rushed from backstage.

Mac didn't look impressed. "Come on, man! We've only got 15 minutes to do this sound check and you're fucking about on your phone!" shouted Mac, he was bright red.

Dex hated making Mac mad but it was also hilarious to see him riled up, he was a big fella and it barely took anything and he was as red as a beetroot! Dex couldn't help but smile but he did well to hide it, he knew that laughing when Mac was in that sort of mood was taking his life into his own hands! Instead he kept his head down. He walked up to his microphone and adjusted the height. Jesse led the sound check, checking all their instruments as Dex belted out a few notes. He sounded good today. He felt well-rested and relaxed and he knew he was really on form. Dex had an undeniably incredible voice but when he was really on his game it really was something else!

As he sang he looked around the huge empty venue. It was quite spectacular, an open-air amphitheatre, in the distance he could see the beautiful Scottish highlands and a pretty little castle. He'd never played a venue with such an amazing view before. It really hit him how lucky he was to be paid to do something he loved whist travelling the world and seeing sights like this one. A year ago he could only have dreamed of standing there.

He pulled his baggy grey sweatshirt sleeves down over his hands and put both hands around his microphone. He closed his eyes and took a deep breath, the cool Scottish air felt so amazing as it filled his lungs and he got ready to belt out his last note of the sound check.

"Thanks guys, that was perfect," said Mac, who had calmed down now. The stage crew began to take away all of their instruments to make way for other acts to sound check. Dex pulled his phone out from the back pocket of his tight skinny jeans; he felt a rush of adrenaline as he saw

One new message

on the screen. *It's her!* he thought, his palms were sweating as he walked backstage he opened the message, excited at what he was about to read.

Hi baby, I'm playing Summer Rocks

Festival, Essex on Friday too! Yay! Can't wait to see you. Love you! <3 Luc xxx

Lucie! Dex felt instantly deflated. His entire body sighed as if the energy had been sucked from him in a split second. It was just from Lucie and even worse than that, she was flying back to the UK on Friday and performing at the same festival they were.

"Awesome," Dex murmured to himself under his breath, he really didn't want to deal with her. With their relationship! She'd only just left him and he was enjoying some uncomplicated time on his own. Mac followed Dex, Jesse, Zach and CJ backstage.

"That sounded awesome guys, good job," he said with a reassuring smile.

"Right, it's 1.20pm, I need you all back here for 4pm prompt, for a 4.15pm rehearsal," he added, looking at each of the guys one by one for their approval and to make sure they were all listening. "Zach?" Mac raised his voice a little.

Zach looked up from his phone. "Huh?" Zach replied, like a deer in headlights.

"Back here 4pm sharp! SHARP!" Mac demanded.

"Yes, I know!" replied Zach, raising his voice with annoyance too; rolling his eyes he looked back down at his phone.

"Right, good, see you all later then," said Mac, dismissing the guys for a few hours of free time.

"We hitting the bar?" asked Jesse.

"Yeah man!" replied Zach.

"Yup," added CJ.

Engrossed in his phone, Dex didn't answer.

"Dex, you coming?" asked Jesse.

Dex looked up from his phone. "Sorry, man. Nah, I'm gonna go see if I can get a couple hours' sleep on the bus," he replied. Lucie had ruined his mood for the day and he just didn't feel like drinking. He knew it wouldn't just be a few drinks with the guys, it would be a constant stream of girls, signing things, posing for photos, talking to countless teenagers about nothing, girls hanging over him, touching him, generally getting on his nerves! After Lucie's text he just felt like taking some time out and being on his own.

"You sure?" questioned Zach.

"Yeah, I got a bit of a headache, I want to get rid before tonight," he lied.

"Okay, man, if you're sure?" replied Zach.

"Yeah, see you later guys," said Dex as he headed off towards the tour bus. Climbing aboard he was pleased to see the bus was completely empty. *Ahhhhhhhh,* he breathed a sigh of relief. He really craved his own space and silence. Something he rarely got in the job he did, sometimes he just needed silence. The bus travelled with lots of people on board and was hectic and loud all the time so quiet time was like gold dust. Dex collapsed onto his bottom bunk, he pulled the curtain across and curled up, hugging his pillow. *Ahhhh,* he let out a huge sigh. It felt good to relax. He pulled back the outside curtain just a couple of inches so he could see outside, the windows were blacked out from the outside so he could watch the world go by anonymously, something he loved to do.

He watched intently as people rushed around outside preparing for tonight's show, other band members carried instruments around, caterers organised food, crew were running around preparing lighting and all of the sound equipment. It was such a fast-moving view from his bunk window, it felt lovely to him to lie completely still, to be totally outside of the bubble for once. As he lay there watching all the preparations his mind turned to the girl. He knew that was probably it now, he had missed too many chances to meet her and find out who she was. She had not text back, maybe her friend was just trying to set her up and she wasn't interested. Maybe it wasn't her number at all. He rolled onto his back and stared blankly at the bottom of CJ's bunk above him. He thought about Lucie, he felt nothing for her anymore. It was purely physical and that just wasn't enough, he had to end things but had no idea how! He hated confrontation and he really didn't like to upset anyone, he was a sensitive guy but he knew he was going to have to man up. Friday was the ideal time to do it; it was going to have to be face to face. If only there was an easier way. He closed his eyes for a minute and tried to switch off from his thoughts.

BANG!!!

Dex woke with a jump as the bus door slammed, followed by laughing and talking.

"Dex, man, it's nearly 4 dude, let's go or Mac's going to be pissed!" said Zach as he undressed.

"Ah thanks, man! I was asleep, Mac would have killed me if I was late again," replied Dex. He grabbed for his jacket, put it on and zipped it up to his chin, shivering. He buried his chin down into his jacket so it was covering his mouth and pulled the sleeves down over his hands holding them in place. He sat down in the seating area waiting for Zach to change his shirt. "Where are Jess and CJ?" asked Dex.

"They…" Zach started, t-shirt over his head. "They've gone straight to rehearsals, I needed to change my shirt, some dude tipped a pint down my back!" said Zach, pulling his shirt down over his head.

"I'm glad you came back or I'd have slept through rehearsals!" said Dex, holding the door open for Zach. As they stepped down from the bus Dex looked at the time on his phone. 4.04pm. "FUCK!… RUN!" yelled Dex. They ran to the side of the main stage where Mac was waiting for them with a face like thunder!

"Sorry, man, my fault!" said Zach, they shuffled nervously past Mac and onto the stage, bracing themselves for a telling off. Mac didn't say a word; he just watched them with a stern look on his face, like a disapproving father with two badly behaved sons.

In position on stage Dex glanced behind at Zach, giving him a little *we got away with that* kind of smirk. CJ counted them in with his drumsticks and they began their rehearsal set. The sun was low on the horizon and the sky looked beautiful, shades of pinks, oranges and purples, streamed across the dusk skyline, beyond the amphitheatre. The last light of the day's sun was illuminating the castle in the distance. Dex felt a little bit like he was in a fairy tale land of forests and castles, he was half expecting a dragon to turn up. There was nowhere like it in the US, not that he'd seen anyway. Open-air venues were the best; he had a feeling the atmosphere at this place was going to be incredible later.

After rehearsing three of the seven songs they were performing tonight the guys finished up on stage and sat out in the bleachers to watch the next band tune up. It was nice to get a tiny insight into what the crowd would experience later.

The catering team came over to them with a trolley full of food.

"Woah! That all looks so good," exclaimed CJ.

"Take what you like, guys," said the lady in a strong Scottish accent. Taking trays of food off of the catering cart the guys sat back down in the bleachers to eat.

"This looks amazing!" said Dex, excited to tuck into his huge hamburger. As he attempted to pick the massive thing up his phone beeped. He put the burger back down on the plate and struggled to pull his phone from the back pocket of his jeans, which became even tighter when he sat down! After struggling for a minute he pulled it free.

One new message

He opened it:

Amelie, who's this?

OH MY GOD, he said loudly in his head, *she's replied!* He was immediately transported back to the night he first saw her, heart racing, sweating hot all over, his spine literally tingled and he could barely contain his ear-to-ear smile.

"Another boo-tay call Mr Rose?" teased Jesse, seeing Dex's smile. Jesse laughed as Dex threw a piece of onion at him, narrowly missing his face.

"Nope," Dex replied, not even looking up from his phone for a second. He read the message over and over again; he had no idea what to reply.

"Come on, dude, fess up! Who's messaging you?" teased Zach. "Ain't Lucie that's putting a smile like that on your face!" he added.

Dex didn't say a word; he looked up at Zach for a second and threw him a cheeky smile.

"Ah I see! I'll get it out of you later, man, when you're all liquored up!" laughed Zach. Secretly Dex kind of hoped that he would, he really wanted to talk to someone about it all and he trusted Zach more than anyone in the world but he couldn't say anything first, it would just sound crazy and he didn't even really feel like he had anything to tell yet. As they watched the other bands rehearse Dex was completely engrossed in his phone. He stared at her message for what seemed like hours, running through various replies in his head. Nothing sounded right.

Approaching dusk an usher came to move them backstage before the fans were let in. They were on stage in 30 minutes and Dex really wanted to reply to her message before he went on. He really couldn't think of anything that sounded right so in a rush to send something he kept it simple.

Dexter Rose

He hit the send button.

"Right, phones and wallets please guys," said Mac. He always looked after their belongings while they were on stage; he was the only person Dex could trust with his phone. He hated not having it with him; he was completely paranoid that it would fall into the wrong hands! Stood side-stage the guys watched the warm-up band have a quick rehearsal. The sun had just set and darkness had begun to fall. Dex leaned forward to see out into the amphitheatre. He swept his hair away from his face as it fell forward, holding it on top of his head for a second he leaned a little further to see the view beyond the amphitheatre.

"Woah," he said. "Look at that view!" he added. Zach, Jesse and CJ leaned in to take a look, the sky was dark but the horizon was glowing with colour, pinks, oranges, purples and reds created the most beautiful backdrop to the stunning landscape. As the moon rose in the sky it shone over the castle as if it was an intentional spotlight set to highlight the castle against its surroundings.

Dex felt his adrenaline building as show time approached, good venues always added to his enthusiasm and he was really ready for tonight. He couldn't wait to get out there but as Mac gave them their 30-minute warning to prepare to go on, the warm-up act were about to play their set, his nerves kicked in at 100 miles an hour as they always did. He felt sick all of a sudden, he needed a drink!

"Mac! Whisky shots please!" demanded Dex.

"Sure," he replied, sending a runner to get them. Mac hated them drinking before going on stage but he knew he had to do what Dex asked. Waiting for the shots to arrive Dex was winding himself up more and more, he hated that the others always seemed so calm, but then he knew he was going to be centre of attention and all the pressure was on him to deliver a good show. His palms were wet, his hair stuck to his forehead. He looked over at Jesse.

"Ya' right man?" asked Jesse. He could see the fear in Dex's eyes. He thought it was crazy, he was one of the most incredible singers the world had ever known, he was born to be on that stage and delivered time and time again. Jesse and the other guys never had a single shred of doubt that things wouldn't go well but Dex just couldn't seem to get a grip on his nerves.

The usher carried a tray of whisky shots up the steps onto the side of the stage. Hidden from view the guys downed their shots, Dex grabbed another one and downed it as quickly as it could.

"Sometimes the road to a good show starts with a drink to calm the nerves," said Dex, shaking his head as if to clear it and bring himself back to reality. The warm-up band were just finishing up their set. With only five minutes to go everyone was feeling the nerves now. Dex paced the side stage, taking in deep breaths, the cool Scottish air really did make his lungs feel better than they ever had before. Zach was bouncing up and down on the spot, feeling really fidgety and itching to get out there. Jesse stood perfectly still, almost in a state of complete mental awareness, he found it always helped him to try to clear his mind and relax his body right before going on stage, it was almost a meditative tool. CJ was the only one who never got nervous, he sat at the back hidden behind his drum kit, he had nothing to be nervous about! The last song of the warm-up act came to an end.

"This is it!" said Dex, he took another deep breath. Mac stood in front of them, he watched for the last member of the warm-up band to leave the stage and turned to face Dex and the other guys.

"In 5, 4, 3..." he began, finishing the countdown silently with his fingers. As he got to 1, he stepped aside and Dex led the band onto the stage. A huge crowd erupted into roars of screaming and shouting. The spotlights were so bright on Dex that he could barely see anyone or anything. He didn't want to move from the spot, he was worried that he would get too close to the edge of the stage and fall off! Both he and Zach had done it... more than once!

As the music started his switch flipped, the lights went down a little, taking his nerves with them. Dex bounced around the stage with ease, never losing his breath and often lingering on single notes for what seemed like an eternity, showcasing just how powerful his voice really was. Striding with arms raised, leading a hundred thousand strong sing along, it felt unreal to hear a mass choir singing his lyrics back at him. He smiled to himself. He loved being on that stage, girls in the front row were crying for him, climbing over each other to get at him, shouting his name, throwing things at him. No matter how many times it happened he never got used to it. Their incredibly catchy music aside they put on an impressive show with a series of dramatic lights-outs, which found the stage frequently pinballing from blindingly bright to pitch black, sending the crowd into a frenzy!

Dex was getting tired towards the end of the 45-minute show, with just one song to go he had to keep his energy levels up. The end of a song gave him a brief couple of seconds to catch his breath and talk to the audience.

"Woah! You guys are awesome tonight," he said through breathing heavily. "This is our last song. If you know the words sing along. We are Craze! Thank you all, it's been fun!" As the first note played from their most well-known song it elevated the venue's energy to fever pitch! Dex could barely hear himself sing over the crowd singing.

Ricco pulled out the dining chair for Millie to sit down. "Thank you, baby," she smiled as he pushed her chair in. Millie looked around the restaurant. "Woah, this place is super posh," said Millie, scanning the room. Large white marble pillars framed the dimly lit room. Dotted between them, intimate tables dressed with crisp white linen and enough crystal to make Millie very aware of how clumsy she could be!

"Only the best for us," joked Ricco, flashing her a beaming white sparkly smile. The soft, gold tinged lighting lit him up like a god. His eyes sparkling against his dark Italian skin. Looking at him Millie took a deep breath to try and refocus as she felt a shiver travel down her spine. *Don't go down that road again!* she thought to herself. She shook her head attempting to shake the thoughts out, but as soon as she looked back at him her mind filled up again. She knew it was perfectly rational; she would be crazy not to want him. His thick, dark, messy hair ironically piled neatly on top of his head with one single strand falling in front of his face. Millie watched as he swept it away from his deep, dark, mysterious eyes, they drew her in every time. His plump pink kissable lips were framed by a five o' clock shadow and his dark Mediterranean skin contrasted with his tight white t-shirt that literally hugged his perfectly toned body. Millie realised she'd been admiring him for quite some time!

"What?" asked Ricco, beginning to feel a little uncomfortable with Millie starting at him.

"Oh, nothing," said Millie, bringing herself back to reality.

"Are you okay?" he asked.

"Uh huh," she replied, playfully biting her lip. Inside her head was a different story. *You're just so utterly perfect!* she said to herself, giving him a cute smile as the words went round in her head. Millie was relieved as the waiter arrived at their table; she was glad of the distraction. It cleared her mind as she thought about what to order.

"Can I get you some drinks?" asked the young waiter.

"Yes, please," replied Ricco, scanning the wine list. "A bottle of champagne please," he added, looking up at the waiter.

Surprised, Millie threw Ricco a wide-eyed expression.

"And anything for the lady?" asked the waiter.

"Just a glass of water please," she replied.

"Ah, yes, a jug for the table please," added Ricco.

"Of course" said the waiter, as he turned to walk away.

"A WHOLE BOTTLE OF CHAMPAGNE?" asked Millie as soon as the waiter had turned his back.

"Yup, I'm going to get you good and drunk," joked Ricco. Millie laughed. "Oh hey, did you get a text today?" asked Ricco.

"Er, a few, why?" replied Millie, puzzled. What an odd question, she always got texts.

"Oh, any unusual?" asked Ricco with a smile.

"Er... I don't think so, why?" asked Millie, becoming increasingly confused at his questioning.

"No reason," he said, burying his head in the menu to avoid Millie's inevitable questions.

Millie pulled her phone from her bag and placed it down on the table. "Oh, I do have a text," she said. She

looked down at the message on the screen.

Dexter Rose

Millie didn't understand it, she swiped the phone to unlock the screen and open the message properly. Picking up the phone from the table and holding it closer to her face she looked at the number it came from. It wasn't anyone she had saved in her contacts, she scrolled up to earlier messages and read the short exchange of messages.

"Well, some clown is texting me saying he's Dexter Rose!" she laughed as she put the phone back down on the table. She hated texting and didn't have the enthusiasm to text back someone who just wanted to wind her up. She glanced back at Ricco.

"I think you should text that one back, babe," Ricco said, trying to keep a serious face.

"Nah, can't be fucked," she replied, brushing it off.

"Babe. I REALLY think you ought to text back," replied Ricco.

Millie looked at him scrunching up her face in utter confusion. "Huh? Why?" she asked.

Ricco sighed, disappointed that he was going to have to give the game up! He really wanted it to be a surprise but Millie just wasn't going to play ball.

"It is Dex Rose texting you… or at least I think it is. I gave him your number at the show last night," admitted Ricco.

"What?" Millie exclaimed. "Whuuu… wuu… what?" she stumbled over her words.

Ricco was about to begin explaining but was interrupted by the return of the waiter with their drinks. "Your champagne Sir, Madame," he said as he filled their glasses.

"Thank you," they both replied in unison.

"And your water," he added, putting the jug down in the centre of the table.

"Thanks," smiled Millie.

"I'll be back shortly to take your order," added the waiter as he left.

"So? Er… what?" Millie quickly dragged Ricco back into the conversation.

"Babes, after the show when I left you alone, I went and gave your number to the band's head security guy and asked him to pass it on to Dexter," Ricco began to explain. "I wasn't sure if he would but it was worth a shot, maybe he did," he added.

Millie didn't say anything; she needed a moment to take it in. She picked her phone up from the table, unlocked the screen and opened the message again. She read the conversation over and over again. "But why would be bother to text me?" asked Millie. Nothing made sense.

"Well you said he looked at you strangely that night at the show, maybe he felt the same as you and wants to talk," said Ricco.

Millie thought for a minute. *Could he?* She thought. Her fingers hovered over the keyboard, lingering over letters of the reply circling in her mixed-up head. She had no idea what to write. She didn't really believe it was him, but she couldn't ignore it, just in case. Nothing in her head seemed like the right reply. Nothing sounded cool yet casual. She sighed, biting her bottom lip as she often did when she was deep in thought. "What should I write back?" Millie asked.

Ricco took a huge glug of champagne. "Mmmm, that's good!" he smiled, wiping his mouth with his napkin. "Er, I don't know, maybe something like I want to have your babies!" Ricco laughed.

Millie leaned over the table and punched him on the arm, loudly clinking a glass with her chunky metal necklace and causing the entire quiet restaurant to look at her. She felt her cheeks go red as she sat back down in her chair. She began to type.

Right. Why would Dexter Rose text me?

She pressed send. She still wasn't convinced and playing it down seemed like the only option in which she wouldn't look stupid if it was someone trying to wind her up!

Sent

She put her phone back down on the table. The waiter came over to take their order.

"Are you ready?" he asked.

"Yes, two feta salads to start please, one lobster and one chicken curry for main please," said Ricco, handing the menus to the waiter.

"Thank you," he said, head buried in his notepad. Millie loved it when Ricco ordered for her; it made her feel like she was on a date with a real gentleman.

"So, what did you think of yesterday?" asked Ricco. "Did you think it went well?" he added, referring to the launch of her bag collection.

"Yeah, it was amazing! Better than I ever expected," gushed Millie.

"My dad said there was a lot of interest from stores all around the world. I think you'll be in some exciting meetings next week," he said.

"Really?" smiled Millie. Ricco nodded. Millie's phone vibrated. Loudly! As it danced along the table she grabbed it quickly, embarrassed that she had drawn attention to herself for a second time.

"You shouldn't bring me to posh places like this," said Millie, clutching her phone to her chest in an attempt to silence it. It stopped. Relieved, she unlocked the screen to read the message. She stared at the screen. Frozen. Not quite able to take in what she was looking at. "What is it, babe?" asked Ricco.

Millie turned the phone around to Ricco, he read the message:

Because he needs to talk to you! ;) D.x

Ps. Here's proof, me and Zach on stage right now in Scotland.

Below was a selfie Dex had taken of him and Zach backstage during the half time break in their show.

"Told you you should text back!" smiled Ricco. He felt his stomach fill with butterflies and he felt a little sick, half excitement and half nerves. He knew he had done something amazing for his girl, but he was terrified of losing her. He knew things were about to change and he knew he would kill Dex if he hurt her. He hoped he had done the right thing. Millie smiled back at him.

"Thank you, baby!" she gushed. "You're amazing," she added. Reaching for his hand across the table, she gave it a squeeze, letting go as the waiter arrived with their starters.

"Aren't you going to text him back?" asked Ricco.

"Later," replied Millie. She was absolutely desperate to text him back but she didn't want it to seem to Ricco that Dex was more important. She was having dinner with Ri, he was important to her too and she knew she needed to give her best friend her time right now. She wasn't the kind of girl to put a guy over her best friend. Even Dexter Rose! But she couldn't wait for dinner to be over so she could reply; she had completely lost her appetite.

CHAPTER 14

Approaching 10pm Dex belted out the final note of the show to an explosion of applause and screams. Exhausted and soaking wet with sweat he breathed a sigh of relief as he stood centre stage, he walked to the front of the stage touching the hands of the girls in the front row he sent them into a primal frenzy! There were so many pretty girls all screaming for him but there was only one girl on his mind tonight. Dex felt happy as he came off stage, almost excited, he hadn't felt that way in a very long time. He just wasn't an excitable person, his mood was mostly sombre, often depressive, but he liked that. He was a happy depressive, it was the state in which he wrote the best songs! But tonight he felt different; he genuinely felt happy and couldn't wipe the smile that was fixed to his face! As he came off stage an usher handed him a towel, he wiped the sweat from his face and brushed his hair back with his fingers.

"Mac, can I have my cell please, dude?" he asked. Mac handed him his phone as he slumped down on the couch backstage. Dex scanned through all his messages, there were always a lot! As he came to the last few his heart sank a little, there was no message from her. He opened the last message he sent her to double check it had sent. It did.

Read 9.05pm. He sighed, putting his phone in his pocket, ignoring the other messages he had got.

Zach, Jesse and CJ were packing up their instruments as stage guys brought them off stage for them.

"Hey, man," Zach called over to Dex. "Drinks?" he added.

"YEAH!" replied Dex, he definitely felt like he needed to drink! He gathered up his stuff and waited for the other guys.

"Hey, Mac, can we go out?" asked CJ.

"Where?" replied Mac, who hated that question! Keeping the band safe out on the town in a foreign country was a logistical nightmare and required a lot of man power.

"Dunno, a bar," replied CJ with a cheeky grin.

"Yes," huffed Mac reluctantly. He couldn't say no, though he wanted to! Mac arranged their security team and called for a taxi. "Back by midnight!" he said sternly.

"Yeeeeeees!" said Zach sarcastically.

After a ten-minute taxi ride they pulled up outside of a very lively looking bar on the main high street.

"YES! This one!" said Zach, watching all the drunken pretty girls dancing around the street outside the bar. A couple of guys from the security team got out first and went inside the bar. Everyone outside the bar was staring at their two-car motorcade. Dex hated it; everywhere they went they drew attention to themselves, when he wanted nothing more than to blend in. Mac got a message on his radio that it was okay inside. Mac got out first, followed by Zach and Jesse. Girls instantly recognised them and began to surround them. Dex put a cap on and his sunglasses and took a second to prepare himself and take in the peace and quiet before the mob began.

"Ready, man?" asked CJ. CJ knew Dex was going to get it the worst! Girls wanting photos with them already surrounded Zach and Jesse; they could barely be seen through the hoards of people.

"Let's go, dude!" replied Dex, taking a deep breath as he slid along the seat to the door. Mac opened it for him and Dex climbed out, followed by CJ. Girls began to scream.

"Oh my god, it's Dex!" screamed one girl the second he emerged from the car. The crowds moved towards him. Mac, together with three security guys from the second car surrounded the band and escorted them inside, a trail of girls following behind, all trying to touch them and talk to them. Girls were pulling at Dex's shirt. It took every ounce of his willpower not to snap. Inside, the security team had got them a private table cordoned off away in a back corner. They sat down at the table surrounded by their security. A waiter brought them a selection of drinks over, there was no way they were going to be able to fight their way to the bar to get their own! Constant streams of girls were approaching the security team who weren't letting anyone near the table. They could finally relax and enjoy some drinks. Dex opened a can of beer and downed half the can.

"Woah, slow down, man!" laughed Jesse. Dex smiled. He was in the mood to get wrecked! The guys chatted amongst themselves; it was good to have some time just the four of them to kick back and have a good time.

Dex got his phone out and scanned through all his new messages, nothing from her. Girls were constantly shouting at them, held back by the security team. That was life now.

"What's the time, man?" asked Dex.

"11.10pm," replied Jesse.

"Fuck, we haven't got long!" replied Dex, and he realised it had been over two hours since he had text her. *Maybe she's not interested,* he thought, opening and downing another beer. He checked his phone again.

"Ya alright, man?" asked Zach, hoping he might get something out of Dex when he'd had a few drinks. Jesse and CJ were chatting on the other side of the table and it was so loud in there Zach knew if he was going to get anything out of Dex it was now.

"Yeah… uh," Dex started. Zach looked right at him intently waiting for the end of that sentence but Dex looked away.

"Problems with Lucie?" asked Zach. Dex looked back at him.

"No… uh, yeah… I dunno," he replied. He really wanted to talk to Zach but talking wasn't his strong point, he felt awkward. *Oh, just do it*, he told himself. Zach had been his best friend for years, if anyone would understand it would be him. Dex looked at Zach, his face was serious, almost sad. Zach was slightly worried about what Dex was about to say.

"I… I kind of met… nah honestly it doesn't matter, dude." Dex couldn't get the words out.

"Nah, come on, man," Zach pushed. "It's just me," Zach added.

Dex was silent for a minute; he went over the words in his head several times. He breathed out heavily. "Okay… I kind of met someone… well no, I haven't met her… woah! This is hard!" he started. "Okay… here goes! So last Friday at the show I saw this girl in the crowd. I didn't know who she was but I sort of felt weird, like I knew her. I don't know, it's all fucked up! She did something to me" Dex tried to explain. Zach listened intently. "Then I saw the same girl again in the hotel in Milan, she was staying in the room next door with some guy," he continued. "I don't really know who she is, her name is Amelie but that's all I know. I can't get her out my head, it's fucking weird, man! It's like some of that love at first sight shit or something." Dex shook his head and laughed, realising he sounded pretty stupid! "Woah! I wasn't expecting that," said Zach. "I thought it was just something to do with Lucie," he admitted.

"I know, fucking crazy eh!" smiled Dex.

"Nah, not crazy, it's kinda cool. So do you have any way of contacting her?" asked Zach.

"I think she text me today, some dude gave Mac a number to pass on to me at the show last night. The note said Amelie Vine and a number, I think that's her," Dex explained.

"Oh cool. Have you spoken to her?" Zach asked. "No, what would I say?" replied Dex.

"Er… I don't know, but I'm pretty sure 95% of the female population would want to get a call from Dexter Rose" Zach joked.

Dex laughed. "Yeah, right." Though it was probably true.

"In all seriousness, I guess just ask her to meet you somewhere for a chat?" Zach suggested.

"Yeah, I guess," said Dex. He pulled his phone from his pocket,

One new message

displayed on the screen. A rush of excitement flooded his body, he was sure this had to be from her. He opened the message:

Woah!. It is you. Hi :) I'm a big fan. Why would you want to text me though? Do you need a suit or something? Call me if you'd like me to hook you up. Millie.x

Dex was both happy and disappointed, he was happy she'd replied but a little disappointed that she thought he was after clothes. He wondered if that meant she wasn't interested. Though she did tell him to call her. *Could he call her?*

"Dude, why don't you just call her and lay it on the line? What have you got to lose?" said Zach, it was as though Zach had read his mind.

"*Should* I call her?" asked Dex. He was slightly terrified of the idea, he was a shy guy, he wasn't one to make the first move, and he wasn't good at talking to girls, what the hell was he going to say? He needed more alcohol!

"Yeah, man," said Zach.

Mac looked at his watch. "Fifteen then we got to go, boys," he said.

"A'ight," replied CJ.

Dex downed another pint and a shot, if he was going to call Millie he needed some alcohol inside him! "What's the time, Mac?" asked Dex.

"Nearly ten to twelve," replied Mac. Dex wondered if it was too late to call her, maybe it was but part of him knew he was just trying to talk himself out of it. Mac began arranging their exit. Dex couldn't even see where the exit was, their table was completely surrounded by girls shouting at them. Only a few security guards stood between them and being completely mobbed!

Millie laid in bed in her hotel room. "Man it's early to be in bed!" she whispered, but Ricco didn't answer. "I can't believe you're asleep already, you lightweight!" she said, talking to herself. Ricco was out for the count! A combination of a very busy week at work and copious amounts of wine! Millie snuggled into him and closed her eyes but she didn't feel tired at all. She was completely on a high from Dex texting her, nothing was going to calm her down tonight. She huffed and turned back onto her back. She grabbed her phone from the nightstand and put the covers over her head so she didn't disturb Ricco with the light.

She scrolled through Craze's Twitter page, looking at photos from tonight's show in Scotland. As she lay in bed looking at a photo of Dex on stage she felt a hot sweat engulf her body, he was texting her then, during that show! When thousands of girls were screaming for him he was texting her! She couldn't help but smile. She knew he was dating Lucie so he only wanted clothes or something, but that didn't matter, she had a text on her phone from Dexter Rose! At least he knew she was alive! Millie opened her messages and stared at the picture Dex had sent her. A number came up on the screen, her phone was on silent but someone was calling her!

"Who the fuck is calling me at 1.15am?!" she whispered

to herself. She slowly pulled back the covers and got out of bed, trying hard to be silent and not wake Ricco. She tiptoed towards the balcony doors as fast as she could before the phone stopped ringing, trying to navigate all the furniture in the pitch-black hotel room. "Ouch! Fuck!" she exclaimed as she walked into a chair, hobbling along with a painful knee she found the curtains, crept behind them and slowly opened the patio doors. She stepped outside, breathing a sigh of relief as she closed them behind her. It was freezing outside! Millie hunched her shoulders up and rubbed her arm with her free hand, she only had Ricco's t-shirt on and her knickers and the night air was bitter. She looked at the phone screen but it had stopped ringing! "Awesome!" she said to herself, but there was no way she'd gone all the way outside in the freezing cold for no reason. She pressed the call back button and huddled in the corner of the balcony, trying to keep somewhat warm!

"Hi," said a man's voice in an American accent. *Hmm,* thought Millie, who did she know with an American accent? She drew a blank.

"Uh... hi," she replied. "Who is this?" she asked. There was a pause.

"Dex," he replied.

"Who?" replied Millie, she didn't twig. It was late, she was beyond cold and she never thought he'd call her in a million years!

"Dexter Rose," he replied, laughing a little.

Millie froze! In both senses of the word! "What!? Dexter from Craze?" In her excitement and nervousness she began to ramble.

"Uh huh, that's the one!" Dex laughed.

Millie was totally lost for words. *I am on the phone with DEXTER ROSE!* she thought to herself. "Wow... uh... hi." Cursing herself for sounding like a dork, she didn't know what to say.

"Hi," he replied. "I think this is going to be the weirdest phone call you've ever received! It's the weirdest phone call I've ever made for sure!" he joked. "I have to admit I'm a little nervous to call you," explained Dex.

God his American accent sounds sexy, thought Millie. "Nervous? Why?" she asked, thinking surely it should be the other way around.

"I'm not good at this," he replied.

"You don't need to be," said Millie.

"I'm sorry to call you so late but I had to speak to you," said Dex. "This is going to sound like some crazy shit but a couple Fridays ago I played a show in England, I saw you there, right?" he asked.

"Yeah," Millie replied nervously. Every inch of her body ached, she wasn't even sure why. She felt every feeling and every emotion possible in that moment, she felt sick with both excitement and nerves! She was numb, suddenly immune to the cold, her whole body engulfed in adrenaline, heat washed over her. She leaned over the balcony railing, looking out over the pretty street below, it was the perfect backdrop to their conversation.

"And I saw you in a hotel, in Milan, right?" he asked. "I… I don't even know how to say this," he began, not giving Millie a chance to reply. "At the show, you saw me looking at you, right?" he asked.

"Yeah… I did, but I wasn't sure it was me you were looking at," Millie explained.

"I felt… uh… I don't even know how I felt but you caught my eye and it totally threw me off, I couldn't sing! No one's ever done that to me before," he continued. "Really?" asked Millie. She couldn't quite believe what she was hearing; it was a dream she was going to wake up from soon, she was sure. She knew exactly what had happened that night but it seemed so unreal, so far from reality, it was her dream playing out, and it couldn't possibly be real.

"Yeah, I know it sounds fucked up but I felt kind of connected to you, like I needed to know you. I've been trying to find out who you are ever since," said Dex. he began to relax, she was easy to talk to. Though he realised that he had barely let her get a word in. The alcohol was talking, continuously.

"This will sound equally crazy," she said. "But I felt exactly the same in that moment," said Millie, barely able to speak through her excitement.

"You did?" asked Dex. "It's fucking weird, right?" he added.

"Yup, I can't quite believe what you're saying but I came home feeling totally strange, I thought it was just an obsessed fan thing," she giggled.

"If that's the case then I'm an obsessed fan of yours!" joked Dex. Millie laughed. "I felt the same thing when I saw you again in Milan, but you were with a dude, I couldn't talk to you," he said.

"That's Ricco, he's my best friend… and my boss… and he's gay!" Millie laughed.

"Good," laughed Dex. "I've had too much to drink tonight, I needed a little courage to call," admitted Dex. "So this probably isn't the best time to talk properly but I just needed to say something to you, to hear your voice, which by the way is super cute!" he laughed. Millie giggled. "I guess I just needed to know I wasn't crazy and that you felt something that night too," he added.

"You're not crazy." Millie began to feel braver. "I've not stopped thinking about you since Friday," she said.

"Me either," admitted Dex.

Millie couldn't believe what she was hearing. It didn't feel like reality, she was waiting for the moment when she would wake up from her dream. "Oh, but wait… aren't you dating Lucie Goldham?" asked Millie. Her heart sank a little as she remembered, what the heck did he think she was going to be if he already had a girlfriend? She wasn't going to lower herself to 'bit on the side' status. With Ricco constantly telling her how amazing and how beautiful she was and with career really taking off she knew she deserved better.

Dex was hesitant to answer. "I... I am. But it's not been working out for quite some time, I'm ending it with her but I have to do it face to face," he explained.

Millie wasn't sure how she felt about it all. Was she going to be in the press as the other woman who split them up? She hadn't even met him but she knew how the media could be. "Er... okay," Millie replied, her mood a little deflated.

"Honestly. I won't mess you around, I'm not that kind of guy," he said. It was as though he had read her mind.

Millie smiled. "Okay," she said.

"I'll leave you to sleep now but can I text you?" he asked.

"Yeah, of course," she replied, he didn't need to ask.

"Rad. Okay, goodnight," said Dex.

"Goodnight," Millie replied. And that was it.

Millie held her phone to her chest, she exhaled deeply and shivers ran down her body at the same time. It was the most surreal moment of her life! She'd just spoken to Dexter Rose on the phone, her... Millie... little Amelie Vine, a nobody from a small city, where nothing exciting ever happened!

There was no way she was going to sleep now! She was wired! She pulled Ricco's t-shirt she was wearing tight around her body. Wrapping her arms around herself for warmth she leaned against the balcony and looked out over a quiet Dublin street. Her mind filled with thoughts of how much her life had changed in the last six months! Just back before Christmas she was really down, she had just split up with Jack, her boyfriend of two years, the love of her life. She spent a rubbish Christmas sulking about him, she had a job as junior designer for one of her favourite high street shops but she had been there for five years and didn't seem to be getting anywhere. She was bored with life, bored with work, bored of men. Oh how her life had changed!

The summer was about to begin and in the short space of time since Christmas she had everything she had ever dreamed of. Her own fashion line of bags, amazing friends and now people were beginning to know her name... Dexter Rose knew her name! After daydreaming for some time she could barely feel her fingers and toes, she needed to go back inside before she froze to death. She slowly opened the patio doors, her fingers hurt from the cold. She could hear Ricco snoring inside; quietly she stepped inside, the warmth felt amazing as it hit her goosebump-covered body. Gently she pulled the doors shut behind her and fixed the curtains back over them. She hated gaps between the curtains. She tiptoed across the room, being careful not to walk into anything. Again!

She approached the side of the bed and lifted the covers back. She sat on the edge of the bed slowly and swung her feet around under the covers about to breathe a sigh of relief that she hadn't woken Ricco when her phone vibrated. Loudly!

"FUCK!" Millie whispered, sitting on her phone to try to silence it. She sat completely still. Ricco's snoring had stopped, she thought for sure she had woken him; he turned over and instantly began snoring again. Millie finally let herself breathe again, she laid down and put the covers over her head, pulling her phone up to her face.

One new message

She opened it.

Hey. Good to speak to you. Will you meet me this Friday? I'm playing a festival in a place called Essex, is that somewhere you could get to? D.x

Millie smiled, she still couldn't believe Dex Rose, worldwide pop-rock star, the man she had fantasised about for the past year, was texting her wanting to meet her! She felt really tingly all over as she read the message over and over, trying to think of what to say.

Hey you! Yes, I'd love to meet you. I'm in Dublin, Ireland right now, I'm flying back to London Friday morning. Essex isn't far so I can be there in the afternoon. Millie

Millie excitedly waited for a reply.

That's chill. I'm on at 7pm, I'll put your name on a VIP list. Watch the show then I'll send someone to get you and bring you backstage. D.x

Her phone vibrated again, she opened it. It was a cute picture of Dex, snuggled up in his bunk on the tour bus. He looked so cute, his sleepy face, messy hair, he was gorgeous! She couldn't quite believe it was him she was talking to.

Great. I can't wait! Thank you. Millie x Ps you're so friggin' cute! ;)

Millie was getting tired, she could barely keep her eyes open, but she didn't want to stop texting him. She took a photo of herself, no make up, hair sprawled out over her pillow, she wasn't sure if she should send it, she hated photos of herself. She just managed to convince herself to press send before her sleepy eyes finally gave up and she fell asleep, phone in hand.

CHAPTER 15

"Wednesday morning, I love you" said Dex as he woke up in his bunk.

"Someone's happy this morning," said Zach, sitting on the end of Dex's bunk.

"I would say someone got some last night! But I know you didn't!" laughed Jesse.

"Ha! I wish!" said Dex. Zach laid down in Dex's bunk next to him, waiting for Jesse to go down to the seating area so he could talk to Dex.

"So, did you call her?" whispered Zach.

"Yeah" he smiled. "So... spill man... come on!" said Zach.

"There's nothing to say!" replied Dex.

"Well? What did she say?" asked Zach.

"Weirdly the same thing about the gig the other night, she felt something strange too," said Dex. He felt stupid every time he said that.

"I think you need to meet this girl and see if there is anything there," suggested Zach.

"Advice? From you?... Really?... Drunken serial fan fucker!" Dex laughed.

"Ha ha! Yeah, alright!" laughed Zach, in agreement that

Dex was right. "Invite her to a gig, bring her back to the bus…" Dex listened, hoping Zach had some decent advice. "and I can fuck 'er!" laughed Zach. "I'm kidding! bring her back, just have a chat to see if there is anything there. It might turn out to be nothing but least you can get it out of your head, man," suggested Zach.

Dex thought for a minute. "She's coming to the festival on Friday," Dex replied.

"That's good, right?" asked Zach.

"Yeah," Dex replied, unconvincingly.

"What? What's wrong with that?" asked Zach. "Uh.. I don't know, it's the whole fan thing I guess," Dex moaned. "Don't you ever worry about that when you bring someone back?" Dex asked.

"Truthfully, no. You can't live your life worrying what if. That's not living, dude. So what if they sell something on you? How can anyone prove it's true, the media already write all kinds of fake shit about us, what's a bit more?" said Zach.

Dex knew he was right, but ultimately all he worried about was what his mom would think. He knew any kind of scandal would disappoint her, embarrass her, it was his biggest worry. He didn't want his fame to affect his family, when truthfully, his parents were so proud of him and so easy going that they wouldn't have cared. They knew him and they knew what was true and what was not and that's all that mattered to them.

"I guess," Dex replied.

"Just keep your guard up and don't tell her anything you wouldn't want printed. At least at first," said Zach.

"Woah! Get you with the sensible advice!" Dex joked.

"Full of it, man!" Zach laughed. "Can't wait to meet her Friday," he added.

"Maybe, but Lucie will be there," said Dex. His face dropped a little, he knew she would be there but saying it out loud sounded worse, it was the sudden realisation that he was never going to get a minute with Millie with Lucie being there!

"You know what these things are like, you'll barely see Lucie, between warm-ups, sound checks and she's on a different stage, don't worry about her, man," Zach said reassuringly.

"Hope so," said Dex. "I need to end it," he added, something he wasn't looking forward to! He hated confrontation and didn't want to break her heart. He had fans sending mail and sending messages through the band's social media on a daily basis telling him he'd broken their hearts and although he knew he hadn't done anything, he still felt a little bad and hated the thought of making anyone unhappy. Even strangers. "Yeah, you do. Do it Friday, get it over with. I'll look after Millie," Zach laughed.

"No way," said Dex, smiling. "You're not going near her!" he joked. Zach laughed. He had a track record for bedding fans!

"Lobby call in ten minutes!" shouted Mac from the front of the bus. Dex knew he had to get up but the warmth of this sheets hugged his half-naked body and the thought of staying right there all day was a much more inviting offer than boring TV interviews back to back all day! He hugged his pillow as if it were a person and nestled his face into it.

"Dexter! Did you hear me?" shouted Mac.

"Yes!" he replied mockingly, lifting his face from the pillow just enough to be heard, then letting his face flop back into his soft warm pillow again. He grabbed his phone from beside him and looked at the screen:

One new message

He opened it. He sat bolt upright and was suddenly completely awake. He stared at the screen, gracing it a beautiful photo Millie had sent of herself last night. He had fallen asleep without seeing it. *Woah!* he thought to himself.

She was gorgeous. He turned the phone around to show Zach.

Wide-eyed, Zach grabbed the phone out of his hand. "WOAH!" Good work man!" exclaimed Zach, Dex smiled. "If you change your mind about her..." Zach teased.

Dex snatched the phone back. *Not a chance!* he thought. Despite her beauty and the intense connection he felt to her, he still felt very cautious about the fact that she was a fan. He was going against everything he stood for. He could hear his mother's voice in his mind. *Are you sure you're doing the right thing? Do you want your private life splashed over the media? You're not messing Lucie around are you?* Though he knew that's exactly what his mom would say, they were genuinely questions in his own mind; he was worried about all those things. Since he became famous he had only dated two girls, Jesse's sister and Lucie, this was brand new territory for him and it made him nervous.

Millie walked along the busy Dublin high street. It was early, all the shops were just opening up. The air felt at its freshest, as if it was brand new, nobody had yet breathed it in. She took a deep breath and filled her lungs, she looked up as a flock of birds flew overhead, tweeting as they went. The sky was already a gorgeous shade of blue and the sun was already warm.

Millie wasn't a morning person but when she had to be up and out early she enjoyed this time of day, the morning hustle and bustle, everyone busying about, starting their days, the shops opening their doors and people on their way to work. She watched people as they went about their business, playing the same game in her head that she played looking out of Ricco's apartment windows. That girl over there in the purple top outside the coffee shop, she's waiting for her boyfriend to arrive, they're having a shopping day, he's treating her for an early birthday present. They'll lunch together, take a stroll along the river hand in hand and... a man caught her eye and her mind was gone... he's on his way to an important interview, he's nervous but today is a good day and he'll get the job and a huge pay rise and his family will be so happy and proud when he gets home tonight to tell them and...

"Millie," said Ricco. Millie was somewhere else. "MILLIE! he shouted.

Millie jumped, stopping dead in her tracks. "Oh my goodness, what?" she replied.

"You're doing it again aren't you!" said Ricco. "Doing what?" She played dumb, knowing full well what he meant.

"You're making up fake lives for people in your head, right?" said Ricco.

"Errrr... no?" she said defensively. *Dammit! He knows me too well,* she thought.

Ricco threw her a cheeky smile and grabbed her hand "Come on, let's hit Salvo's and see if they have your bags in," he suggested, pulling her along the street.

"YES!" she replied, excitedly. And off they hurried down the street. Salvo's wasn't far. Millie loved walking around arm in arm with Ricco, she knew people would look at them and assume he was her boyfriend. She liked people thinking that, he was one of the most gorgeous men alive! He was literally like an Italian god, Millie felt great on his arm. She knew if he was straight she would never pull a guy like him, he was way out of her league.

Ricco caught a glimpse of Millie in a shop window, she had a huge smile on her face, it was the happiest he had seen her in ages. He turned to her and smiled; pulling her by the hand in close to him he kissed her on the forehead.

"You're happy today," he said.

"I know," she grinned.

"Ms Vine! What are you no telling me?" he said in a

slightly stern, very sexy Italian accent. Millie loved when he got English sentences just slightly wrong; it was so cute and endearing.

"I no tell you nothing!" she mocked him in her best fake Italian accent, giggling after.

"Come on! Stop that," he replied. Millie stayed silent, grinning from ear to ear. Ricco stopped walking and stood right in front of her. "Fess up!" he pleaded. Millie laughed. "Fine! I had a middle of the night phone call last night," she teased, giving nothing away.

"From who?" Ricco asked.

"I'm sure you could hazard a guess, I'm pretty sure I have you to thank for it!" she said.

Ricco smiled. "Dexter?" asked Ricco, playing dumb.

"Of course from Dexter!" she smiled.

"Oh my! What did he say?" he asked enthusiastically.

"Oh my god, Ri! Never have I heard a sentence so camp come out your mouth!" she laughed.

Ricco stopped walking. "Shut up! Come on! Tell me!" he pushed.

"He invited me to a festival he is playing at this Friday," Millie replied, not wanting to give too much away. She needed a little bit of secrecy, even from Ricco.

"Well that's good isn't it?" he asked as he took her hand and began walking along the pavement again, navigating through the growing crowds of morning commuters.

"It's more than good, it's incredible!" gushed Millie. "Thank you, baby!" she said, leaning into his arm. "I owe you!" she added.

"You owe me nothing" he said with a smile.

Arriving outside Salvo's Millie couldn't believe how big it was! It was bigger than their main London store. It was set in an old-style building with big stone steps up to the door and huge stone pillars in front. It seemed nothing like a clothes shop from the outside. To Millie it looked like a museum or something of equal architectural importance.

Hanging into Ricco's arm and looking down at her feet with every step she took, she climbed the steps. This was the kind of thing that she dreaded as one of the world's clumsiest people. She breathed a sigh of relief as she took the final step through the doors; the store was quiet this early in the morning. Ricco went ahead, he turned into director the second he walked through the doors. His dad's stores were his babies and one day he would take over and own them all, so it was important to him that every store was perfect! Looking around he spotted a broken light.

"Browse, I'll come find you in a minute," he said as he hurried off to find someone to rectify the imperfection. Millie didn't envy the person who was on the receiving end of Ricco. In work mode he could be very fiery! It was the Italian passion in him!

Millie wandered around the store, browsing the clothes. She recognised some pieces that had been through the design office. She meandered through the shoe section. *Bags must be somewhere around here,* she thought to herself. As she turned the corner, there they were!

Her stomach instantly filled with butterflies as she rushed over to the beautiful display, it was much like the display at her launch in the London store. A huge beautiful distressed vintage-style white vanity table stood alone on the floor, covered with her beautiful faded rose design. Pale pink rose petals were laid over the top of the table and her bags were each placed in their own spot on the table. The large oval mirror on the back of the vanity table had *'A. Rose x'* scrawled across it, written in pink lipstick. She walked briskly to the stand, looking on in awe. It still hadn't sunk in that these were HER bags! She could barely contain her excitement, she looked around for someone to tell but she was alone.

She picked up one of the bags and gazed at the gorgeously girly tag that hung from the handle. She placed the tag in the palm of her hand and pulled out her phone to discreetly take a photo, feeling like she was doing something wrong, or at least silly. She jumped a mile as someone tapped her on the shoulder.

"Ahhh," she said as she turned quickly to see who it was. "Ricco! You fucking scared me!"

"Haha sorry! Found your bags then," he said. Millie smiled. "Come on!" he said, pulling her in close and holding his phone out in front of them. "We need to take some selfies with your display," he said.

"Oh," Millie rolled her eyes, secretly loving the idea, but not letting on that it was anything more than daft and self-indulgent as she posed for a picture… and another… and another! Her phone began to ring 'mid-selfie', she scrambled around in her bag to find it. "Hello," she said, rushing to get the phone to her ear in time.

"Hello… Ams?" Only her mum called her that.

"Hi, Mum," Millie replied. She felt instantly uneasy by the tone of her mum's voice, she knew something was wrong!

"Everything okay?" Millie asked.

"It's your sister, Lexi… Lexi's been in an

accident!" her mum was choked up and struggled to get her words out.

Millie's heart sank, she just managed to stop herself from being sick. *Please be alive, please be alive!* Millie said to herself, crossing her fingers without even realising she was doing it.

"Oh my god! Mum! Is she okay?" Millie asked. Her eyes began to well up before she'd even got an answer.

"Ams, she was hit by a car! She's going down to surgery soon, she's not good," said her mum, fighting back the tears.

"Oh shit! Okay, mum, I'm coming home. I'll get a flight,"

replied Millie, wiping away tears. She knew after all her luck lately something had to go wrong!

"Okay, darling," said her mum.

"Bye, Mum," she replied, completely choked up. Ricco was worried, he had no idea what had just happened but he put his arms around Millie. As she took the phone down from her ear she burst into hysterical tears, her legs turned to jelly and she couldn't stand. Ricco held her up, holding her tight in her his arms. "What's the matter? What's happened?" he asked. He felt sick himself, he knew something was really wrong.

"My... my... mm..." she couldn't speak through her tears. "My sister," she sobbed.

"What's wrong with your sister?" Ricco instantly thought the worst.

"She was hit by a car, she's in a bad way. She's going into surgery." Millie could barely breathe, it took all her energy to get the words out.

"Oh, babe." Ricco didn't know what to say, he just squeezed her tight, wiping the tears from her face and brushing the hair away that had stuck to her wet face. "Is it Aria or Lex?" He asked.

"Lex" she replied her head nestled into his neck.

"Let's get you home, sweetie," said Ricco, walking out of the shop still holding Millie up. Ricco dialled for a taxi to the airport. He sat Millie down on a bench outside the shop whilst they waited, he then called the hotel and arranged for their belongings to be flown home. Ricco had enough money and power to make things happen. Within five minutes he had transport to the airport, booked new flights to a different destination airport closer to home, made plans for their belongings they had left in their hotel room to be sent home and cars to collect them for when they arrived home. He sat down next to Millie and pulled her in close to him, gently stroking her tear-stained cheek.

"She'll be okay babe, she's a fighter, like you are," Ricco said, trying his best to find the right words. Millie didn't need him to say anything, just holding her and getting her home was enough.

"Yeah," Millie half-heartedly agreed, hoping to god he was right. "Thank you," she smiled at him,

grateful for all he had done for her.

"Don't mention it," he replied as the taxi pulled up. Ricco opened the door and helped Millie into the back, before getting in the front. "The airport please," he told the driver. "As quickly as you can," he added.

"Yes, sir," replied the cabby. The taxi sped away through the city centre.

"Oh no! What about our passports?" said Millie as it dawned on her that she had left it in her hotel room.

"I've got them," Ricco reassured her. "I don't leave my passport anywhere!" he added. Millie was relieved, she didn't want anything holding her up, she needed to get to her little sister.

Approaching the airport she looked at the time on her phone: 10.26am. She had several new messages on the screen but they weren't important right now. She text her mum to let her know she was getting on a plane.

The taxi pulled up at the terminal, it was busy today and she couldn't even see the doors through the crowds of people all trying to make their way inside. Ricco paid the driver and got out of the taxi, opening the door for Millie and holding out a hand to her.

"Thanks, babe," she said, still sounding pretty choked up. Inside the airport it seemed to take forever to check in. "Why does everything take so long when you're in a hurry?" Millie groaned as they joined the back of a very long queue.

"It's alright babe, it won't be long," replied Ricco, rubbing the back of her head.

Millie was irritable, she needed things to move faster. *Don't they know I need to get home? Like now!* she thought to herself, getting frustrated. Millie felt as if someone had zapped the life from her, just standing in the queue was a stretch for her exhausted body's capabilities, her legs were still like jelly and she felt as though her body was too heavy to be supported by them. She leaned against Ricco's shoulder and he put his arm around her and kissed the top of her head. She managed a half-hearted grateful smile.

Despite only a 40-minute wait, boarding the plane seemed to Millie to take a lifetime; she looked down at her watch for about the 10th time since they checked in. "Come on!" she moaned under her breath, she felt helpless and utterly defeated at not being able to get to her sister or be with her distraught family. As she climbed the steps onto the plane she felt a slight relief that at least she was now on her way.

The plane thundered down the runway but for the very first time Millie wasn't holding onto the armrests for dear life. She didn't care that she was flying, adrenaline and an instinctive need to get to Lexi had taken over and suppressed her fears.

Ricco felt uneasy next to her, he didn't know what to say or how to comfort her. Usually he could read her mind, he always knew the right thing to say to her, but not this time. He sat in silence for nearly the entire flight, running over things to say in his head time and time again and them determining that it wasn't the right time to say it. Maybe this was bigger than him, he thought. Maybe he didn't need to fix this like he did with everything else in her life. Maybe this was something Millie needed to deal with alone and he would just be there to pick up what was left of her afterwards. He watched her out of the corner of his eye as she looked at her watch every 30 seconds, then out of the window as if she was looking for landmarks to see if she was getting closer, but there was a vast nothingness behind the window.

The flight was quickly over and Millie rushed to get off

the plane. Stuck in a queue of people in the central aisle she could feel herself getting anxious, everyone seemed to be going so slowly. *Come on!* she said to herself, willing the people in front of her to hurry up and gather their belongings and get moving. Millie hadn't even given Ricco a second thought, he was some way behind her further down the aisle. At last the other passengers began moving slowly to the exit, Millie shuffled forward a few little steps, sandwiched between two strangers. She was annoyed that her arms were too restricted to see her watch.

A few more passengers stepped off of the plane and Millie could finally see outside. *Nearly there.* Her mind was racing, the sick feeling in the pit of her stomach had intensified and she felt dizzy. She managed to navigate the steps as if her body was on autopilot and walked briskly towards the terminal building. She was glad she had no luggage to collect and rushed to get outside to the car with Ricco chasing behind trying to catch her up.

"Here, baby," he called to her as he spotted his driver waiting across the road in the black Mercedes company car. Ricco caught up with Millie as she crossed the street, he grabbed her hand but she pulled it away. Ricco stopped. He was taken aback, he'd never had that reaction from her, she was always so loving towards him and usually loved that he was there for her. Millie barely even realised and kept walking briskly towards the car. Ricco slowly followed behind her, feeling rejected and pretty useless.

Millie opened the car door and climbed in the back, Ricco wasn't long behind her. He opened the passenger door and looked in.

"Hi, Tim," said Ricco. Tim had been driving for Ricco's dad since Ricco was a kid, the fifty-something, white-haired, softly spoken Bristolian felt almost like family to Ricco.

"Where to, fella?" Tim asked.

"Eden Park Hospital, please," replied Ricco. "Hospital?

Everything okay?" asked Tim.

"Millie's sister has been involved in an accident," he replied.

"Oh," replied Tim. Millie hadn't heard any of the conversation, she was completely inside her own head imaging the horrible news she might be arriving to. *What if she's paralysed? What if she's brain damaged? What if... what if she... dies?* Thought Millie. Her eyes welled up again and she felt a single tear trickle down her cheek as she stared blankly out of the window.

It wasn't long before the hospital was in sight in the distance. Looking at her phone again to check the time, nine new messages displayed on the screen. Millie ignored them, none of them mattered right now. She had completely forgotten about Dex, her bags and just about everything else in her life. All that flooded her mind today was getting to her sister.

The car pulled up and Millie was gone in a flash. "Thanks, Tim," said Ricco.

"Not a problem, kid," replied Tim.

Ricco stopped and thought for a minute. "Actually, I'm not going to go in, I think she just needs her family right now," said Ricco, knowing that he was right but feeling slightly deflated that he wasn't what Millie needed. He couldn't make this better for her like he did with everything else.

"Are you sure?" asked Tim.

"Yeah, she wouldn't even notice if I was there!" he replied. "Can you take me back to Salvo head office, please?" asked Ricco.

"Sure thing, kid," replied Tim. The car sped away, Ricco watched out of the window as the hospital got further and further from view. He hoped he was doing the right thing by Millie, he knew he probably was.

"Mum!" shouted Millie as she ran down the hospital

corridor. She threw her arms around her mum, who burst into tears. "How is she?" asked Millie. She leaned back from her mum's embrace to see her face, she'd never seen her mum look so tired, so fragile, so old! She was usually so glamorous and happy; Millie couldn't remember a time when she'd ever seen her mum looking so vulnerable.

"No news yet, she's still in surgery, they say she might be in there for up to 8 hours! She's broken her neck and her back," explained her mum. Millie burst into tears.

"Oh my goodness, Mum!" said Millie, putting her hands over her mouth. It sounded so serious! "What happened?" asked Millie, fighting back the tears to speak.

"She was walking to university early this morning in the city centre. A car's brakes failed, he swerved to miss another car and hit Lexi on the pavement, pushing her along the ground," Her mum explained.

"Oh my god! Lex!" Millie's eyes began to fill again, her poor sister.

"She's very lucky the car didn't run right over her! She's very lucky to be alive," her mum added, speaking calmly though visibly distraught.

The rest of her family had had time to come to terms with it but it was just hitting Millie. Her mum put her arm around Millie's shoulders. Wiping away her own tears with her other hand she led Millie down the corridor to where the rest of the family were.

"Dad!" She said as she ran towards him,

throwing her arms around him.

He kissed her on the cheek. "Alright, my darling," he said, with a half-hearted smile. He gave her a squeeze. Aria stood up to hug Millie.

"Aria," said Millie as she embraced her big sister who was visibly upset. Her face was bright red, black makeup streamed down from each eye, her eyes were red and her hair a mess. She was dressed in her white therapist uniform and had rushed to the hospital straight from work.

"Hey, Mil," said Aria. They leaned back to look at each other's faces, they both managed a smile before hugging each other tightly again. It was obvious at that moment they were both very appreciative of having each other.

Millie turned to see Nate, Lexi's boyfriend, sat on a chair in the corner of the room. He was all alone, his face in his hands. Millie hadn't really taken to Nate since Lexi had started dating him a year ago. Lexi had barely turned 18 and he was 33! Millie thought the age gap was too much and worried about him taking advantage of her little sister, she was beautiful! Gorgeous long blonde hair, olive skin, a perfect figure, long legs to die for that Millie had always been jealous of. She was doing well at university, studying creative arts. She dreamed of being a dancer in a West End show, she had her whole life ahead of her and Millie felt like he would hold her back. A waiter in a bar by day, a wannabe rock star playing in a local band by night, he was going no where fast. Even his name irritated Millie; he was Nathan but went by Nate, who on earth goes by Nate in England! It was so Americanised! It fitted in perfectly with Millie's perception of him, a 33-year-old wishing he had made it in a rock band ten years ago, not quite managing to let go and move on from his failure.

Millie could see what Lexi saw in him, he was good looking, a bit rough around the edges, every bit the rock star look, but he was never going to be good enough for her little sister or for a successful rock band! Right now she put her thoughts about him aside. She glanced over at him as he looked up from his hands, he looked so pale, almost ill. If he wasn't genuinely concerned for Alexia he was putting on a show-stopping performance of the doting boyfriend.

"Alright?" he muttered to Millie. He knew full well Millie didn't like him but his sad puppy dog routine was working,

Millie *almost* felt sorry for him. She rolled her eyes and breathed out deeply. *Be nice,* she told herself. She walked towards him and sat down beside him. He looked up at her as though surprised to see her next to him. It took every ounce of her better nature to be nice. She patted him on the back awkwardly.

"How ya doing?" asked Millie. She wasn't even bothered what the answer would be, it just seemed like the right thing to say, it was at least what Lexi would have wanted.

"Alright," he replied. He didn't look up at her, his eyes were fixed on the floor.

"She'll be okay, she's a tough cookie," said Millie, trying to reassure him. And herself!

"Yeah," he replied.

Wow, thought Millie. *It's like getting blood from a stone!* Feeling unable to converse with him she went to sit with her family across the room. She sat down next to her sister, Aria reached across and held onto her hand. Millie hated the waiting, she was desperate to hear something. Every time the door opened her heart skipped a beat but it was only nurses coming and going. It had been over an hour since Millie arrived, most of that time everyone sat in silence, each entertaining their own thoughts of Lexi, occasionally making small talk.

"How was your trip?" Aria asked. "Ya know, until this happened," she added.

Millie really didn't feel like talking about it, it seemed wrong to talk about happy things at a time like this. She felt almost guilty that she had been away having a good time when the accident happened.

"Umm, it was good. Ricco and I had dinner in a fancy restaurant last night, this morning he took me to Salvo's in Dublin and I saw my bag display! That was pretty awesome," she smiled.

"I bet!" Aria smiled back. She was so proud of her little sister, she loved her job as a beauty therapist but always felt like she should have tried harder. Millie was making a name for herself as a fashion designer, Lexi was a really talented dancer and though still young, Aria knew she would make it to that West End stage, or at least she was heading that way before the accident. Aria never pushed herself, she just settled. She was more interested in boys and going out when she was younger, she was never academic and knew she could have done something far better with her life.

"So, are you dating him yet?" asked Aria.

Millie looked at her, confused. A panic came over her. She didn't know about Dex, did she? How could she? Only Ricco knew, had he told Aria? He couldn't have, they barely knew each other. "Who?" Millie asked, feeling her cheeks getting hotter and hotter.

"That Ricco fella," replied Aria.

Millie laughed, feeling a huge relief. "Ha! No, Ricco is gay!" said Millie.

"Ohhhhh, is he? What a waste!" joked Aria.

"I know, right!" agreed Millie, giggling. It was a thought that filled her head at least 10 times a day! *At least I've seen him naked,* she thought to herself.

Millie's smile soon faded with the silence and she was brought back to the reality of the situation, she felt guilty for even smiling.

"Millie, Aria, Nate, we're going to be here a long time. Why don't you all head home and we'll call you if there's any news?" suggested Millie's mum.

"No, I want to stay," said Millie.

"There's no point us all sitting here, she may be in surgery until 9 o'clock tonight," their mum added.

Millie didn't want to leave. "We'll stay while you and Dad go and grab some lunch, it's nearly 3 o'clock and I bet you guys haven't eaten today. Then when you come back we'll go home for a while," suggested Millie.

"Okay," agreed her mum.

"I'm gonna go grab a coffee, Mil," said Aria. "Do you want anything?" she asked.

"No, I'm good ta" Millie replied. Left alone with Nate, the silence was awkward; Millie had no idea what to say to him, they'd never taken to each other so they had never gotten to know each other. Trying to be discreet Millie looked at him out of the corner of her eye; he sat lifeless staring at the floor.

"Why don't you go home and get some rest, Nate?" said Millie.

Nate looked up at her. "Nah, I want to be here," he replied. "You know, in case she wakes up and I'm not here," he added.

Millie said nothing. To her it still all seemed like an act. Millie rested her head on her shoulder and closed her eyes.

She woke sometime later to someone shaking her shoulder. "Ams," said a voice.

Millie opened her eyes, it took a moment for them to adjust. When they focused she saw her mum looking down at her.

"Ams, go home, honey. Get some rest, Lexi will be in surgery for some time yet. I'll call you if there's any change," said her mum.

Millie didn't want to go but she was feeling so tired, so reluctantly, she agreed.

"I'll drive you home," said Aria, standing to follow Millie. "Nate, do you want a lift home?" Aria asked.

"No, thanks, I'll stay," he replied.

"Okay, Mum, call me if you hear ANYTHING!" said Aria. Both girls kissed their mum and dad goodbye and left.

CHAPTER 16

"Man, what a day!" Groaned CJ as he climbed aboard the tour bus; they'd done back-to-back TV and radio interviews for 11 hours straight!

"I've never talked so much in my fucking life!" said Dex, following behind him. They all slumped down in the seating area, exhausted.

"Mac, crack the beers open!" said Jesse. Dex pulled his phone from his pocket. He hadn't heard from Millie all day, she'd not replied to his last message. He was dying to text her again but he didn't want to seem too keen. He wasn't going to chase her, as much as he wanted to get to know her he wasn't that kind of guy. He was a little shy, he definitely wasn't a ladies man! He needed her to come to him. He opened the photo of Millie she had sent him and just stared at it. Man, she did something to him! Just looking at her sent shivers down his spine, he could feel the hairs on the back of his neck stand up. He couldn't get his head around how he could feel like that from just a picture, he'd barely felt like that with a girl in person! He could only imagine how intense it would be to actually be with her in the flesh. Though the thought of it made him nervous. "I'm heading to bed guys, I'm beat," said Dex.

"Yeah, I won't be long either," replied Zach, "I'm exhausted too," he added. His phone rang so he went outside the bus to talk in private; it was his girlfriend Emma calling from the states. Dex hated that he cheated on her so much. Emma was one of the nicest girls he had ever met, she was one of very few girls Dex felt completely comfortable with, he could talk to her about anything. He totally felt like he was betraying her knowing about Zach's numerous infidelities whilst on tour, but he knew he couldn't say anything. He had been best friends with Zach for years and his loyalties had to lie with him, he hated feeling in the middle of it.

Ten minutes later and lights were out on the bus, all the guys and crew were in bed. Dex looked at the time on his phone: 8.49pm, lights out this early was nearly unheard of, clearly the day had taken its toll on everyone! Dex was pleased, he craved peace and quiet, time inside his own head. His life was one constant noise, surrounded by people and chaos 24/7, he wanted nothing more than time to think, time to just chill. He lay in his bunk cuddling his pillow, browsing the band's Twitter feed. He wasn't a social media fan but sometimes it was nice to read nice things about himself. He was ridiculously popular amongst their fans, every other tweet was about him, and it certainly gave him an ego boost. As he read through them all he wondered what these girls would think if they knew he was reading their tweets.

"Hey, Mac," Dex whispered, loudly! Led by Zach a choir of shushes followed. Zach laughed.

"No Dexter, you're not having another beer!" replied Mac, anticipating his question.

"No, that's not it. Mac, I'm bored, can I do a Twitter question and answer session on the Craze page?" The others often did this, the fans loved it, but Dex had never done it before, he had never been interested in doing it before but with his feelings towards Millie his attitude towards the fans was changing somewhat and for some strange reason he felt like doing it.

"If you want to, but don't say anything stupid!" replied Mac, he was already worried about the damage control he may have to do afterwards. Dex was unpredictable.

@CRAZETHEBAND Dex here. Let's do a QandA! Hash tag #AskDexRose Go!

Immediately the band's twitter page went mad! Fans were in a frenzy to get their questions in, there were literally hundreds within seconds!

"Do you even know how to work Twitter, dude?" Zach teased.

Dex smiled to himself in the dark, ignoring him as he read through the tweets and began to answer some. Zach started laughing to himself, the bus was pitch black and Dex had no idea what he was doing. Zach logged into the band's Twitter too, sending Dex wind up tweets and answering fans questions stupidly as Dex.

Millie looked at the clock in reception as she and Aria arrived back at the hospital, 9.07pm.

"She should be coming out of surgery by now," said Millie, feeling really nervous. She was dying to see Lexi, no matter what the prognosis or the outcome of her surgery, she just wanted to hug her little sister.

As they walked down the corridor Millie smiled as she saw her parents at the other end. Her dad was asleep in his chair. As she got closer the corridor opened up into a waiting area and she could see Nate, asleep, laid across several chairs. Her mum smiled and stood up to give her daughters a hug.

"Alright, mum?" Millie asked.

"Yes, honey, I'm alright," she replied with a warm smile.

Smiles quickly faded as the doctor came out to see them. Millie's mum nudged her dad to wake him up, Millie shook Nate's shoulder to wake him too, they all stood up to hear the news. Millie felt her heart beating in her mouth; she held her breath in anticipation of bad news. Watching as her dad grabbed her mum's hand and pulled her closer to him, Millie couldn't imagine what her parents must be feeling right now, with their baby girl lying in that hospital not knowing if she was paralysed for the rest of her life, her dreams of being a dancer and all she had worked towards her entire life, shattered in a split second of bad luck and bad timing.

"I'm doctor Freeman," he said. "Alexia is out of surgery. The surgery itself went well, we had to put some pins in to help her back to heal but she's very, very lucky! The breaks although in serious places were fairly minor and there is no obvious damage to the spinal cord or anything major. Fingers crossed there will be no permanent damage," the doctor smiled.

Millie's mum burst into tears and threw her arms around her dad. Millie sighed. What a relief. She looked at Aria and smiled, Aria leaned forward and gave her a hug and kissed her on the cheek.

"Thank god," said Aria quietly. Millie let go of Aria and glanced over at Nate, he was smiling, tears were rolling down his cheeks.

"Hey, Nate, come here," said Millie, feeling sorry for him stood there all alone. Nate looked up, feeling a bit uneasy about what Millie might want him for. Slowly he walked over to her, she threw her arms around him.

"See, I told you she would be okay!" smiled Millie, Nate managed a smile. It was moments like this that really put life into perspective. Maybe she should just let go of her feelings towards Nate, after all she had seen a different side of him today. He'd sat by himself for over 12 hours waiting for news of his girlfriend, Millie thought that showed some kind of commitment on his part. Maybe he needed a chance, she thought.

"Can we see her?" asked her mum.

"You can all have five minutes with her before you leave but she's still heavily sedated and most likely will sleep it off till morning now. Plus visiting hours ended at 9pm, so you can see her properly in the morning," explained the doctor.

"Okay, thank you. Just five minutes now would be lovely," her mum replied. The doctor led them all through the doors and into the intensive care unit where Lexi was being kept overnight.

As they approached her bed Millie wasn't quite prepared for what she saw. She gasped, putting her hands to her face as her eyes welled up. Lexi was nearly unrecognisable. Her beautiful face was swollen all over, her eyes bruised shut, her face was covered in scratches and one side was completely black with bruises. She had a bandage around her neck, her arms were covered in cuts and bruises. Millie noticed she had stitches all up one elbow. She was wearing a gown and had sheets up to her chest so Millie couldn't see much of her body but what she could see was horrendous, she was in a bad way. Her mum went straight over and kissed her cheek, brushing her hair from her face. Her dad stood at the foot of the bed completely still, as if he was frozen to the spot. Her dad wasn't one to share his feeling but as Millie looked at him she saw tears roll down his cheeks for the first time in her life! Lexi looked lifeless as she laid there in a deep sleep.

"It looks far worse than it is" said the doctor, trying to reassure a visibly distraught family. "It's mostly just external swelling and bruising, it will have gone down a lot by tomorrow," he added. "I'll give you five minutes".

Millie and Aria sat on the end of Lexi's bed clutching each other's hands, Millie held on to Lexi's hand with her other hand.

Millie watched as Nate walked over to the side of her bed. Millie could tell he really wanted to be with her and touch her but he was hesitant, like he felt he didn't have as much of a right to be there as the rest of the family.

"Let's give Nate a minute alone with her, eh?" said Millie, she winked at Nate.

Her mum and dad both kissed Lexi on the forehead. "Bye, darling, we will be back first thing in the morning," her mum said.

"I love you, sweetheart," said her dad. She could see the hurt in his eyes.

Millie and Aria both gave Lexi a kiss on the cheek. "See you in the morning, Lex," said Millie. "Love you," she added.

The family left together. As Millie held the door open for them she glanced behind at Nate, he looked at her and silently mouthed *thank you*. Millie smiled as she closed the door behind her.

"Woah, what a day," said Millie as Aria pulled up outside her house.

"I know! At least Lex is going to be okay," said Aria.

"Yeah, what a relief," agreed Millie. "Thanks for the lift home, Ari," said Millie as she got out of the car.

"No sweat chick, I'm going to stay with Mum and Dad down here tonight so if you need a lift to the hospital tomorrow, let me know," said Aria.

"Ah thanks. Goodnight," Millie replied, leaning back in the car to give Aria a kiss.

On her doorstep Millie fumbled around for her keys, before pulling them from her bag. She quietly tiptoed inside, trying not to wake Amber, she went to bed early most nights as she had to leave for work at 5.30am. She crept into the kitchen and turned on the light.

"What are you doing here?" said a voice from behind her.

Millie jumped a mile; turning around she saw Amber stood in the doorway. "Jesus fucking Christ, Ambs!" cursed Millie. "You scared the shit out of me!" she added.

"*You* scared the shit out of *me*!" said Amber. "I wasn't expecting you back yet, I thought you were away until Friday," said Amber.

"I was, but I flew home this morning. Lexi was in a terrible accident! I've been at the hospital all day," Millie explained.

"Oh my goodness! Is she okay?" asked Amber.

"I think so, she's been in surgery all day, she's broke, her neck and her back," said Millie.

"OH MY GOD!" exclaimed Amber.

"Sounds horrendous I know, but her surgery went well and doctors say she'll make a full recovery," said Millie.

"Thank god!" said Amber, breathing a sigh of relief. She gave Millie a hug. "Right, babe, I'm off to bed, are you sure you're okay?" said Amber.

"Yeah, fine, thanks, goodnight babe," Millie replied. She couldn't wait to get in bed herself, it had been a very long, emotionally draining day and she wanted nothing more than to snuggle in her own bed. She made a sandwich and poured herself a glass of water and carried it up to her room, she took her clothes off, threw on a t-shirt and climbed into bed. Eating her sandwich with one hand she picked up her phone with the other.

12 new messages

She barely had the energy to read 12 messages, let alone reply to 12 messages. She was too exhausted; she put her phone down on her nightstand. They could wait until tomorrow; nothing was going to be half as important as her sister today.

She closed her eyes.

CHAPTER 17

10.12am Thursday morning and Dex was still asleep. This was unheard of for him, usually the commotion of the bus parking woke him, the sound of the reversing alarm was etched into his dreams. But not this morning. The bus had arrived in Essex and parked at 6am but it was quiet, no one was stirring yet. Dex was a morning person, he rarely slept past 7am and if he woke up, he had to get up, he wasn't the kind of person to just lie in bed, he felt like it was a waste of his life. Dex had recently started running, he loved nothing more than to hit the street at 7am, the cold, crisp morning air of even the warmest cities filled his lungs and made him feel alive. He had given up smoking not too long ago and he felt like it was some kind of compensation for his lungs. He was giving something back to them for years of abuse. It was also a good way to see the places he visited. The streets were pretty quiet at that time, he didn't need security, it was just him and the road. It cleared his mind and gave him alone time to think and he could really see the cities properly. Sometimes he got lost, but he didn't mind that, sometimes that added to the fun. But not today, today he had missed his morning run. He had missed breakfast, he had missed lobby call!

As he began to stir he was confused by the silence, he felt around on the bed beside him for his phone. Lifting it to within an inch of his eyes he squinted to see the time, he could barely make out the numbers, his eyes hadn't quite adjusted to being awake yet. It looked like it said 10.15am but it couldn't be, he looked again. "Jesus! Is it really 10.15am!" he said to himself. He sat up and rubbed his eyes, looking at his phone one last time. It was definitely 10.15am! Pulling back the covers he reached for his shorts on the floor and pulled them on. He got up out of bed and looked down the bus, it was empty, everyone was gone, all of the bunk curtains were pulled back and he could see that they were all empty. He leaned over his bunk and pulled back the outside curtain. Outside seemed quiet too, he could see the back of a stage in the distance, lots of buses and vans were parked closely and a few people dressed in black were walking around. He was backstage at a festival. His brain kicked in and he remembered they were in Essex to play the Summer Rocks festival tomorrow. He pulled the curtain back across and stood back up. Grabbing his hoody he made his way to the door, walking through the bus it was evident that there was absolutely no one on the bus! Why had no one woken him?

He pushed the door open and the sunlight hit him, it was so bright! He put his arm up to shield his eyes as he walked down the steps. He had no idea where everyone was so he headed towards the stage. There were people running around looking busy, getting everything ready for the festival. Caterers were setting up their food pitches, stagehands dressed all in black were setting up the lighting and sound cables that trailed off the stage, there were other tour buses parked in rows next to Craze's bus. As he got closer to the stage it got much busier, there were a lot of people gathered around the stage, both bands and crews. Dex scanned the crowds for his band and crew but couldn't see anyone; he didn't have his contacts in! He pulled out his phone and dialled Zach's number.

"Hey sleeping beauty!" said Zach as he answered the call.

"Where the fuck are you, man?" asked Dex. "Instrumental sound check, dude," replied Zach.

"Why did no one wake me?" asked Dex.

"You didn't need to be here for this so Mac said to let you sleep," said Zach.

"Oh," replied Dex. "Where are you guys?" Dex asked.

"Far side of main stage," replied Zach. "But go chill on the bus dude, enjoy the peace!" said Zach. "You're not needed until 11.30am," he added.

"Okay, thanks man," replied Dex. He turned and made his way back to the bus.

Sitting down in the seating area on the bus, the quiet was blissful. He pulled his phone from his pocket:

16 new messages

Dex scrolled through the messages, ignoring most. As he got to the last few he was disappointed that there was still nothing from Millie. Maybe she wasn't interested after all.

Dex wrote out a text to her. His finger hovered over the send button but he couldn't bring himself to send it, he put his phone back in his pocket to avoid temptation. He grabbed his sunglasses from his bunk and climbed down off the bus again. He didn't want to be alone this morning, he was thinking too much and he could feel himself entering his depressive state. He needed to stay busy, so we went to find the guys.

Approaching the stage he could see Zach, Jesse and CJ sat in the front row seats at the far side of the stage. He walked across to meet them, as he got closer Jesse spotted him.

"Good morning, sleeping beauty," Jesse laughed. Dex rolled his eyes. He was often teased by the band about his good looks. He had perfect skin, almost baby-faced, girls always commented on his looks giving the other guys plenty of ammunition.

Dex sat down in the bleachers with the rest of the band and crew, as Mac handed out bacon sandwiches.

"Oh yes, Mac!" said Zach, grabbing a

sandwich from the tray and shoving half of it in his mouth. They watched as other bands rehearsed and sound checked their instruments on the main stage. The sun was already warm, it was going to be a lovely day. The atmosphere at a festival was always so much better when the weather was good. It put everyone, bands and fans, in a much better mood. Dex hoped the weather was this good when they played tomorrow evening.

"What time does this thing start, Mac?" asked Jesse.

Mac looked down at the folded paperwork in his hand. "Uhh… campers are let in at 5pm this evening, there are a few acts on tonight but it kicks off officially at 2.30pm tomorrow. You're on the main stage at 7pm," explained Mac.

"Okay, cool," Jesse replied. "I'm totally stoked for this one. This place is rad!" he added.

The guys sat there all day, eating, drinking and watching the other bands in between their own sound checks and rehearsals. Dex looked around him, his best friends were all laughing and having fun, it was times like this he felt grateful to be living the life he was. Life was good.

He hadn't even checked his phone all day.

CHAPTER 18

Millie arrived at the hospital at 5.30pm. She had spent the day at work, despite having the day booked off. She wasn't away in Dublin so she thought she should go in. She was pleased she did, she spent the entire day in meetings back-to-back which had totally taken her mind off her life for a few hours. She didn't have the chance to worry about her sister or think about Dex, she hadn't even had the chance to see Ricco all day. She was very glad of the distraction and it felt nice to get back into work and feel like she was doing something she was in control of.

Walking down the corridor she approached the door to the intensive care unit. She put her hand to the door to push it open but instead took a deep breath and paused for a moment. *Please be okay,* she said to herself. She pushed the door open, Lexi was lying awake in her bed with her mum sat beside her. She looked better, brighter, but still black and blue. Her eye swelling had gone down slightly and her eyes were open, her face was still swollen and she didn't look like herself. She smiled when she saw Millie.

"Lex!" said Millie, sympathetically; she walked towards Lexi's bed, picking up her pace. "Hi, Mum," she said, giving her a hug and kiss on the cheek. "Hello honey" her mum replied.

Millie leaned over the bed and kissed Lexi on the forehead. "How are you feeling, Lex?" asked Millie in an almost baby-like voice.

"Sore," Lexi whispered, her voice was painfully coarse. She tried to smile but her face was too swollen to show any expression, it hurt to talk, or move at all, she was cut and bruised from head to toe, her whole body ached.

"I'm not surprised, you had us all so worried!" smiled Millie, gently stroking Lexi's forehead. "The doctor says you'll make a full recovery," said Millie, trying to be upbeat. She could tell Lexi was trying to smile. Millie looked up at her mum.

"Any more news, Mum?" she asked.

"Just more of the same, no major damage, thank god. She's going to be fine." Her mum looked down at Lexi and smiled. "Millie, if you're going to be here for a

little while do you mind if I pop home and shower quickly? I don't want Lexi to be alone but I haven't been home all day," said her mum.

"Of course," said Millie.

"I'll be back later, sweetheart," said her mum, stroking Lexi's cheek.

"Okay." Lexi struggled to get the word out.

Millie went around to the other side of the bed and sat in her mum's chair. Looking at Lexi it didn't look like her baby sister lying there, she didn't know what to say to her.

"Nate's been here a lot," said Millie. "He actually seems like quite a nice guy," she added. Lexi knew Millie's opinion of him, but this time she was being genuine. Lexi didn't answer. Millie wasn't sure if it was something she didn't want to talk about or if it was just too painful to speak. She thought it best to change the subject anyway. She tried to think of something interesting to talk about.

"Hey, Lex, you'll never guess who I'm meeting tomorrow!"

said Millie excitedly. She saw Lexi's eyes turn to look at her. Millie pulled out her phone and found the photo Dex had sent her, she noticed she had a new message from him but couldn't read it or reply right now. She turned the phone around for Lexi to see. Lexi's eyes widened in shock as she looked at the photo, she gestured to Millie to bring the phone closer to her face for a better look.

"Dex?" Lexi muttered, her voice shaky and obviously pain-ridden, Millie could only just make out what she said.

Millie nodded enthusiastically. "Yep!" she replied. Lexi managed a weak smile. "We've been texting and he's invited me to the Summer Rocks festival tomorrow, it's an odd and long story and I'll tell you EVERYTHING! As soon as you're better, I promise!" said Millie.

She heard the door open behind her, someone came up behind her and kissed her on the cheek.

"Hey, girl!" It was Ricco, carrying two huge bunches of flowers. He handed one to Millie, walking around the other side of the bed he placed the other bunch on top of the cabinet next to Lexi's bed. He smiled at Millie.

"Good god! You don't do things by half do you babe!" he teased. Lexi's smile broadened a little. Millie was pleased to see him, she always felt safe in his presence. "So, any cute doctors?" joked Ricco.

Millie could always rely on him to lighten the mood no matter how bad the situation, he was just that kind of guy. He could see the good and the fun in any situation and had a knack for making people feel better. "Just a flying visit I'm afraid, I'm on my way back to the airport, flying out to Tokyo tonight," he said. Millie's smile quickly faded, she looked at him and he gave her an apologetic look.

"How long for?" asked Millie. Ricco could tell she was mad at him. He cleared his throat awkwardly before he spoke.

"I'm not sure babe, at least a few days, possibly a week.

There's some kind of issue with production in Tokyo, so I have to go and sort it. I'm sorry babe, I know we had plans," he replied.

"Oh," said Millie, gutted he was leaving. She really wanted him to come to the festival with her, he was the only one who knew about Dex and the person she trusted the most in the world. She knew Amber, Holly or Cate would come with her and she did trust them but girls could be judgmental, she didn't want them to think badly of her that she was meeting Dex when he was dating Lucie and she didn't want them to act star struck and embarrass her. She needed to be cool. She just wasn't ready to tell her friends about him yet, she needed some time to figure things out in her own head first.

Ricco said his goodbyes. "I'll call you, Mil," he said as he closed the door behind him.

Millie turned to watch him go. She looked back, Lexi had gone to sleep. Millie sat down on the chair next to the bed and got her phone out, it was the perfect opportunity to text Dex and let him know what had happened and that she couldn't wait until tomorrow. She began to type a message as the door swung open again, sending a whoosh of cold air into the room. Millie looked up.

"Oh, hi, Nate," she said, sliding her phone back into her pocket; her text would have to wait until she got home.

"Hello," he replied. Millie was surprised by how clean he looked for once, he'd been home to get showered and changed and it was blatantly obvious. He scrubbed up pretty well!

"She's asleep but I'm going to head off now, give you some time alone," said Millie.

"Okay, thanks," replied Nate.

Millie stood up so Nate could have the chair. She kissed her sister on the cheek and stroked her arm, her skin felt so rough as Millie gently ran her fingers over the maze of cuts.

"Mum and Dad will be back shortly," said Millie as she walked towards the door.

"Okay, goodnight," Nate replied.

It seemed to take forever to get home, traffic was awful this time of evening. Millie seemed to get stuck in every traffic jam. 48 minutes later she arrived home. Opening the front door she threw her bag down on the hallway floor and kicked off her shoes, man it felt good to take them off and let her tired feet breathe! She'd been in heels for nearly 12 hours! Every step she took on the cold wooden floor was bliss for her sore, aching feet. She unhooked her bra clasp and did one of those fancy manoeuvres, pulling it out from the sleeve of her grey blouse.

"Ahhhhhhhh," she sighed. "That's better." She wandered into the kitchen to make something to eat. On the kitchen work top was a note on a piece of paper, folded to stand up like a tent. Millie approached it to see what it said.

Mils, had to run, late for spin class, made you a lasagne in case you got back late from the hospital and didn't feel like cooking. See you later, love you! Amber xxx

Ps Hope Lexi is ok. X

"Aww bless her," Millie said to herself. She knew she had some really great friends, she was truly grateful for Amber's gesture. She was right, she really wasn't in the mood to cook, it was nearly 7.45pm and all she wanted was a hot shower and her bed! It had been an exhausting few days both physically and emotionally. Her arms and legs felt heavy, she needed a decent night's sleep and maybe now she knew Lexi would be okay her mind would let her switch off and sleep tonight.

She warmed up the lasagne in the microwave and carried it up to her room, something she rarely ever did but she just needed the comfort of her own room and her own bed.

She put her dinner down on the nightstand, switched on

her TV and sat down on her bed to eat. Looking up at the TV every so often she struggled to keep her eyes open. She finished her dinner and put the plate on the nightstand next to her bed, then turned off the TV with every intention of getting in the shower. She put her head down on the pillow for a second… and was out like a light.

Amber arrived home an hour later. Holding onto the door handle as she closed the front door she kicked off her trainers. She heard a beeping noise, she picked up Millie's bag from the floor and it beeped again. Reaching inside she pulled out Millie's phone:

One new message

displayed on the screen. Amber walked through into the kitchen looking for Millie. The kitchen was empty, the note she had left was laid on the kitchen side. She walked through into the lounge, silence. She walked up the stairs quietly calling Millie. She approached her bedroom door which was slightly ajar. Amber pushed the door open slowly, just enough to stick her head inside. She could see Millie laid on her bed with her back to the door.

"Mil," she called quietly. Millie didn't move. Amber pushed the door open a little more and squeezed herself through the gap. She walked around to the other side of the bed. Millie was fast asleep, still in her work clothes. Amber switched Millie's phone to silent and put it on the nightstand next to her, she grabbed a blanket that hung over the foot of Millie's bed and covered her over. Taking her empty plate she turned out the light and pulled the door closed behind her. Amber knew things were catching up with Millie, she needed a rest.

Dex, Zach and Jesse sat side stage watching the last band of the evening finish their set. The place had filled up fast with over 50,000 people arriving to camp for the weekend since 5pm, with another 100,000 expected over the course of the weekend. It had completely changed the atmosphere from the quiet, relaxing, near empty fields from earlier in the day to a jam-packed, ear-piercingly loud, chaotic scene. Dex liked both. The day had been lovely just relaxing with the guys. Not having to perform meant Dex could totally relax and have a good time with his friends. Though nothing beat the happy festival atmosphere, come night fall Dex loved to see a huge crowd, dancing, singing, drinking and having a great time, he felt like that was what life was all about. He looked at his phone, annoyed with himself that he had text Millie a second time without reply. He cracked open another beer, determined to not let it ruin his mood.

His phone vibrated in his pocket. His entire body flooded with excitement, she'd text him back, he could barely open the message where his hands were so shaky. He looked down at the screen. Squinting, he tried to make his blurry eyes focus; he'd had one too many beers.

Hey gorgeous! Can't wait to see you tomorrow. Call me if you're not on stage… Luc xxx

He felt the ultimate comedown, rivalling his teenage drug dabbling days. The excitement he felt was instantly replaced by anger and complete resentment for Lucie. "Oh go away," he muttered to himself, pushing his phone back down into the tight back pocket of his super skinny black jeans.

Zach heard him. "Alright, man?" he asked.

"Just fucking Lucie!" he replied.

"Get rid, man!" said Zach. Dex was absolutely determined tomorrow had to be the day.

The next morning the guys were all up early for an 8am lobby call. They had media interviews and competition winners to meet and greet this morning; they made their way backstage to the media tent. Mac went over the rules of the interviews with the presenters before allowing the guys to come onto the TV set.

Dex's phone beeped.

"Turn that off, Dexter," Mac shouted over. It was as though

his ears had been finely tuned to seek out mobile phone noise. Mac was of a different generation, he hated mobile phones and younger people being constantly glued to them. He was pretty strict with the band about when and where they could use their phones, though Dex and Zach rarely took any notice.

Dex turned on silent mode and opened the message, his face instantly lit up as he read the name at the top of the message.

Hey you, sorry for being distant.

My little sister had a nasty accident. Broke

neck+back! Been with her in hospital.

Got your message about how to meet you. Excited! Can't wait.

Millie x

As he read the message he could feel his entire body turn to jelly. Inside his head tingled, his palms began to sweat and just holding his phone was a challenge.

"Right, let's go guys," said Mac, gesturing for them to come onto the set for their TV interview.

"Oh for fuck sake!" muttered Dex, quietly under his breath, sliding this phone back into his pocket. They walked out onto the makeshift TV studio that had been set up backstage for live TV interviews with the bands throughout the festival.

"Okay, so Dex, you sit there. Zach, in the middle. Jesse, on the end. No swearing, no girlfriends!" Mac instructed.

The hair and make up team swept in, busily coating them in powder and hairspray. A guy from the crew handed them microphones. Dex noticed a tall blonde lady with a microphone walking over towards them.

As she approached them she held a hand to shake Dex's hand. "Hi," she said with a friendly smile and

a firm handshake. "Dex Rose, right?" She said.

"Yeah," he replied with a half-hearted smile. "Great! Zach?" she said, moving along to Zach and offering a handshake once again.

"Yeah," replied Zach.

"And Jesse?" she said, shaking Jesse's hand. "Is there a fourth still to come?" she asked.

"No," said Jesse. "There's CJ, but he's our touring drummer, he isn't actually a member of the band," he explained.

"Ah I see," she replied. "Well, my name's Rachel and I'm just going to ask you a few questions if that's okay? We are live so please don't swear." the guys nodded.

As the interview got underway Dex got into the swing of it. He was unusually chatty and upbeat, even funny at times. It was obvious someone had lifted his mood, not an easy feat for anyone!

As it came to a close the interview had gone well. Mac was pleased, they had come across well and he didn't have to do any damage control for once!

When it had finished the competition winners were brought in. They posed for photos, signed things and chatted a little and by 10.15am they were done for the day, or at least the media was done for the day. "Good job, guys," said Mac, patting each of them on the back as they walked past him to exit the media area. "Right guys, stay in the bands area, no going out front of stage, no mingling with fans, NO BRINGING ANYONE BACK!" groaned Mac, directing his glance at Zach. "Let's give me a break today, eh?" he added. He didn't have the easiest job in the world, looking after a band of three stubborn rule breakers and risk takers was rarely easy and Mac was getting on a bit now.

"Yessss," they replied in a chorus of sarcasm. They headed back towards their bus.

"Do you know when Lucie is arriving yet?" asked Zach.

"She text me earlier," said Dex unenthusiastically. "She's

being choppered in straight from the airport at around 7pm," he added.

"Oh. When is she on?" asked Zach.

"8pm, I think, on the Radio Stars stage," Dex replied.

"She probably won't be around until late, then," said Zach, trying to sound optimistic.

"Yeah, maybe," Dex replied.

"Hey, how come we don't get choppered in?" asked Zach, changing the subject as he opened the tour bus door. They were greeted by the sound of CJ snoring… loudly! "Let's shave his eyebrows off!" suggested Zach, excitedly!

"Ha! No thanks, Ellie would murder us!" replied Jesse. Ellie was CJ's fiancée back home. She was already not happy that CJ had recently started drumming for Craze and left her to tour all summer, pushing back their wedding, and suggestions like Zach's were exactly why she didn't want him to go! Guys were stupid, they did stupid things and she didn't want CJ involved in it all, not to mention how much she hated all the attention he got from girls!

"I'm going back to bed for a few hours," said Dex.

"A'ight man," said Zach. "Good luck sleeping with the steam train down there!" Zach joked.

He was right; sleeping anywhere near CJ was a challenge. Dex climbed into his bunk, drawing back the outside curtain just a couple of inches so he could watch the world go by. He loved nothing more than chilling out in his bunk watching all the crew outside rushing around and busying about getting everything ready for a show. He watched as people carried cables and amplifiers; his eyes followed a young girl with a clipboard, rushing around talking to people, trying to organise something; he watched other bands wandering around. He could just see the side of the main stage from his bunk; it was going to be a great view later once things kicked off. In his people-watching suddenly it dawned on him that he hadn't text Millie back. Lying on his stomach, resting his phone against his pillow he began to type. Just texting her sent his stomach into a frenzy of butterflies.

Hey! Woah! That's rough! Hope your sister's ok? Can I do anything? Can't wait to see you later. D.x

He wasn't one for kisses but felt compelled to type one. He turned onto his back and threw his phone down beside him; staring at the bottom of the bunk above him he began to overthink it like he always did! He started to feel nervous, not about the show; though he knew those nerves would follow later. He was nervous about seeing her! He still wasn't sure he was doing the right thing, the whole 'fan' thing still stuck in the back of his mind; he would never feel comfortable with it. Sure he was excited, he still thought about her every minute of the day and every time he thought of her his entire body filled up with the same adrenaline he felt that first night he saw her. But what if she was nothing like he expected? He worried that he'd let his guard down and let this girl into his life and she'd be like all the others, using him for his fame and money. He shook his head, he had to get out of his own thoughts or he was going to talk himself out of it. He snuggled into his pillow and closed his eyes.

It was 5.30pm. As Dex climbed down from the bus the music was loud, the festival was in full swing. After a shower and a change of clothes he felt even more nervous about Millie being there. Now he was ready it seemed even closer, it wasn't even just meeting her but performing in front of her made him feel sick to his stomach! How was he ever going to concentrate and remember all the words? Standing outside the bus waiting for everyone he felt fidgety, re-tucking his perfectly white t-shirt into his super-tight, ankle-grazer, skinny jeans again, putting his arms down he let his shirt hang open over the top. His long, dark, floppy fringe fell in front of his face, running his fingers through he pushed it back off his face, only for it to fall over his eyes again minutes later. His forehead was sweaty and it was becoming difficult to sweep the hair away from his face as he brushed it back again with his fingers. The bus door swung open, smacking back into the side of the bus. Zach emerged, can of beer in hand, followed by Jesse and CJ. Zach stomped down the steps.

"LET'S DO THIS!" Zach yelled.

Dex laughed, Zach had clearly had a few too many already, but Dex liked drunk Zach, he was one of those guys who got nothing but funnier with every drink.

Mac and two other security team guys emerged behind them.

"Right, come on then fellas," said Mac. "That's enough beers," he added, grabbing the can from Zach's hand.

"MAAACCCC!" Zach groaned.

"Come on," said Mac, gesturing for them to follow him. He showed them to where they had to wait backstage. As they climbed the steps up to the back of the main stage the band before them were just going on stage, so Craze had about an hour's wait before it was them.

There were several sofas and armchairs in a chillout area for the bands to wait in; Jesse noticed a buffet table at the back and next to it a table of various beers and shots.

"I'm there!" said Zach, setting eyes on the alcohol table, a silly grin from ear to ear as he wandered off towards it to Mac's dismay.

For a while Dex watched the band on stage from the side of the stage. He could never eat before a show, he would almost certainly throw it back up on stage! He already felt sick enough. His nerves completely abolished any appetite he had. From where he was stood he could see part of the crowd.

"Woah," he said to himself, it was one of the biggest crowds he had ever seen! He couldn't actually see where the crowd ended, the festival site was huge and the field of people stretched to as far as the eye could see! Dex tucked his t-shirt in again for about the 20th time since he got dressed less than an hour ago. He couldn't relax, he needed to do something to distract himself or the nerves would drive him insane. He needed to get out of his own head. He pulled his phone out.

One new message

He hadn't heard his phone over the loud band and intense shouting and screaming coming from the crowd.

Hey you! I'm FINALLY here! and I'm in!

Thanks for sorting that, I felt like a VIP skipping all the queues! :) Can't wait till you're on.

Millie x

Millie had finished work early and been on the train all afternoon. She had planned to land in London from her Dublin trip, it was only a 30-minute cab ride to the festival from London but with her sister's accident changing her plans she was travelling to the festival from home, over three hours away! But there was no way she was missing it for the world.

Dex couldn't help but smile, he shivered reading the text, he felt like a kid. He still had his apprehensions but excitement had prevailed in his mind. He was going to see HER, talk to her, the girl that had been in his head continuously since the moment he laid eyes on her. The girl that had him up every night, just wondering where she was or what she was doing, wondering about her life, the people in her life. He'd laid awake at night picturing what her life might be like, what his life might be like if she were in it. He'd spoken to her a hundred times in his mind, he'd touched her soft skin, stroked her silky hair, put his arms around her, felt her breath on his skin but then he'd fall asleep and wake up alone again. Tonight, tonight would be different, she was there. Actually there. He already liked her. He liked the feeling of liking her. He was beyond nervous about meeting her face to face. He could feel his body quivering as the time flew by and it got closer to going on stage, but he was insanely excited too, he knew that contained exhilaration was not nearly as exciting as its release.

On in 5. Nervous! See you in a minute :) D x

He replied.

"This is our last song, you've been an awesome crowd," said the lead singer of the band on stage. Dex took a deep breath and counted to five, trying to stay calm. Zach, Jesse and CJ returned from the buffet table, Zach still stuffing a sandwich into his mouth.

"Here ya go, man," said CJ, handing Dex two shots of whisky.

"Ah thanks, dude," replied Dex. He really needed something to calm his nerves.

In what seemed like only a few seconds the band on stage were finished and walking off stage. "Have a good show guys" said the lead singer as his band passed Craze waiting to go on.

"Cheers, dude," replied Dex, giving him a friendly fist bump. "This is it!" Dex whispered to himself. Counting in his head to slow his breathing down, he began to recite lyrics, he knew them inside and out but he always worried he would forget when he got out there. Zach, Jesse and CJ downed the last of their drinks as the stage crews were on stage setting up their instruments for them. Dex bounced up and down on the spot, his energy at boiling point, ready to explode the minute he got on that stage. It was time!

The last member of the stage crew came off stage, giving Dex the thumbs up to lead the band onto the stage.

"This is it, boys," said Dex, turning quickly to high-five the other guys.

"YEAH BABY!" yelled Zach, drunkenly, as he high-fived Dex.

Dex laughed. He stepped out into the view of the crowd

and was instantly greeted by an eruption of deafening screams! He gave the guys a minute to get ready with their instruments, he looked out and couldn't quite believe the size of the sheer mass of humanity spread out across the field. Never had he ever seen so many people in one place! He took a very quick scan, he couldn't see Millie. There were too many people, packed so tightly together that all he could see was a sea of heads.

CJ started the drumbeat and the crowd once again erupted at hearing the familiar beat of the start of one of their well-known songs. The screen behind them displayed the music video in between cutting to live shots of them on stage; the lights began an impressive laser show overhead as Dex prepared himself to belt out the first line. His showman switch had flipped and he was on fire as usual.

Millie stared up at him in awe. It was like a different person up there, that was world-famous pop-rock star Dex Rose, hopping about the stage in front of hundreds of thousands of people, not the man that had text her just five minutes ago, not the man she had talked to on the phone just a few days ago... definitely not the man she was there to meet after the show! She was so close, only a couple of rows from the front. She looked around at the hundreds of girls that surrounded her, she felt really out of place and really old! Most of them looked about 15! And most of them were screaming for Dex, some held signs with messages on for him, one girl close to her was crying her eyes out that she couldn't get any closer to him. *Woah! This is crazy!* thought Millie. If things went well tonight this may be something she needed to get used to, sharing him with the world. She tried not to think about it, she didn't want to jump the gun, she hadn't even met him yet!

As Dex bounced around the stage with endless energy, his voice sounded incredible, with what could only be described as the sound of a modern-day Freddie Mercury. Millie was impressed, she'd never heard anyone sound so amazing live. He hit every note effortlessly whilst a dazzling display of stage lights entertained behind him, making it feel more like a theatrical stage show than a pop-rock festival. Transfixed on Dex, Millie felt a drop of rain on her face. She wiped it away with her finger, she felt another, then another.

"Oh fuck! I'm going to get soaked," she said to herself with impeccable timing as the heavens opened, giving the entire 170,000-strong crowd a communal mud bath! *Brilliant!* thought Millie, meeting Dex Rose in soaking wet clothes, hair ruined and makeup streaming down her face was not part of her plan! As the song came to an end Dex took to the mic to talk to the crowd, a usual part of his stage routine.

"Are you guys okay?" he asked, genuinely concerned that they were all getting drenched by the sudden downpour. He was greeted with an ear-piercing collective of cheers. Dex smiled, they didn't care they were getting wet. Well... all but Millie who had spent hours doing her hair and make up this morning!

Dex was an impressive front man, a natural, with a commanding presence up there, he seemed so different to Millie than he had on the phone the other night, it was hard to believe it was the same man. When Millie was talking to him he was a little shy, softly spoken and nervous. Up there on the stage he ruled the world, he gave everything he had every time he stepped on that stage and always pushed himself to deliver his best. For someone who was fairly shy and borderline antisocial he commanded the audience of thousands, he had nearly everyone on their feet, singing, dancing and generally engaging the entire crowd in the show.

Millie kept looking at Dex, hoping he would notice her crammed in between hundreds of other festival-goers. By the end of the third song he still hadn't seen her.

"Jesus! Give me a minute... to... catch my... breath," said Dex, leaning on the mic stand. The song he had just sung was the hardest, lots of long, high notes to hold. He hit every single one with ease but it took everything out of him, he was always pleased to get that one over with at the start of the show. As he began to get his breath back he stood up straight. As he looked up she caught his eye, the hugest smile washed over his face, hers too. It literally took her breath away for a second. He winked at her. Millie completely melted, her legs turned to jelly as a shiver of excitement waved down through her entire body. There was just something about him Millie couldn't put her finger on, no one had ever made her feel the way he did, without even touching her. Sure he was gorgeous, famous, talented, probably pretty wealthy, and wanted by half the female population but Millie didn't care about any of that, there was something else. It was just a look, it was all in his eyes.

Seeing Millie had the opposite effect that Dex was expecting. Rather than making him nervous and putting him off his game, this time he felt more confident knowing she was watching him. He upped his already incredible game even more, pushing his vocal range to new limits. He was only singing for her now and he felt good, he knew he was delivering a mind-blowing show so far and he wasn't about to stop. He wanted to look at her but tried not to, she looked so pretty soaking wet. He was always conscious of where she was and every now and then he glanced at her out of the corner of his eye, still just about managing to maintain his showman alter-ego and carry on delivering a good show. Usually he loved being on the stage and didn't want the show to end but tonight he was counting down the minutes until he could come off the stage and see her properly.

After 40 minutes Dex came to the end of the penultimate song. He walked up to the front edge of the stage, beyond the canopy that covered them on stage, and held on to the mic stand, leaning in to the mic. He was getting wet from the rain.

"You guys are fucking awesome! You could be anywhere in the world right now but you chose to be here with us, getting totally drenched! That's pretty awesome!" he said to an eruption of cheers, wiping away the hair stuck to his wet rain-covered face. "This is our last song guys, sing along if you know it," Dex said. As he looked away he winked at Millie again, smiling and biting his lip suggestively.

Millie had to breathe through her excitement, which she tried to hide as girls in front of her turned to see who Dex had winked at. Her smile disappeared quickly and she tried to blend in, feeling slightly uneasy to be in the middle of all of Dex's fans. She'd heard about the crazy things fans do through jealousy which made her feel somewhat vulnerable, though in reality no one could have known she was the object of his affections. No one would have believed her even if she'd told them! It was getting dark and Millie was glad that the show was coming to an end; she didn't like being alone in the dark, miles away from home. She wished so much that Ricco could have been there to look after her. She could have asked Amber, Holly or Cate to come but she just wasn't ready to tell them anything about Dex yet. She knew they would ask questions, questions she didn't know the answers to herself yet, plus she wanted to meet Dex alone and didn't want to be an awful friend and abandon a friend there, so she had gone alone. Craze's set came to an exciting end with a final light show to accompany Dex belting out the last lines of the song, interchanging between an impressive, blindingly bright display of golden lights and dramatic light-outs, ending with one final light out when Dex ended the final note, leaving the stage in complete darkness. The crowd were louder than ever and the atmosphere was really intense, the entire 170,000-strong crowd left wanting more. A few seconds and the lights came back up, Dex was stood right at the front edge of the stage.

"Thank you! You've been an amazing crowd tonight, the biggest we've ever played to I think," he said, turning around to get dome confirmation from the other guys. Zach nodded in agreement. "See you next time," he added as he followed the rest of the band off the stage.

Millie wanted to squeal with excitement, this was it! *What do I do now?* she thought, completely trapped in the middle of a huge tightly packed crowd. No one was moving! They were waiting for the next act to come on.

Completely sandwiched by people all around her Millie managed to wiggle her arm down into her bag and grab her phone. She text Dex.

Err.. I'm stuck! x

Coming off the side of the stage crew members were waiting to hand Dex and the guys towels and water. "Thanks," said Dex, taking the towel and drying the sweat and rain mixture from his head and neck. His t-shirt was completely soaked to his chest, he wasn't sure if it was sweat or rain! He took a huge gulp of water and breathed deeply, trying to calm down and catch his breath.

"Mac, I need my phone, man, please," said Dex, desperate to have it back. Mac handed it to him.

"Good job tonight, Dex, that was a great show," said Mac. "All of you. Really good job tonight," he added.

"Thanks," Jesse replied. Dex didn't even hear him, he was completely immersed in his phone. After a second, he looked up from it.

"Ah, welcome back to reality," joked Mac.

"Mac, I need a favour" Dex smiled.

Mac knew he wasn't going to like whatever it was going to be. "Whaaaat?" asked Mac, in a sarcastic tone.

"I need a security guy to escort someone from the crowd up to here," Dex smiled sweetly, he knew Mac wasn't going to he pleased at the request but he knew he would convince him.

"What? Who?" asked Mac, who was as he predicted

suitably unimpressed by the request.

"Umm... a girl," smiled Dex, sheepishly.

"What? Why? What happened to Lucie?" asked Mac. "You better not have ditched her after I went through hell and a lot of stress with her here last week!" said Mac.

"No, I haven't ditched Lucie, she's err... a friend," said Dex.

Mac knew full well what Dex's intentions were. Mac had helped to sneak back many a '*friend*' for Zach over the past few months. Mac sighed, shooting Dex an angry face. Dex knew he wasn't really angry with him. Dex was fairly close to Mac, he was like a son to him, he knew Mac had a soft spot for him.

"Fine!" said Mac. "Where is she?" he huffed, as if it was a lot of trouble.

"Come, I'll show you," said Dex. He led Mac over to the side of the stage. The next band were already on stage, Dex hid just out of sight of the crowd. Mac stuck his head out. "Right, look front right, about four rows back, dark hair, denim jacket," Dex started.

"Are you fucking kidding me?! It's dark and there are a million dark-haired girls!" replied Mac.

"Wait for the light to be up, just look, man!" Dex said impatiently.

Mac scanned the crowd. "That one?" asked Mac. Dex waited for the lights to be at their brightest again. "Yeah that's her," he replied.

Mac walked behind the stage and around to the opposite side, he walked to the edge of the stage and whispered into the ear of one of the stewards down on the floor in front of the stage. Dex watched from the opposite side of the stage as the steward went over to the railing and leaned over into the crowd to get Millie's attention. The steward helped to part the crowd so Millie could push her way through, the people in front of her tutting as she pushed past them. The steward held her hand and helped her climb over the barrier. Mac crouched down, holding out a hand to pull Millie up onto the stage. The nearby crowd watched intently, wondering why SHE was allowed on the stage!

"I'm Mac, Craze's security manager," he said. He put his hand across her back and led her off to the back of the stage.

"I'm Millie," she said nervously as she followed him. It felt surreal to be backstage; she walked past famous bands as they waited backstage until their time to go on. Approaching the opposite side of the stage Millie could see it opened up into a seating area. She felt sick with nerves, made worse by the fact that she was drenched from head to toe, her hair and her clothes were completely stuck to her and she didn't want to even think about the mess that her makeup must be in! A few steps further and she spotted Jesse and CJ laid out on one of the sofas. Mac led her past them, both of them looked up at the gorgeous girl following Mac.

As they approached the exit, Millie followed Mac past the buffet tables. Zach was getting a drink with a crew member from the alcohol table, as he turned to go and sit with Jesse and CJ on the sofas he caught a glimpse of Millie. He smiled at her "Woah!" he smiled to himself. Millie was stunning, even when she looked like a drowned rat! "Dexter you dawwwwwg!" he added,

with no one else in earshot, giggling to himself.

Mac led Millie out of the backstage exit and down some steps. Millie wondered where he was taking her, she kept trying to look beyond Mac to see if she could see anything. As she stepped off the last step onto the floor, Dex stepped out from underneath the stage scaffolding.

"Thanks, man," winked Dex, giving Mac a fist bump. Mac just nodded, silent in his disapproval. He headed back up the steps to the back of the stage.

There he was.

Pop-rock star Dexter Rose, the guy she'd been in love with in her head for a year, the guy she fantasised about every night! He was stood a foot in front of her. He was even more perfect than she had imagined he would be. He had changed into dry clothes. She looked him up and down for a second, he looked gorgeous in his tight black skinny jeans. His baggy grey sweatshirt swamped him, the sleeves pulled down covering his hands, holding them there with clenched fists. His hair fell over his eyes. She watched intently as he brushed it back with his fingers, his gorgeous smile complete with gleaming white teeth. He was like something out of a movie.

"Hey you," he smiled, biting his lip nervously as he took a step closer to her. Millie could feel her entire body trembling. She was relieved that the lighting was dim down there, the only light filtered down the steps from up on the stage which made her feel slightly less self conscious about the fact that she was drenched and looked far from her best. She wanted so badly to look perfect for this moment. All week she'd thought about what she would wear, how she would do her makeup and her hair but right now she didn't care. It was what it was and she wasn't going to dwell on it and ruin her moment.

"Hi," she smiled, nervously. "I'm sorry about the state of me," she added, looking down at her soggy clothes that hung heavily from her body. She felt the need to apologise as if she was a disappointment to him. Dex reached for her hand and pulled her closer to him, his touch made her shiver.

"You look pretty amazing to me," he smiled. It was that look again, those eyes, they did something to her that she couldn't even begin to understand. "Like a beautiful, drowned rat!" he joked, trying to break the ice. It worked, Millie smiled. "Thanks," she replied shyly.

"So this is kind of weird, huh!" said Dex.

"Yeah, just... just a little bit," Millie replied. She tried to relax, her breathing was so heavy and erratic that she stumbled over her words. She tried to concentrate on what he was saying but all she could think about was the fact that he was rubbing her hand with his thumb.

"I just want you to know that this is the first time I've ever done anything like this, I've never had any kind of personal relations with a fan, of any kind! But from the moment I saw you I just felt like… like I knew you, or that I had to know you," said Dex. It was important to him that she knew he didn't sleep with fans all the time like some of the other guys did, his parents brought him up to be a gentleman and to be respectful and he needed Millie to know that.

Even though he felt bad sneaking around, texting Millie when technically he was dating Lucie, he knew that as long as he didn't have a physical relationship with Millie until he had ended it with Lucie then he wouldn't have gone against everything he believed in.

Millie didn't take well to lovey-dovey talk, it just wasn't her. She loved hearing him say those things but she couldn't say them back. "I never thought in a million years I'd be stood here with you! Things like this don't happen in my life," replied Millie. "I've had a crush on you like forever," she added, cringing at herself as she forced herself to admit it.

Dex smiled. "Good," he replied, "Cuz I've had a crush on you too… for like two weeks!" he joked.

She could see him gradually edging closer to her it made her whole body feel weak. She wanted to be closer to him, she'd waited forever to touch Dex Rose. Now with him stood inches from her, she couldn't move, her limbs felt heavy. He was going to have to take the lead.

His smile quickly faded, replaced by a look that Millie couldn't determine if it was seriousness or sadness. He looked her in the eyes as he spoke.

"I have no idea what I'm doing, my heart is totally ruling my head right now. Where do we go from here? What do you want to do?" he asked. She could tell he was confused about the whole situation. He almost looked scared.

Millie squeezed his hand a little in reassurance. "You've got far more to lose than me, it has to be your call," said Millie, though in her head the answer to his question 'what do you want to do?' was simply 'you, on the floor, right here, right now'.

Dex looked at her stood there in front of him, he had an overwhelming feeling of *'she's the one'*. he'd never felt anything like it before, he didn't even believe in stuff like that but as he looked into her mysterious dark brown eyes it was clear to him there was something deep there, he had to give in to this. It was now or never. He took another step closer, lifting his free hand to brush her hair away from her face.

Oh my god, he's going to kiss me! thought Millie. She braced herself; she was borderline hyperventilating as he leaned in. She closed her eyes and in less than a second felt his cold lips touch hers softly, just slightly, then he pulled back as if to seek approval on her face before going any further. She looked up at him with a sultry glance, clearly giving him the green light as he leaned back in, this time with more force, letting her hand he was holding drop back down beside her as he moved his hands up to the sides of her face. He stepped into her, pushing himself up against her, through her thin, charcoal grey, jersey pencil dress she could feel all of his body. He wasn't an overly tall guy but with just her converse trainers on he towered above her, making her feel like he was in complete control. Adrenaline kicked in and she bravely put her hands on his waist, holding onto his belt she gently pulled him closer into her.

She could feel an intense power between them. Whatever the feeling was it hit her in a second like a thunderbolt.

Feeling awkward, he was clumsy. Starting slow he lingered on her bottom lip, pulling away slightly, then going back a little rougher each time, his fingers entangled in her wet, messy hair. Dex's body ached as adrenaline pumped through his veins, making him feel powerful like he was about to fight to the death. He felt amazingly uncomfortable as an overwhelming pressure filled his abdomen. He had never felt anything so intense, certainly not from a kiss. It was beautiful and messy, a feeling he could dwell on later, he didn't want his head filled with thoughts right now, he was just content to feel her breath come and go with his.

"Zach, have you seen Dex?" asked a female voice from behind him. Sat on the sofa with the other guys, Zach turned his head. Lucie stood behind him; she rubbed his hair in an annoying childlike way. "Dex? Do you know where he is? He's not answering his phone," she added.

"Err... no, let me go see if he's in the guys' bathroom," said Zach, getting up. Zach knew Dex was somewhere with Millie. As he walked away from the sofa area he glanced back, Lucie had sat down on the sofa with Jesse and CJ, luckily with her back to the direction Zach was heading.

As he approached the steps he took one more quick glance back at her, she wasn't looking. He snuck down two steps and glanced down, he saw Dex and Millie kissing passionately. "Oh fuck!" he whispered to himself, now he was going to have to keep Lucie away. He walked back over to her.

"No, not there. Come on, Luc, I'll help you find him," said Zach. Jesse looked at him strangely as he led her off in the opposite direction.

The passion was becoming too much and Dex knew that as much as he didn't want to, he needed to stop before things went any further and he wasn't able to stop. He didn't want anything more to happen underneath the stage, it wasn't right. She deserved better from him. So did Lucie. Somehow among all the dizziness he found enough willpower to gently slow down, touching her soft lips gently a few times with his before completely pulling back. He held onto her tightly, not wanting to let her go. Leaning back so he could see her face, he breathed out deeply, exhausted. She smiled at him, biting her lip, she looked so cute. Looking into each other's eyes they knew they were both feeling the exact same thing, something inside them both had changed, irreversibly turning them both inside out.

Dex leaned up against a wall, pulling Millie in close he wrapped his arms around her. He felt fiercely protective of her already, he didn't want to let go of her, he loved the way she nestled her head into his chest.

Closing her eyes she took in the beautiful smell of his sweat with every breath, his touch sent shivers down her spine as he softly stroked the back of her head. She could feel him breathing in her hair. They were both silent, neither needed to say a word. He would never bring himself to admit it. But he knew!

He was in love.

He didn't believe in love at first sight, he didn't believe in love at second... or third sight! He always thought love grew over time as you got to know someone. He knew nothing about Millie, or at least not a lot, and had spent only around 15 minutes with her. To be in love with her went against his rules but he felt it whether he believed it or not.

Mac came stomping down the steps. "Right, that's it, Dexter, we have to go," he commanded, with no sympathy towards them at all.

Millie jumped, letting go of Dex and quickly stepping away from him as if she was 15 years old again and her parents had just walked in on them. To Mac this was just another one night stand with a fan, which he didn't agree with at all.

"Okay, two seconds," Dex replied. His heart sank at the thought of letting her go. He pulled her back into his chest, kissing her on top of her head and squeezing her tightly. Millie felt so safe in his arms; Ricco was the only other man who could make her feel that way. She never thought she would ever find someone to rival the way Ricco made her feel but in the 15 minutes she had spent with Dex, he had exceeded it. She didn't want him to go.

He put his hand to her chin and lifted it to kiss her again; he closed his eyes, heart throbbing in his chest. "Will you see me again?" he asked.

"Of course," Millie replied. Growing in confidence she reached up and kissed him.

"I'm sorry you travelled so far and I have to go so soon," he said, gently stroking her cheek. "I have to be in the states in the morning," he added.

"It's okay," Millie replied, sadly. "You were worth it," she added with a cute smile.

"I'll call you later," Dex said, grabbing her for one last kiss and cuddle before he had to go. "Mac will escort you out," said Dex.

"Okay," Millie replied, feeling absolutely gutted to be leaving him already, even more so that by the morning he would be thousands of miles away in another country, but she knew that if she got into this with him, that was going to become her reality.

Millie walked up the steps to where Mac was waiting. As she got to the top she turned and shouted down to Dex, "Colpo di fulmine!" A phrase Ricco had

taught her.

Dex was confused. "What?" he replied.

Millie giggled. "Look it up!" she said as Mac walked her away.

Dex waited a few minutes, he needed some time to get himself together and come down from the high he was on. He got out his phone; he had eight missed calls and several texts from Lucie. He'd forgotten she was even there! Ignoring them all he typed what Millie had said into Google, or at least his best attempt at spelling it!

He clicked on the first link:

Colpo di fulmine; The thunderbolt, What the Italians call love at first sight, love strikes you as suddenly and as powerfully as lightning would.

Dex smiled to himself, he couldn't have put it into words better himself.

CHAPTER 19

The other guys were already gone so Dex walked back to the bus alone. As he approached the coach park the bus doors were open and he could see Lucie was aboard the bus. In his head he started going over excuses about where he had been. Lucie saw him coming and stepped down from the bus, closing the door behind her. Her face lit up.

"Hey baby!" she said, throwing her arms around his neck. "I've missed you!" she added.

Dex stared blankly ahead at the side of the bus, waiting for her to let go. He felt absolutely nothing in seeing her and even cringed a little at her touch. At that moment he had no doubt whatsoever it was over. Finally releasing him from her embrace she stepped back and looked at him, his face was expressionless.

"What's wrong, Dex?" she asked, confused by his behaviour and despondence. Dex looked at the floor. "Dex?" she asked again.

He sighed heavily as he looked up at her. "Luc, it's over, I'm sorry." His heart sank. He hated confrontation, he hated hurting people. His emotions were all over the place, going from total euphoria with Millie ten minutes ago to utter anguish.

Lucie's face dropped, her bottom lip quivered a little as she tried to speak. "What? Why!?" she asked, her voice shaky.

"I'm sorry, I'm just not feeling it anymore and it wouldn't be fair to you to carry on." Knowing he was doing the right thing made Dex more confident in his words.

Lucie stepped towards him, tears began to roll down her cheeks as she tried to put her arms around him again. He stepped back, taking her wrists in his hands to stop her, gently he pushed her arms down.

"Luc. No. Don't make this any harder," he said. Lucie was completely taken aback; she thought for sure she could change his mind. She was a beautiful, world-famous pop star, of course he would want her. But as she looked into his eyes, she knew that was it. He had never looked at her like that. There was nothing in his eyes, not anymore.

Lucie burst into tears. She put her head in her hands, expecting Dex to at least comfort her, but instead he walked straight past her and opened the door to the tour bus. He knew engaging in any kind of sympathy would only complicate things, he wanted a clean break. He was too old for the drama. He leaned in the bus door. "Mac, can you walk Lucie back to her security team please, I don't want her walking back alone in the dark, but I can't do it," he said.

"Uh, sure," replied Mac, looking confused at Dex's odd request.

A weight had been lifted from Dex's shoulders. She was gone.

On the plane home Dex felt emotional. He'd had one of the best but hardest nights of his life, it felt bittersweet sat on a plane going in the opposite direction to Millie. He knew any future with her would be tough. They lived on different continents, he travelled almost constantly and she had a busy life in England. He didn't know how he was going to make it work but all he knew in that moment was that he wanted to try.

He wondered if he should text her, not wanting to come on too strongly and scare her off. He knew his lifestyle wasn't going to be easy for her to deal with, he needed to give her time to decide if it was something she wanted to be involved in. His past girlfriends had received death threats and all sorts from fans, so he wanted Millie to be 100% sure!

Less than an hour into the flight his phone beeped,

One new message

He smiled hoping it was from Millie, it wasn't. Instead he was greeted with an angry text from Lucie, calling him every name under the sun, threatening to ruin any future relationship he had and telling him what a shit boyfriend he had been. It all just reiterated that he had made the right decision; Lucie was not only young in age but incredibly immature too. He was too old for the drama; it wasn't something he wanted in his life at 31!

His body felt heavy and he was emotionally drained, closing his eyes for a split second, he fell asleep.

Getting home seemed to take forever, two trains and a drive home later Millie yawned as she unlocked the front door, desperate for her bed. Inside she glanced at the hallway clock. 1.23am! Never had she been so pleased at the thought of tomorrow being Saturday, a weekend off! She noticed Aaron, Amber's boyfriend's shoes on the floor, he must have stayed over. She kicked off her own shoes and tiptoed up the stairs by the light of her phone, tripping over someone's shoes. She banged against the wall to save herself.

"Fuuuuuuuuuuck!" she whispered to herself. Freezing on the spot for a second she listened to see if she had woken Amber. Silence. She crept to her bedroom door, quietly went in and closed it behind her, breathing a sigh of relief as her phone beeped... loudly!

"Oh for fuck sake!" she whispered, hugging her phone to try to silence it. After a few seconds she slowly pulled the phone from her chest.

I look at you and I see the kind of person I want to spend my life with, I may sound crazy but I've never been able to look at anyone in that way. D.x

As she read the words she was instantly taken back to underneath the stadium steps with him. The butterflies, the lighting, the intensity. Closing her eyes she could still taste him on her lips, she could smell him in her hair, every bit of her ached for him.

She undressed, after a long day it felt amazing to finally take her bra off! She threw on a t-shirt she found on the floor and climbed into bed, clutching her teddy bear, as she closed her eyes. She needed a minute to pull herself together.

How am I going to sleep tonight when you send me things like that? x

She replied. *Life can't get any better*, she thought to herself as she fell asleep.

Dex was woken by a huge thud as the plane hit the tarmac at Newark airport. Thrown forward in his seat by the impact he hit his head on the seat in front of him. His phone fell out of his pocket into the floor and slid under the seat in front of him.

"Owww fuck! What was that?!" he groaned. Leaning forward to look out of the window he was pleased to see they were on the ground!

"Just a bad landing!" said Jesse, looking out of the window beside him. The band had flown hundreds of times and never had a landing been that... painful! Dex touched his head.

"Jesus, man! You're bleeding!" said Zach, sat the other side of him. Zach got up to go and get something to put on Dex's head. An air hostess rushed down the aisle towards him.

"Sir!...Sir! You need to sit down sir, the fasten seat belt signs are still on, sir!" she said frantically as she met Zach half way down the aisle.

"No, I need a First Aid kit, my friend's head is bleeding after that awful landing!" explained Zach abruptly!

"Oh, okay, I'll fetch one right away, but please take your seat!" she said, her look of disapproval changing to one of concern as she walked briskly back up the aisle into the stewards' area. Zach went back to his seat.

"Are you okay, bro?" Zach asked.

"Yeah, it's fine, it's nothing," Dex replied. A line of blood ran from his forehead to his cheek.

"The air hostess has gone to get a First Aid kit," said Zach.

The guys began to gather their stuff together ready to disembark the plane. It was nearly 2am in New York, after leaving the UK at midnight the time difference meant they'd flown back in time! Dex always thought that was kind of cool, it was like getting the chance to relive time you've already lived, a concept he found magical.

The aisle began to fill as people got up from their seats and began to gather their baggage. The air hostess pushed through the crowds of people who had gathered in the aisle, finally reaching Dex.

"Are you okay, sir?" she asked, her voice a little shaky as she looked right as him. Recognising him she tried to maintain her professionalism.

"Yeah, fine, thanks," he replied. He just

wanted to get off the plane.

"Can I take a look?" she asked nervously.

"I guess," he replied, thinking the quicker he cooperated the sooner he could get off the plane. He leaned forward to let her look at the cut on his forehead, the bleeding had stopped.

"It's not too bad, would you just like an antiseptic wipe to clean it up?" she asked, handing him a small white packet.

"Sure, thanks," he replied.

CHAPTER 20

The plane began to disembark and in minutes they were in the terminal building joining the back of the queue for immigration control.

Dex got the wipe out and cleaned up his face before they faced the media. Splitting up with Lucie on the same night he got home, face covered in blood was a story for the media that wrote itself!

Surprisingly as the band emerged into the arrivals terminal it was quiet. They could see a few paparazzi waiting outside of the main terminal doors but there were no crowds. The airport was calm with only a handful of people inside, none of which seemed at all interested in the band.

"Awesome!" said Dex as Mac led them outside to a waiting car. The double automatic doors opened and immediately the flashes started, Dex thought surely these people would rather be in bed at nearly 3am!

With no fans holding them up they were in the car and on their way in minutes! Dex's parents only lived ten minutes from the airport and he was going to stay with them, he had four days off before a festival in Chicago on Thursday and he was looking forward to some quiet time with his family somewhere he could completely relax and wouldn't be bothered by fans or paparazzi. Plus the thought of his mom's home cooking was pretty appealing too!

Zach was dropped off first at his girlfriend's apartment in Manhattan. A few minutes later the car pulled up outside of Dex's mom and dad's house. It was dark and quiet as he grabbed his bags from the boot. He leaned into the car.

"See you Thursday, guys," he said to CJ and Jesse. CJ was asleep.

"Bye man, enjoy your days off!" replied Jesse as he shut the car door.

Monday morning arrived early for Millie but for once it wasn't the sun that had woken her. Instead it was an intense rainstorm lashing against her window. She loved the rain. Looking at her phone she was pleased to see 6.41am displayed on the screen, she had time to lie in bed and listen to the rain until her alarm went off. She felt odd this morning. After an eventful week, a fun weekend shopping, drinking and dancing with Amber the reality of Monday morning hit her like a brick! She rarely felt down but this morning there was something eating away at her, but she had no idea what. She had a lot to look forward to, a meeting with Mr Salvatore about designing her own shoe collection, celebrities coming into the office today to discuss designs for dresses for Cannes Film Festival, Millie had been beyond excited for weeks to design for such high-profile people and at such a high-profile event, but this morning her enthusiasm escaped her.

Laid in bed she had a browse through Twitter as she did every morning when she woke. She was disappointed to not have any messages from Dex, she'd not heard anything from him since the early hours of Saturday morning as he left for America and thoughts had begun to fill her head. *Did he make it home okay? Did he just do this with fans all the time? Was he in love with Lucie and just wanted a bit on the side?* She knew he was busy and lived a chaotic lifestyle but with each hour that had passed Millie began to lose hope of seeing him again. Maybe he had changed his mind; she knew he was struggling with the idea of dating a fan.

It took all her willpower not to text him; she was determined not to be *that* girl. She wanted to play it cool, she had learned from past relationships that the less contact with him the more intrigued he would be by her, though not hearing a word from him she began to wonder if she was doing the right thing.

The drive to work took forever, traffic was horrendous and it always was on a rainy day! She turned the radio on and her eyes welled up a little. She just wanted to rewind, she had pinned all her hopes on Friday being the beginning of her relationship with Dex, she hadn't even contemplated it being the last of it. Pulling down the sunshade she looked in the mirror, she was a mess, the rain had already got the better of her hair this morning and her watery eyes had un-set her eye makeup. *From smoky and seductive to woeful panda! Brilliant!* she thought.

Finally arriving at work (late!) she sat in the car for a moment to pull herself together. She felt teary, but she had no idea why. She eventually got out of the car to a second drenching. Luckily as she pushed open the door to Salvo's head office Sophie was on the phone, Millie quickly rushed past her desk and into the lift, breathing a sigh of relief that she didn't have to stop and listen to Sophie's life story or a play by play of how she bought, cooked and ate her dinner last night!

PING!

The lift opened. Millie was pleased to see the corridor was empty, she hated small talk with people in the morning. She wasn't a morning person and having to pretend to be friendly and chirpy that early in the day was more energy than she could muster! Closing the door to her office behind her, she turned off her mobile and switched her office phone to answer machine. She just felt like being alone today, the past week had sent her emotions all over the place with the highest highs with work and Dex and the lowest lows with her sister. She'd had a strange and exhausting week.

Despite the promise of exciting things ahead, Monday morning back in her 9-5 brought a reality check Millie hadn't anticipated. Just one week ago she was a globe-trotting fashion designer, attracting attention from the world, kissing a pop-rock star she'd been in love with forever. And this week Millie sat at her desk alone, the same desk she had sat at every day for the last five years, the room silent. If she didn't know better she would have assumed last week was a dream.

Picking up a pencil she began to draw. Drawing was when Millie felt at her most content, it was in her blood. She could sit down with a sketch pad and a pencil and completely lose herself, the entire world could just fall away around her and she wouldn't notice. So it wasn't surprising that as someone knocked on her office door she nearly fell off her chair, dropping her pencil on the floor. She snapped back to reality, gazing up at the door to see Sophie's little round face pressed up against the glass panel in the door, smiling enthusiastically at her. She couldn't help but smile, gesturing for her to come in.

"Ricco's on the phone for you, I couldn't get hold of you from downstairs!" squawked Sophie.

"Yeah... my... uhhh... phone's playing up," lied Millie.

"Oh... I'll get someone to look at it," said Sophie. "Ricco's on line 5," she chirped.

"Okay, thanks," replied Millie, picking up the phone. She waited until Sophie had left and the door was closed. "Hey, Ri," said Millie.

"Hey, darlin'," he replied. A smile crept across Millie's face, it was so good to hear his voice.

"How's Lexi?" he added

"She's doing alright, recovering slowly….I miss you!" she said.

"oh, good. I'm missing you like crazy too, doll," he said. "But… I am done here, I'm coming home tonight!" he added.

"Really? When?" she asked, her mood lifted a little, excited that she would get to see him soon.

"Late, about 2am," he replied. "But anyway… come on! Spill! I want to know everything about Friday!" he said.

Millie was silent for a minute.

"YOU DIDN'T SLEEP WITH HIM ON A FIRST DATE… DID YOU?" began Ricco's interrogation.

"NO!" declared Millie, enthusiastically.

"So? Come on then!" Ricco pushed.

"We just kissed," admitted Millie, shyly.

"Just?!... You JUST kissed Dex Rose! Do you actually know how incredibly lucky you are?" he added. "Yeah, it was… incredible!" she gushed, beginning to feel the hairs on the back of her neck stand up as she relived the moment in her head.

"So… come on! How was it, was he good? What did he do? What did he say?" asked Ricco, excitedly. "Woah, slow down, babe!" laughed Millie. She took a moment to collect her thoughts. "It was in…CREDIBLE!" she began. Ricco listened intently. "I got there late, but managed to be near the front. I watched him perform, they were more amazing than ever before! Then their security guy just came and picked me out of the crowd and pulled me up onto the side of the stage!"

"NO WAY!" interrupted Ricco. "Every single other girl there must have been jealous as fuck of you!" he continued. "Sorry, carry on," he added.

Millie smiled to herself and continued with her story. "So, this guy led me backstage and down some steps underneath the stage and there he was," said Millie.

"And?! You can't stop there! We're just getting to the juicy bit!" joked Ricco.

"We talked a bit and then he kissed me," said Millie.

Ricco was silent for a moment, frustrated with her less than insightful account! "Are you trying to be annoying?" he replied. "And?!" he pushed.

"And... oh, Ri! It was beyond words. The best moment of my life so far, I am ridiculously in love!" she gushed, not at all embarrassed to tell him. She felt comfortable to say it out loud now, no matter how stupid it sounded!

"You're so fucking lucky! He's a babe!" said Ricco. "Was he a good kisser?" he asked.

"Yeah, awesome! Kind of awkward and... err... messy! But strangely that made it more amazing," Millie explained.

"He's awkward on stage too! That must just be his thing," said Ricco. "So what now? Are you dating him?" asked Ricco, feeling unexpectedly gutted by his own question.

"No, he's dating Lucie Goldham still!" exclaimed Millie.

"What? Still?! So what's he doing meeting you? I won't let you be his play thing!" said Ricco, in a serious tone, feeling overprotective of her.

"I won't be, don't worry. To be honest, I think that's it. I've not heard from him since that night!" said Millie.

"What?!" asked Ricco, confused. "He text Friday night after I left him and that was the last I heard from him," she explained, saddened by the reality of hearing her own words.

"That doesn't sound right to me, there has to be a genuine reason why," said Ricco, trying to reassure her. "Maybe after meeting me I just wasn't what he expected! Plus I looked awful, I got caught in a rain storm!" said Millie.

"Don't be silly, that's not it. I bet you looked HAAAWT even if you were soaking wet!" said Ricco.

"Oh I don't know," said Millie, apathetically, picking up her pencils and continuing to sketch. Ricco took the hint, she was done with this conversation.

"I've got to go now, babes, go and stay over at mine after work so I can see you when I get home" he said.

"Okay," she replied automatically, she had entered a state of concentration she liked to refer to as a sketch coma!

CHAPTER 21

Approaching 11am Millie walked along to the canteen to make a coffee, she had a long afternoon of meetings ahead and needed a little caffeine boost!

"Ah, Amelie, just who I was coming to see." Millie jumped at the sound of a deep voice behind her, she turned around.

"Hello, Mr Salvatore, what can I do for you?" she asked.

"The first celebrity client has arrived, the design team are meeting with her in the boardroom in five minutes. Can you join us?" he asked.

"Yeah, sure, give me two minutes to grab my things and I'll be there," replied Millie, rushing to make her coffee.

"Thank you, dear," said Mr Salvatore pouring himself some coffee. Millie took a quick sip of coffee as she left the canteen. She stopped.

"Do you know who it is?" Millie asked, poking her head back around the canteen door.

"Uh, she's a young singer. Uh, Lucie something. Goldman?" he tried to recall.

Millie froze. "Lucie Goldham?" she asked, her heart began to race.

"Yes! That's it" he replied.

"FUCK!" Millie mouthed to herself silently. In that second her excitement to design for celebrity clients had turned into a living nightmare, she was minutes away from being face to face with Dex's girlfriend! She felt so sick as she walked along the corridor to her office. She grabbed her portfolio folder, her sketch pad and pencils and turned to walk back out of the door. She stopped on the spot for a moment, closed her eyes, took a deep breath and tried to calm her nerves, she needed to be confident. *She's just a client, she's just a client,* she told herself over and over again. She breathed out. *Let's do this!*

She nervously pushed open the boardroom door, wishing so hard that Ricco was there beside her like he normally would be. Of all the times for him to be away! Several people from her design department were already sat around the table. A young girl sat with her back to the door, her long white-blonde hair cascaded down the back of the chair. She turned around as Millie walked in, shooting her a perfect smile that stood out against her pale porcelain skin. She didn't look real, she was like a doll. Millie had only ever seen her in pictures but she looked more perfect in the flesh than she did in photos. She had the most stunning sea-green eyes Millie had ever seen but all she could think was *Woah, she looks young!* If Millie didn't know better she'd have guessed she was around 14! She couldn't imagine Dex being with her yet all she could think was *she sleeps with Dex!*

Millie walked around to the opposite side of the table and sat down, right in front of Lucie.

"We're just waiting for Mr Salvatore then we can begin," said Silvio, Mr Salvatore's personal assistant. "He's just grabbing a coffee," added Millie.

Lucie turned to look at Millie as she spoke, making eye contact. Millie looked away quickly feeling awkward.

Mr Salvatore appeared at the open door, he walked into the boardroom, closing it behind him.

"Right, let's get started," he said, putting his coffee down at the head of the table. "Firstly, welcome to Salvo's, Ms Goldham, we're very pleased to have you here," he began, wandering around the table. "Let me introduce you to our design team," he said. "This is Giovanna, head of design," he started, standing behind each person and gently touching them on the shoulder as he introduced them, as if they were at school. "This is Anthony, he's our stylist. This is Amelie, Millie is a senior designer here."

Millie was surprised and delighted at being introduced as a senior designer, she was employed as a junior designer and had no idea when or how that had changed, but it was a change she would happily get used to, it made her look more impressive in front of Lucie if nothing else!

"This is Katarina, our pattern maker and Stefano, our knitwear designer," said Mr Salvatore. "You'll also be working with my son, Ricco. He's director of design but he's unfortunately on a business trip in Tokyo at the moment," he added.

"Thank you, Mr Salvatore," said Kelly, Lucie's representative. "So shall we start?" asked Kelly.

"Please," replied Mr Salvatore as he took his seat, taking a sip of his coffee.

"Ok, so Lucie is attending Cannes Film Festival in two weeks and we need a dress. Lucie has some ideas of what she would like so we're hoping you can take them and come up with something," explained Kelly.

"I'd like it to be white," said Lucie quietly, she not only looked 14 but sounded it too. Millie was surprised by the immaturity of her voice.

"Okay, anything else?" asked Millie.

"It needs to be full length and I like sparkly," said Lucie. Millie looked at Anthony, rolling her eyes. It was like getting a brief from a five-year-old.

After 45 minutes of throwing ideas and sketches around, the team had come up with a design Lucie liked.

"We'll call it a day there, I know you have to get away to some other engagements, Ms Goldham," said Mr Salvatore, as people around the table began to get their paperwork together.

"Amelie, could you please take Ms Goldham to the studio and take her measurements?" asked Mr Salvatore. *Oh for fuck sake! Why me?* thought Millie.

"Of course," she replied politely. "This way please Ms Goldham," said Millie, gesturing for Lucie to follow her to her office. She led the way down the corridor, Lucie trailing behind. Millie held open her office door for her; she could feel her fingers shaking, she was nervous to be alone with her, what if she knew something? She looked Lucie up and down as she approached. Millie had never noticed how tiny she was, her thin white legs looked washed out against her white denim shorts, a black oversized baseball t-shirt, the words 'New York' across the front hung off her hiding any figure she had underneath.

"Alright, so, I need to take your measurements, is that okay?" asked Millie.

"Sure," replied Lucie.

"I'm going to need you in your underwear for that," said Millie awkwardly.

"Okay." Lucie began to take her top off.

"Ah! Hang on! Not here, if you go behind that screen and get undressed, I'll come in when you're ready," said Millie.

"Oh, okay," said Lucie. She walked towards the other end of the office and disappeared behind the screen. Millie took a moment to get herself together, the image of Dex was permanently transfixed in her mind, part of her felt gutted that that was the girl he touched, the girl he kissed, the girl he slept with! But another part of her secretly couldn't get the words out of her head *I spent Friday night kissing your boyfriend!* A smile crept across her face, she knew it made her a bitch but it gave her a tiny bit of satisfaction. She walked over to the screen.

"Are you ready?" asked Millie.

"Yes," replied Lucie.

Millie walked behind the screen, avoiding eye contact. Lucie stood in front of her in her skimpy white underwear. Her figure was almost boyish, no waist, no hips, her tiny lacy shorts hung from her protruding hip bones. Millie walked towards her with the tape measure, putting her arms around Lucie she pulled the tape measure around her waist, her hand lightly grazed her stomach. Lucie jumped.

"Sorry, my hands are cold," said Millie, as she crouched down to measure her thighs, feeling like she ought to make some polite conversation. "So, are you performing tonight?" asked Millie.

"No, I've got a couple of days off," replied Lucie.

"Ah that must be nice," said Mille, faking an interest.

"Yeah, I'm flying out to America this afternoon to see my boyfriend, he lives in New York," said Lucie.

Millie dropped the tape measure! *What? She's flying out to be with him tonight!* she thought to herself. She instantly felt sick, a burning feeling filled the pit of her stomach, rising into the back of her throat. It all made sense now, she was just a bit of fun, he was still very much with Lucie, all the pieces began to fit together now. Millie felt stupid, she believed every word Dex said to her. She believed the emotion he felt underneath the stage that night, she believed he was going to leave Lucie for her and now she felt pretty stupid! She could finally see things clearly; of course he wasn't going to leave his perfect little pop starlet for Millie.

A nobody.

"Oh, wow, must be difficult to find the time to see each

other with such a busy lifestyle," said Millie, fishing for more information as she measured Lucie's bust.

"Yeah it can be hard, he's in the same industry so he is super busy too, but I only saw him last Friday so it's not been too long," she smiled at Millie.

He'd been with Lucie on Friday too! Millie was crushed. It was the worst kind of pain as Millie smiled back to stop the tears from falling. "All done!" she said, swallowing the lump in her throat. "Go to the end of the corridor, take a right and you'll be back at the boardroom," said Millie, avoiding eye contact. She knew Mr Salvatore would be mad that she didn't escort her but she couldn't face a moment longer with her.

"Thanks," said Lucie as she walked out of the door. Millie burst into tears. How could she have been stupid enough to believe his lies?

Monday morning Dex woke up to a familiar smell. He knew that smell, he had smelled it a hundred times before and every single time it was better than the last! He took a minute to adjust to being awake; he finally opened his eyes and looked around the room, a smile washed over his face as he remembered where he was. Home.

"Dexter! Breakfast!" Shouted his mom.

Man he had missed that! "Okay, thanks, Mom," he called back, feeling like he was 12 again. He couldn't have been happier to be back at his parents' house, even if only for a few days. He had forgotten how amazing his mom's cooking smelled in the morning! He laid in bed for a few minutes taking everything in, he knew in a couple of days it would all be gone again and he wasn't sure for how long. The windows were open and the sun was shining. A cool, refreshing spring breeze came softly through the window, brushing his face. He took a deep breath, filling his lungs with the fresh morning air. Kicking back the covers he sat up. Reaching for his t-shirt on the floor, he threw it on and looked over at the clock. It was 9.36am, he always slept like a baby at his parents' house. His first thought was the same every morning. Millie. But he no longer had her number! Or a phone. He was desperate for the mail to come, the airline had found his phone that he dropped and left on board on Friday night, he felt completely lost without it. He had spent most of the weekend trying to get in touch with her, calling, texting, even using social media, which he couldn't stand! To try to find a way of getting her number, he'd left Ricco numerous messages on his Twitter account but he'd heard nothing back! But he was just thankful someone had found his phone and posted it back to him. Having someone able to see the contents of his phone made him feel physically sick! It was his worst nightmare. That phone contained his life! He had messages from Lucie, Millie, family and other celebrities, private photos, his family's phone numbers as well as a whole host of other private things. If someone had got hold of all that and released it, his life was over!

"Morning, Mom," he said with a huge smile as he walked into the kitchen. His mom was stood cooking pancakes, Dex took a deep breath, the smell was utterly divine.

"Good morning, Son," said his mom. She was so pleased to have her boy back, even if only for a short time. He wasn't going to have to lift a finger whilst he was there, his mom swept right back into 'mom' mode, cooking his meals, doing his laundry. She seemed to forget he was a 31-year-old man now, but Dex didn't mind, he could use a rest.

"Parcel came for you there, Dex," said his mom, pointing to a small brown package on the kitchen work top.

"Ah great! Thanks, Mom," he replied, tearing apart the wrapping paper. There it was! A huge sense of relief embodied him. He turned the phone on, after a minute the beeps began, message after message after message came through! He sat down at the breakfast table, wishing everyone would just leave him alone for a couple of days, days off never seemed to truly be 'days off' anymore. With one hand he began to read through the messages whilst tucking into some pancakes with the other.

Nearly every message he opened was from Lucie, threats to take private information to the press, he was this, he was that, followed by begging him to reconsider his decision. The messages only helped to make him more sure that he absolutely did the right thing! She was immature and needed to learn how to be in an adult relationship, more so how to behave when it ends. Dex had begun to really dislike her, though he didn't like anyone or anything that caused him hassle and she was certainly doing that! His phone beeped with another message, opening it he was excited to see Millie's name across the screen.

I've just spent the day with Lucie, she came into my work for a dress fitting. She told me all about how happy you guys are and that she's flying out to be with you tonight. Least I know the score before I got in any deeper. I won't go to the press with anything, don't worry. I'm not that kind of girl. Delete my number and we can forget anything ever happened. Millie

A feeling of panic spread through his abdomen, what had Lucie been lying about now? He could put up with the constant stream of abuse and threats from Lucie, it was his own fault for getting mixed up with a little girl! But if she was going to start screwing with his friends, his family! Millie! That wasn't going to fly with him. He immediately dialled Millie's number, desperate to find out what lies Lucie had told her and to explain the truth that he had broken it off with Lucie after being with Millie on Friday night but she was too childish to accept it and just walk away.

Millie's phone rang for a couple of minutes. No answer. He quickly wrote a message:

Millie, please call me, whatever Lucie told you is lies, I ended it with her. D.x

He waited a few minutes, no reply. Sat at the kitchen table he rested his chin on his hands, he had completely lost his appetite and could feel a gut-wrenching sense of loss in the pit of his stomach.

"Something wrong, Son?" his mom asked, it's like she had a sixth sense to what her kids were feeling.

"Nah, I'm alright, Ma," he replied, unconvincingly.

"Come on, Dexter," she replied, tilting her head sympathetically. He was close to his mom and could talk to her about almost anything but he just didn't think he could explain what he was thinking or feeling this time, he didn't even understand it himself.

"Have you and Lucie fallen out again?" she asked. "No, Lucie and I have gone our separate ways," he admitted.

"Oh no! How come?" she asked.

"It just wasn't working out, my heart wasn't in it anymore," he said.

"To be honest, Dex, I'm not surprised. The age gap was just too big, and you both have such busy lives what with all the travelling you both do. It was going to be hard to make that work, Son," said his mom diplomatically.

"Yeah," he replied.

"That's not what you're sad about is it?" she asked, concerned by her son's woeful response. She knew there was something more than that to it.

"No," he admitted, his mom had a knack for getting things out of him! Wiping her hands on a tea towel she came and sat down beside him at the kitchen table.

"What's bothering you, Dex?" she asked, rubbing his back affectionately.

Dex hesitated, he wasn't sure how to explain the situation he had got himself into, nor was he sure he wanted to tell his mom about it. But he did feel like he needed to talk about it and there was no one in the world he trusted more than his mom. He counted to three in his head...

"I met someone," he blurted it out quickly before he could talk himself out of it.

"Okay...?" his mom replied, waiting to hear more. "Her name is Millie, she's in England, she's 26, she's a fashion designer," he started.

"Okay. So, if you're not with Lucie anymore what's the problem?" asked his mom.

"I think...." He stopped himself, reconsidering his next words in his mind. He breathed out heavily, "I think I... I'm in love with her!" he admitted, feeling slightly embarrassed by his own admission. His mom smiled.

"And that's a bad thing, Son?" she asked, slightly confused.

"Well, kinda, she's a fan. I barely know her, I've only met her once, barely more than a week ago, it's just crazy!" he explained. His mom laughed, rubbing his back again reassuringly.

"It's not crazy, darling. That's what love does! It hits you when you least expect it and there's nothing you can do about that," said his mom.

Dex looked at her. "Do you think?" he asked. "Yes, just look at me and your dad. I knew I loved him the first time I saw him, well actually the second time. The first time I saw him I thought he was a jackass!" she laughed. Dex smiled.

"But you guys weren't famous, what if she's just in it to sell stories? I don't know if I can trust her," he said, talking himself out of it.

"That's a risk you take, love! And if you get burned you get burned, you'll never experience anything if you don't take a few risks, Son," she said with a smile.

Dex thought about what she had said. He didn't know how she did it but his mom had a knack for fixing anything in his life.

"Go get her!" his mom said as she got up from the table to finish cooking breakfast. Dex sat in silence for a minute, his mom's words resonating in his mind.

"I don't think she wants me to, Lucie has been telling her lies that were still together and that she's flying out to spend the night with me," explained Dex.

"That's the trouble with the young 'uns, always drama!" said his Mom. "If you think you love her go and fight for her love, sort it out, face to face," she added. She was right! He had to go get her! "Your brother's flying to London early tomorrow morning, why don't you go with him, you have a couple days off, right?" his mom suggested.

"Yeah," he replied, thinking about what she said for a minute. Could he just show up? It seemed like a pretty good way to make things up to her rather than just calling her.

"I'm gonna go, Mom!" he said, suddenly feeling a rush of nerves and excitement.

"Good for you, Son!" she replied, happy to see her son fight for the girl he loved. She knew she had brought him up right, he'd grown into an amazing man. Dex went to call his older brother Felix. "Thanks, Mom," he said, kissing her on the forehead as he left the kitchen.

His body was pumping full of adrenaline, he was really going to do this! A chapter in his life was going to end tonight, a new one to start tomorrow. He couldn't decide how he felt, excited, nervous, sick all rolled into one.

He made some calls, to his brother, the airline, to Mac. He ran up the stairs, throwing some clothes into a bag. He had never done anything like this for a girl before but he was really going to do this!

CHAPTER 22

Millie pulled up outside Ricco's apartment. The day's rainstorms had given way to a glorious sunny evening. Millie had had a horrible day, she couldn't wait to get out of her work clothes, throw on something cool, grab a glass of wine and chill on the balcony.

After the elevator opened up into his stunning penthouse apartment, Millie poured herself a glass of wine and headed straight for her favourite place. The balcony. The sun was still warm; Millie slouched down into the chair, taking off her work shirt to reveal a lace-trim black vest top. As she tried to unwind Lucie's words went round and round in her head. She felt emptiness, all of her hopes, all of her excitement had been zapped from her body, leaving her feeling a little disorientated.

Tonight she wasn't going to dwell on it, work was going amazingly well and she had a lot to be thankful for in her life. She sat for a few minutes; there was something about a warm evening that Millie loved. Standing, she walked over to the balcony railing, standing quietly alone she watched as the world below her went by. The sun had begun to set and the sky was a beautiful mix of yellows and oranges.

She felt deflated, confused, where did she go from

here? She was happy in her life generally but she just felt like something was missing, something she couldn't put her finger on. She looked down at the people on the street and watched as a couple walked hand in hand down the road, laughing and smiling together. He held the door open for her as they entered a pub, Millie wondered what their evening would be like, where would they go next, was he 'the one', would they get married some day? Once the couple was out of view Millie's attention moved to a guy walking alone, smiling, looking down at his phone and dodging people as he typed something out. Millie wondered who he was texting and who had made him smile. Completely caught up in other people's imaginary lives Millie jumped a mile as her phone beeped and vibrated loudly across the glass table behind her.

She caught her breath and turned around, picking it up and turning back to lean over the railing she clutched the phone to her chest for a minute, whoever it was could wait. The street seemed empty now, people were going home and the city was quieting down before filling again later with party-goers out for the evening in the city's bars and clubs. It was a life that wasn't for Millie. Sure, some nights she liked a cocktail with friends but she was a home bird, she preferred to spend her evenings snuggled up on the sofa, sketch book in hand. That was her contentment, that was her joy in life. Forgetting about the message she went inside for a shower. Millie threw on one of Ricco's t-shirts and cracked open a bottle of wine. Dragging a blanket out on the balcony she felt surprisingly pleased that Ricco wasn't there, she hadn't realised how physically and emotionally drained she was, what with work being so hectic, her sister's accident and everything with Dex and Lucie. She was surprised to be enjoying her own company, she hadn't seen much of Cate and Hollie, even living with Amber they had become like ships that passed in the night lately. She considered inviting them round for the evening but talked herself out of it, maybe a night on her own to chill was just what she needed. She put

Craze's album on quietly on her iPod and popped inside to get her sketch pad and pencils. It was the perfect place to draw, she felt inspired and her best work was born out of spontaneous moments like these.

Drawing, sipping her wine, snuggled under a blanket watching the city as it came alive for the evening had turned into a pretty perfect place to be, it was exactly what she needed. The sun had set and the city was aglow with street lights. The pavements began to fill with people, talking, laughing, enjoying the warm summer evening. Millie loved the sounds of the city, the people, the traffic, she loved the sound of the hustle and bustle, everyone going about their business. She picked up her pencil, laying her sketch book on her lap she began to sketch a rose. Her eyes felt heavy, she closed them, just for a minute, and that was it, she was out like a light!

Ricco arrived home just after 1am. As the elevator opened into his apartment he expected Millie to be in bed, she wasn't one for staying up late. The light was still on out on the balcony, he went out to turn it off, and as he opened the door to the balcony he was surprised to see Millie, snuggled up in the chair with a blanket on her. It had been raining, she was soaking wet. Her notebook and pencils strewn about, all completely wet through! Her phone sat next to an empty wine bottle on the table. He quickly dried her phone in his t-shirt and slipped it into his back pocket. Slowly picking her up, blanket still wrapped around her, he carried her indoors and put her in his bed, covering her up with a blanket. He went back outside to salvage what he could of her work, knowing she would be gutted in the morning to see it all ruined!

He took inside as much as he could save. Turning the lights off, he went back to his bedroom. Millie was sound asleep. Her clothes were soaked through, he didn't know whether to wake her so she could change into something dry or just leave her asleep.

He took his clothes off, turned out the light and climbed into bed. She felt freezing to the touch. He snuggled into her, pulling her into him to try to warm her up with his body heat. Her clothes, her hair, her skin, all soaking wet. Wrapping the blankets around her he held her as tightly as he could. He had just spent the last few days secretly away with a man he really cared for, but laid there with Millie with just a wet t-shirt between them he couldn't understand why he felt like he was holding himself back. As he laid in bed his mind was all over the place. He gently stroked her back while she slept, relieved that he was so tired, he fell asleep quickly.

"Ouch!" Thought Millie as she woke with a pounding headache. The room was still quite dark, the sun wasn't shining through the curtains and annoying her like it did most mornings. She turned over to see if Ricco was still asleep but was confused to see the bed empty beside her. The bed covers were untucked and scruffy, a half-drunk glass of water stood on the nightstand beside the bed. He had slept there, but now he was gone. Millie turned onto her back, glancing up at the clock on the wall, 7.54am!

"Jesus fuck! I'm going to be late!" she said to herself. She couldn't remember the last time she slept in that late! Sitting up in bed she rubbed her eyes and yawned, she could hear the rain lashing down on the windows. She couldn't remember going to bed, her hair was damp and tangled, she couldn't find her phone, and nothing made sense this morning! It was as if she had taken a trip through the wardrobe and woke up in Narnia!

Holding the blanket around herself she got up and walked over to the window. Pulling the curtain back a tiny bit she was greeted with torrential rain, the street below wasn't filled with commuters like a usual morning, instead the pavements were deserted! She watched the traffic go by for a minute or two, letting the curtain drop back into place she wandered out of the bedroom to find Ricco. The apartment was quiet, the open-plan lounge/kitchen/diner was empty, all she could hear was the sound of the rain beating down on the full-length windows, it looked horrendous out there! Though she found watching it from inside one of the best ways to relax, it really made her entire body feel free, there was something about cool raindrops that made her feel alive! But still she wasn't looking forward to driving to work in it. She walked to the kettle and flicked it on, noticing a note on the kitchen side

Mil,

Had to go into work early. Didn't want to disturb you. See you there,

Ri xx

Ps you fell asleep out in the rain you nutter!

Millie smiled, she couldn't remember a thing, which could probably be blamed on the entire bottle of wine she managed to polish off alone!

She made herself a cup of tea and took some paracetamol. She was getting too old for drinking, she suffered for days afterwards! Sipping her tea she went back through the bedroom to shower.

9am and already Ricco had been at work for over two hours. Sat at his desk, feeling really stressed out, he'd only had four hours sleep and felt exhausted but he had meetings back to back all day and needed to do some prep after being away.

Millie rushed through the office door, soaking wet, something that had become a daily occurrence in her life. She'd hoped with it being six days into May that the April showers would have subsided by now, but no such luck!

"Fucking rain!" she groaned as she passed Sophie's desk.

"Good morning, Millie," said Sophie, with no less chirp, despite the weather!

"Morning," Millie shouted back as she ran up the stairs.

Approaching the third floor she began to wish she had taken the lift! Completely knackered and feeling very unfit she knocked on Ricco's office door.

"Come in," said a stern voice.

"Morning, Mr Salvatore," she said as she opened the door, rushing straight past him to the other side of the office.

"RICCO!" she shouted, he stood up as she smacked into him, full force, throwing her arms around his neck.

"Morning, Mil," he said, laughing at her enthusiasm.

"I've missed you!" She said.

"You'd have seen me sooner if you hadn't drank too much and passed out!" he joked, still wrapped up in her embrace.

Millie let go of him abruptly. "Have you seen my phone?" she asked.

"Errr…" Ricco thought for a second, suddenly remembering putting it in his pocket last night. "Oh, shit, yes! You left it out in the rain, I put it in my jeans pocket!" he said. "I'll go home at lunchtime and get it for you," he added, knowing she couldn't be parted from it!

"It's alright, don't worry, I don't need it," she said.

Ricco was confused, normally Millie couldn't even be parted from her phone to have a wee!

"Ooh, come with me a sec," she said, grabbing him by the hand and pulling him out of the door, out of earshot of Mr Salvatore. "Guess who was here yesterday!?" whispered Millie, pulling Ricco right up against her.

"Who?" he asked quietly.

"LUCIE GOLDHAM!" said Millie.

"What? Why?" asked Ricco.

"She's one of the celebrities we're dressing for Cannes!" she replied.

"No way! Bet that was awkward, what was she like? What did she say?" he asked.

"She was errr… really small! She's still with Dex, she flew out to be with him last night in New York!" said Millie, trying to sound like she was totally over it, which couldn't be further from the truth! She fought hard to stop her eyes from filling with tears, not wanting Ricco to feel sorry for her, she felt stupid, how could she have fallen for his act, admitting that she loved him when he wasn't in the slightest bit interested. She was annoyed with herself for letting her guard down, normally something she never did!

"What the fuck? Are you sure? What an absolute prick!" said Ricco. His fiery Italian temper had been activated. "He'd better keep away from me!" threatened Ricco.

"It's alright, at least it ended before it started, before I got in any deeper," said Millie, trying to play it down, when in reality her aching heart had been pulled from her chest and stamped on.

"Don't be so easy on him! You deserve to be treated better!" said Ricco, pulling her head into his chest, kissing her on top her head.

"Thanks, babe," she said with a smile.

"Now go and do some work!" Ricco joked.

"Yes, boss!" she replied, playing along. He slapped her on the ass as she walked away, making her squeal in the girliest, most ear-piercing, high-pitched sound he had ever heard.

Millie sighed as she sat down at her drawing desk in her office. Since yesterday she had been trying to convince herself that she was fine, she was happy and had good people in her life and good things to focus on, she didn't need him. It would never have worked out with their work schedules anyway she told herself, he was better off with Lucie, she would flit off here and there with him whenever and wherever they wanted.

Millie was tied to a 9-5 job, she couldn't be off around the world at the drop of a hat. It's for the best, she told herself, picking up her pencils to sketch shoes for her forthcoming collection. She should have been beyond excited, her fashion dreams were coming true on a fast, unimaginable scale but she just wasn't feeling it, usually her heart was in her work but right now it was somewhere else entirely!

As lunchtime approached Millie had been attempting to draw shoe designs for her collection for over two hours. Looking down at her page one single pencil line stared back at her. All inspiration had evaded her. She couldn't do this today. Grabbing her jacket from the back of the chair she left to get some lunch in town.

Ricco held the office door open for her. "Where are you off to?" he asked.

"Town, for some lunch," she replied.

"Oh, I'm going home to get your phone,

want to come with me? I'll make us some lunch at home," said Ricco.

"Thanks, but I fancy getting out in the fresh air," she replied as she passed him going through the door. "Okay," said Ricco, "I'll see you later then," he added, raising his voice to be heard as she walked away. "Uh huh," she shouted back, approaching her car.

Driving home Ricco wasn't sure how he was going to fix this one! He knew the *'I'm fine'* was an act, it was obvious to him that she was heartbroken! Dex had let her down big time and he knew she was going to have to get worse before she got better. The act wouldn't last for long, Millie pretended to be strong but Ricco knew she wasn't, she would cave at some point and he would have to be there to pick up the pieces when she fell. He felt so much hate for Dex, he never gave her a chance, if he had Ricco knew he'd have fallen for her for sure, it was impossible not to! She was one of the rare ones. She was a nice girl, genuinely nice! She was always happy and smiley, she brightened up any room she walked into. She was never bitchy, she liked everyone and everyone got an equal shot with her. Plus she was effortlessly beautiful inside and out. Ricco really admired the drive in her to succeed and he knew she would get where she wanted to go, he'd never seen anyone push so hard for anything.

She had such passionate ambition, it was impossible not to love her for everything she was. It was completely Dex's loss! He had no idea what he had passed up, Lucie might be a pretty pop star but without even having met her he knew she wasn't a patch on Millie.

He unlocked the door to his apartment and walked straight through to his bedroom, he had left his skinny, black Armani jeans on the bedroom floor but Millie had tidied up as usual, he dug them out of the washing basket and riffled through the pockets, pulling the phone from the back pocket. He switched it on and almost immediately it started beeping with messages coming through, he knew he shouldn't look at them but feeling the urge to protect Millie.

He opened her messages. Five new messages, all from Dex. One by one he read them, feeling a huge sense of guilt at invading her privacy.

Millie please call me, you've got it all wrong Lucie is nuts. It's over I swear! D.x

Lucie's been harassing me since I broke it

off. She's threatening to take things to the press. It's all lies. D.x

Millie, I'm getting on a plane to England

now. Please tell me where you are.

I need to see you. D.x

Please let me come and explain things face

to face. If you never want to see me again after that I'll fly home and I won't bother you again. Please give me a chance. D.x

I land in England at 6.40pm UK time, I'll call you then in the hope you will talk to me and tell me where I can find you. D.x

You have missed calls. DEX ROSE (3)

Ricco looked at his watch. 1.12pm, Dex was already going to be in the air and would be in the UK in a few hours! He had no idea how to tell Millie firstly that he had read her messages and secondly that Dex was coming to England to see her! He didn't want him here, he wished he would just go back to his celebrity world and leave Millie alone.

Ricco sat down at the dining table to think. He was sure Dex was messing her around, he probably had to come to the UK for work anyway, or to see Lucie and was just hoping for a little bonus one night stand! Ricco had encountered these pop star types before, after as much as they could get for as little as they'd have to give in return. He did start to think Dex was genuinely different when Millie first started to mention him but it had become increasingly obvious that he was completely as Ricco had first assumed. The further away Ricco could keep him from Millie, the better.

Ricco's finger hovered over the 'delete all' button; surely it was for the best she didn't see them, it would only mess with her head and give her false hope but he wondered if she would forgive him for keeping it from her if she found out.

He put Dex's number in his own phone and after a few minutes of battling for and against in his head he turned off Millie's phone and slipped it into his pocket. He couldn't do it.

He grabbed some food from the fridge and left the apartment to go back to work. As he drove back his phone rang. He struggled to get it out from the pocket of his skin-tight jeans with one hand, trying to concentrate somewhat on driving at the same time.

"Ciao, Ricco," he said, putting the phone

to his ear.

"RICCO!"

Scrunching up his face he pulled the phone away from his ear, he shook his head, cautiously putting it back to his ear. "JESUS FUCKING CHRIST, SOPHIE!" he

started. "Why you have to shout all the time?" he asked. She had a loud, shrill voice that made his balls jump back up inside his body.

"SORRY! Anyway, Mr Salvatore, your Dad, Mr Salva...." she talked at 100 miles an hour!

"Yes Sophie! I know who he is... what does he want?" said Ricco, unenthusiastically.

"WELL... he asked if you can drive up to the London store and collect something for him?" said Sophie.

"Oh for fuck sake! Now?!" he asked, not feeling overly excited about a three-hour drive there and back again just to collect something!

"Yes, he said he needs it today," said Sophie. "Fine, I'm on my way," he replied.

"He said he will call you shortly and explain what you need to pick up," said Sophie.

"Yes! Okay," he replied.

"Thanks… b…" Sophie was interrupted.

"OH SOPH... can you put me through to Millie please?" asked Ricco. "Sure, one second," she replied.

"Design department, Amelie speaking," said Millie.

"Mils, I am really sorry, I collected your phone but Dad's sending me straight to London now. I'll drop it off on my way home tonight, sorry babe!" Ricco braced himself for Millie's reaction, she couldn't usually breathe without her phone in her hand! He knew she wasn't going to be happy.

"Okay, no worries," she replied.

Ricco was confused at her calm reaction. "You sure?" he asked.

"Yep, I don't need it, babe," she replied.

"Oh, good, okay... see you later then, ciao," said Ricco. Someone had kidnapped the real Millie for sure! "See ya," she replied, putting the phone down. *That was odd*, thought Ricco.

CHAPTER 23

Dex felt nervous as he sat on the plane approaching the sixth hour into his seven and a half hour flight. He'd never done anything so impulsive, his head was spinning with thoughts. Was this a bad idea? Would he regret it? Would he even find her? She had ignored all his messages and calls, which he knew meant she probably didn't want to be found.

He tried to mentally prepare himself for rejection, he knew that the romantic moment after travelling across the world to see her was probably in reality going to be an awkward argument and another seven-hour flight back home. The only thought keeping him going was that he had to try, if he was back on the plane to New York in a few hours at least it would be knowing he did everything he could and if she sent him packing, that was her decision. He hadn't even considered the fact that he was going to be alone in a relatively unknown country to him, with none of his security, none of his bandmates, no one at all, once he got to London. Felix was working there so he was going to have to go it alone from that point. As he thought more about it he began to feel anxious, he was a shy guy and he was going to have to deal with all the fans, the screaming, being mobbed, without anyone to save his ass! As much as Mac drove him nuts with all the rules and regulations, Dex wished he was with him right now.

"Fe, are you awake?" asked Dex, poking his brother in the arm.

"Ouch! I am now, Dex!" he groaned.

"Sorry, man. How long til we land?" he asked.

Felix pushed himself up so he was sat straight in his chair; he pulled back his sleeve and looked at his watch. "Uh, around an hour," he replied.

"Thanks," replied Dex, his nerves were building and he couldn't help but fidget in his chair. His hands wouldn't keep still as he rubbed them together in his lap, his restless feet tapping on the floor.

"What's up, man?" asked Felix. "You seem anxious, everything okay?" he asked. He'd seen Dex nervous plenty of times, he'd been to his shows, he'd seen him in an awful state of anxiety before performing on TV shows and at awards ceremonies. He knew his brother suffered badly with his nerves but he didn't have his band with him so he wasn't going to perform in the UK, Felix didn't understand why he was so edgy.

"Uhh… yeah, just not looking forward to being here without my security," admitted Dex.

"What are you even coming over for all on your own, why aren't the rest of your band coming?" asked Felix.

"It's… uh, more of a personal trip," said Dex.

"Ah, you're going to see Lucie?" said Felix, wondering why he would be nervous about that. She would have her security team ready for him at the airport, she was a pop star too, she knew the drill.

"Not exactly," Dex said, praying for Felix not to interrogate him.

"I'm lost, man!" said Felix, bewildered, his forehead wrinkled.

Dex sighed at the thought of having to explain it... again! "I broke it off with Lucie" he started small.

"Oh, why dude?" asked Felix. To him, on the outside Lucie was perfect. He was a little bit jealous that his brother had landed such a gorgeous girlfriend. Felix was the more obviously attractive of the two. Sure, Dex was a good-looking guy, but he was short and thin, and in contrast to his brother's confident personality Dex was shy and sweet, almost childlike. Felix shared a lot of Dex's features, it wasn't hard to tell they were brothers but Felix was tall and he worked out, his big strong arms framed a masculine chest and hard washboard stomach, his short dark hair and deep brown eyes gave him an almost Mediterranean look about him. He could never quite understand how his little brother got so much female attention, girls literally threw themselves at him wherever he went. He had marriage proposals from strangers, declarations of love on a daily basis and it was totally wasted on him, Dex hated it! It seemed beyond incomprehensible that Dex would let Lucie go, to Felix, she was perfect!

"She was too young, too immature, I just wasn't feeling it anymore," said Dex.

"Oh," replied Felix, thinking for a minute. "So why are you coming to the UK then?" asked Felix.

"Uhhh," he hesitated. "I kinda met someone else," he admitted.

"Oh. In London?" asked Felix.

"Uh, in England. I don't think she's from London, I actually have no idea where she lives!" said Dex. As he said it out loud it sounded even more ridiculous to be travelling all this way to find someone when he had no idea where she was, but naively he figured England was pretty small, he'd find her.

"Right," said Felix, sceptical of Dex's plans. He wasn't going to pry, with only a year in age between them they'd been close growing up but they had drifted apart in the last few years. Dex had been away travelling with bands more often than not for several years and Felix was a music producer, working in both London and New York he constantly travelled back and forth and they rarely got to see each other anymore. Dex could definitely feel a distance between them that hadn't been there growing up.

As the plane came in to land at Heathrow airport, Dex braced himself, still sore from the last landing he had endured. It had made him a little apprehensive. The plane landed softly without a hitch and Dex breathed a sigh of relief as his tense muscles relaxed. Though his relaxation was short-lived as reality hit him, he now had to get off the plane, to undoubtedly hoards of girls jumping all over him. The thought alone made him sweat!

The plane came to a halt in its parking bay and the fasten seat belt signs pinged. People began to get up and collect their baggage from the overhead bins. Dex pulled his cap down low and put his sunglasses on, he stood up in his seat, keeping his head down to avoid anyone recognising him and making a scene.

He switched his phone on while he waited for the plane to start disembarking. It beeped immediately with a message. He gasped in anticipation that it would be from Millie, instead, displayed was a message from an unknown number. He would normally have just ignored it, he got loads! But boredom waiting for the passengers to get moving prompted him to read it.

It's Ricco Salvatore, Millie's friend.
I saw that you're flying to England,
Could you please give me a call as soon
as you land, before you speak to Millie.
It's important. Thanks.

I wonder what he wants, thought Dex, intrigued and slightly worried at how and why Ricco would want to speak to him. With the plane doors still not open he slouched back down in his seat and pressed call on Ricco's number. The dial tone was odd in England he thought.

"Ciao, Ricco Salvatore," said the voice on the other end. Dex stuck a finger in his other ear to block out the noise of the people on the plane.

"Hi, it's Dexter Rose, you wanted me to call you, man?" asked Dex.

"Yeah. Listen dude, I know your plan is to come and see Millie but I think it's best you just leave her alone now. Go and see your girlfriend instead, I'm sure she'll be happier to see you," said Ricco, in his stern fiery Italian voice.

"What?" said Dex, confused. "I don't have a girlfriend, man. I've come here to see Millie, I need to speak with her," said Dex.

"Come on, man. Guy to guy, we both know you're dating Lucie Goldham and you're only after one thing from Millie," said Ricco, getting more wound up. *This guy sounds like a jerk,* thought Ricco, *with his pretty-boy American accent.*

Dex was slightly taken aback, is that what Millie thought? This guy had to be getting this from somewhere. "Dude, you got this all wrong!" said Dex, getting fired up at this foreign-sounding dude on the other end of the phone getting involved in his business. "Look, man, I don't give a fuck if you believe me but I am not dating anyone! I've flown thousands of miles to spend the one day I have off from work with Millie and you're not going to stop me from seeing her so do me a favour and butt out!" said Dex.

It took every ounce of Ricco's willpower and every bit of his love for Millie not to fire into Dex; he wanted to rip his poncy American head off! "No, I won't fucking butt out, dude! I don't care if you're famous, I will do everything in my power to stop that girl from getting hurt!" said Ricco. He could feel his palms starting to sweat. Slightly worried that people could hear his heated conversation, he stuck his head out of the office door, he was glad that nearly everyone had left the Salvo's London store.

"Hurt her?" said Dex, calming himself down. He realised he was drawing attention to himself as he made his way down the aisle of the plane. He brought his voice down almost to a whisper. "Dude, I won't hurt her... I..." Dex started. "I love her," he admitted, feeling pretty

embarrassed that he had just admitted that to another guy, a guy he didn't even know! Praying none of the passengers around him heard, that would certainly be a story to sell to the papers!

Ricco was silent, wondering if he had heard right. He breathed out deeply, calming himself down. "What?" he asked, needing some clarification.

"You heard me man! I'm not saying it again!" said Dex.

"You love her?" asked Ricco. "Seriously?" he added, taken aback by Dex's admission, he wasn't expecting him to say that. He was so sure Millie had fallen in love with him but he was only in it for some action. Millie always threw herself in the deep end with guys, she fell in love easily and gave her heart away too quickly, often getting hurt by non-reciprocation.

"Yup," Dex replied, feeling very uneasy.

Ricco didn't know what to say. "Oh," he replied. "Look man, I've come all this way, I need to see her, do you know where she is?" Dex asked.

"Yes," said Ricco, dropping his guard. "Where are you? I'll take you to her," he added, reluctantly against his better judgement.

"Really? Thanks man. I'm at Heathrow, just stepped off the plane," said Dex, his nerves began to turn to excitement at the thought of seeing her, Ricco had just solved half his battle, it was a huge weight off for Dex, now he just had to survive the mobs of fans in the airport!

"I'm working about 10 minutes from Heathrow, I'll come get you," said Ricco.

"Thanks, dude! I might be a while though, I have no security!" said Dex, "I'm probably going to get mobbed!"

"I'll sort security," said Ricco.

"Thanks, dude," said Dex, feeling more relaxed now.

"I'll call you when I'm at the arrivals gate, Ciao," said Ricco.

Dex slid his phone back into his pocket, he pulled his cap down lower over his eye. The tunnel into the terminal building was cold, he pulled his sweatshirt up over his mouth and the sleeves down over his hands, holding the ends together. His ankle-grazer jeans stopped short of his white Converse sneakers, leaving his ankles exposed to the cold. It was a chilly evening; the sky was a dark grey, it was obvious the heavens were going to open at any point and there was a chill in the air. Dex wasn't prepared at all; he hadn't packed for the prospect of rain! Or cold! He was used to heat! New York was generally in the 20s in May, he hadn't considered stepping off the plane to a chilly 9-degree evening in London!

Inside the terminal they joined the back of a long queue to passport control. Dex kept his head down but out the corner of his eye could already see people ahead in the queue pointing and whispering. He felt vulnerable. "Stand in front of me, man," he said to Felix. Felix looked around and spotted the people in the queue staring in their direction. As he moved in front of Dex, he knew it was too late and that they had already spotted him and knew exactly who he was, but at least hiding might stop more people recognising him. It seemed to take forever to get to the front of the queue, Dex was getting more and more frustrated, worried about the walk through the open terminal building and more worried about Ricco having to wait ages for him. He was fully aware that the dude didn't like him but being close to Millie, Dex had to keep him sweet!

Finally through the checkpoint, Dex's bag was first off the baggage carousel, Felix had kept his bag with him in the cabin. Dex walked swiftly through the baggage claim area towards the arrivals gate, avoiding eye contact with anyone, Felix hurrying to keep up behind. At the sliding doors that led out into the main terminal building Dex stopped.

"I'll have to leave you here, man," said Dex. "Why?" asked Felix.

"I need to wait for security before I go out there," Dex replied.

"Oh, okay" said Felix.

"Was good to catch up man, have a safe trip. I'll see you at home in a couple of weeks," said Dex, putting his arms around his brother.

"Yeah, good to see you bro, good luck! See you soon," smiled Felix.

Dex watched as he walked out through the sliding doors and was gone. The arrivals hall looked packed, which didn't fill Dex with joy! An airport security guard approached him.

"Dexter Rose?" he asked in a deep British accent. "Yeah," Dex replied.

"Ah, good. I'm Paul, head of high-profile client security. I've been instructed to escort you through the airport to your vehicle, son," said the security guard.

"Awesome, thanks," replied Dex.

"They know you're here, someone's tipped your fans off. There's a lot of them screaming for you out there, just so you're prepared," said Paul. "You ready?" he asked.

"Yeah," Dex replied, feeling apprehensive.

Paul grabbed hold of the back of Dex's sweatshirt and walked right up behind him, almost touching him. It was a total invasion of his personal space, something Dex was a little funny about people being in, but on this occasion he was pleased to put up with it. The sliding doors opened to crowds of people waiting in arrivals. He kept his hat down low and walked looking at the floor. Two more security guards spotted Paul escorting someone and came to help part the crowd. Dex heard girls to his left screaming his name, cameras were flashing ahead of him, a journalist stuck her dictaphone in his face.

"Where's Lucie?. Is she travelling with you?" she asked.

"Lucie who?" he replied, playing dumb. He didn't usually answer any journalist questions but with Lucie being such a bitch to him lately he wanted the world to know she was no longer anything to do with him! He was completely surrounded by people, arms waving in his face, girls pulling at his clothes, touching him anywhere they could reach, he felt like an animal. He didn't understand how people felt they had the right to touch him, it's not like they would go up to a stranger in the street and put their hands all over them, so why did they feel it okay to do it to him? It was one of the cons of the job, but one he was willing to endure for the pros. He looked up briefly and could see they were close to the entrance, just a few more minutes and he would be free from it. As he passed through the doors the cool outside air hit him. He took a deep breath, filling his lungs. The crowds made him feel so claustrophobic, they surrounded him all the way to the car, pushing him around, grabbing at him. Someone reached out to try and touch him, catching their watch on his eye. Dex put his hand to his eye, there was blood on his fingers!

After what seemed like a lifetime they had reached the side of Ricco's car. The security guys moved the chorus of screaming girls to allow the car door to open. Dex finally looked up from the floor at the car, *Woah!* he thought, it wasn't quite what he expected as he clocked eyes on the impressive gleaming white Lamborghini in front of him. The passenger door was open, Dex could see the luxurious interior with big black leather seats. He leaned down to get in, looking over at the driver. He recognised Ricco instantly, that was the guy he'd seen in Milan with Millie, he looked every bit the owner of a Lamborghini! He smiled a near perfect smile, with his brilliant white teeth set against his tanned Italian skin. His dark messy hair looked perfectly tousled as if he had just rolled out of bed. Dex's eyes followed his face down to his masculine jaw line, he fitted the part of millionaire business man sat in the driver seat, an expensive-looking designer charcoal grey suit jacket hung open over a black shiny shirt, buttoned half way up revealing a tanned, toned chest. Dark blue skinny jeans clung to his muscular thighs. Dex felt very inadequate sat next to him.

"Thank you, Paul," said Ricco, leaning over Dex to hand money to the security guard.

"You're welcome, buddy," he said, closing the door. Ricco put his foot down and they were gone. "Woah! Awesome car, dude!" said Dex.

"It'll get us home quicker, anyway," said Ricco, flashing that Colgate smile again.

"Thanks for the ride, man, and the security guys, appreciate it," said Dex, genuinely grateful.

"No problem, Paul looks after my dad when he travels," said Ricco, looking at Dex out of the corner of his eye. *Seriously? This guy?!* he thought. In the flesh Dex was nothing like he had imagined. He could sort of see the appeal, he was cute and cool, with a laid-back American vibe, but he was a scruffy looking guy, his hair long and messy on top his head, swept to one side. It annoyed Ricco that he kept brushing it away from his face. He looked a lot younger than Ricco expected, his jeans were tighter than any Ricco had ever seen on a guy before. Ricco couldn't help but think he looked a little bit weedy for a pop-rock star!

"So how far away do you guys live?" Dex asked. "About two and a half hours' drive," said Ricco. "Oh man! That far?!" said Dex, not expecting that at all.

"Yeah, but maybe two hours in this car," smiled Ricco. He put his foot down and the car flew down the motorway. Ricco's car phone rang, Millie's home phone number appeared on the dashboard.

"That's Mil," said Ricco. "She doesn't know you're coming. She left her phone at my house, so I've had it all day, I think she will love the surprise," said Ricco. Dex suddenly felt sick in the pit of his stomach. Ricco turned to him, with his finger to his lips. "Shhhush," he gestured, pressing the button to answer the call.

"Ciao babe, what's up?" said Ricco, he felt some kind of power over Dex that Millie was close to him.

"Hey babes, where are you?" she asked.

The moment Dex heard her voice his body flooded with adrenaline. A shiver zigzagged down his spine, disappearing into his legs. His bottom lip began to quiver in excitement, he writhed around in his seat, even her voice sent his mind into a spin. He was suddenly overcome with nerves, he felt sweating hot, pulling his jumper out from his neck to let the air go down onto his chest.

"I'm on the M4, doll," he said.

"That means nothing to me, babe, does it!" joked Millie. Dex laughed quietly to himself.

"I'll be about another two hours. Missing your beloved phone?" Ricco teased.

"No, I'm missing you of course," she said. "No, I'm lying, I just miss my phone," she joked. Ricco laughed.

"Where are you? Your place or mine?" asked Ricco.

"Mine, Amber came with me after work to visit Lexi, we've just got home," said Millie.

"Okay, babe, see you about 10-ish," said Ricco. "Okay, see you soon, mwah," said Millie, making a kissing sound down the phone. She hung up and the radio came back on.

Dex sat looking out of the window, deep in thought. The rain had stopped and the sun had just set on the horizon, the British countryside looked beautiful at dusk, even at 100mph!

"How ya feeling? This has got to be kinda nerve wracking, right?" asked Ricco, trying to break the awkward silence.

"Yeah," Dex sighed. "I feel sick, man!" he admitted.

"You'd better not be sick in my car!" joked Ricco. Dex laughed. "Nah, I'm good," he replied.

"It'll be alright, man. Millie's pretty chilled, she'll love you just turning up, it's so romantic!" Ricco assured him.

The remainder of the car journey was a mixture of awkward silences and forced conversations. Ricco was very relieved to be 20 minutes from Millie's house, not long and he could kick this dude out of his car!

Driving through the city Dex vaguely recognised it, he remembered the river that ran through the city centre. He had no idea where he was but he knew he had been there before. His emotions were all over the place knowing that he was close to her, she'd walked these streets. This was where it all started, in the club, in this city. If someone had told him two weeks ago when he arrived here to play that the sequence of events that had unfolded were going to he'd not have believed it in a million years, he didn't think for one second that he would be back in this city two weeks later chasing a girl! It was like something out of a movie, it wasn't real life. Except it was. And he was here. And it was all about to happen.

"Not far now," said Ricco. It started to rain again, hard.

"Awesome," replied Dex. He counted to ten in his head as he breathed in and counted for ten as he breathed out, trying to stay calm. He felt much the same as he did before he went on stage, except on stage he knew what he was doing and exactly how it would play out. He had no control over this and no way of knowing what would happen. He could feel his cheeks getting hot, it was a familiar signal that his nerves were reaching panic attack level, a level he had reached many times before a performance. He closed his eyes and concentrated on his breathing, counting in between breaths, a technique his therapist had taught him years ago. He scratched at the inside of his elbow, a habit he had picked up as a child. Whenever he got really nervous he scratched the same spot, often to bleeding point. He hated it, it made his arm look like he was a junkie! But he just couldn't break the habit.

"Right, we're here. Mil lives on this street, just down here," said Ricco.

Dex looked down the street. It almost looked American, rows of pretty little detached houses lined each side of the street, with gardens in front of the houses. Trees lined the road on each side, it reminded him of the street he grew up on where his parents still lived. Ricco pulled up outside of Millie's house, her bedroom windows were open and he could see her bedroom light was on through the gap in her curtains, which were blowing in and out of the open window in the breeze.

"That's Millie's bedroom there with the light on," said Ricco, pointing. "Can you give her this?" asked Ricco,

pulling her phone from his pocket and handing it to Dex. "Sure," he replied, struggling to slide it into his tight pocket. "I'm going to get soaked, man!" said Dex watching the rain hammering down on the car windscreen.

"Yeah, but it'll be worth it. You've travelled thousands of miles, it's taken you like, what 12 hours to get here, what's a bit of rain!" said Ricco. "Plus, Millie loves the rain!" he added.

"She does?" asked Dex.

"Yeah, she's a nutter!" he replied, laughing.

Dex smiled. He suddenly felt calm. He knew whatever the outcome he was about to do the most amazing thing he had ever done! And he knew he would remember this night for the rest of his life. "Here goes!" he said, swallowing the lump in his throat. He got out of the car, at least the rain cooled him down. He was sweating profusely, the rain drops felt blissful as they bounced off his warm skin, it was so refreshing.

He leaned down into the car, his hair already soaked and stuck to the side of his face. "Thanks a lot for your help, man," said Dex, holding out a hand. Ricco shook his hand.

"I'd do anything for her, she's one in a million," Ricco replied, letting Dex know he did it for Millie not for him. "Go get her!" said Ricco.

Dex shut the door and Ricco sped off. Dex walked slowly towards the front of her house. He was already drenched to his skin, his sweatshirt was soaked through and hung heavily off him. As he walked, slowly, he went over and over what he was going to say in his head, nothing sounded right.

He stood on the grass out the front of her house just below her window, trying to get the courage to do something or say something. The rain was pouring down his face. *Just do it!* he told himself. The only thing he knew how to do was sing, so he did, though the adrenalin coursing through his veins made his breathing shallow and erratic causing his chest to tighten, forcing the words out in a kind of shouting mess!

Millie looked at the clock, 10.38pm. She was beginning to get frustrated with not having her phone, Ricco was late and she needed a cuddle. She hoped he was going to stay over, Amber was staying over at her boyfriend's. She hated being at home alone at night, especially with the rain, it was so heavy she was nervous it may turn into a thunderstorm, a prospect that terrified her. She laid on her bed watching some rubbish TV show. She could vaguely hear music coming from somewhere outside, it was annoying her with the TV being on.

"Who's playing music at this time of night!" she groaned

as she got up to shut the window. She pulled back the curtain and gasped.

Her heart seemed to stop.

"Oh… my… god!" she exclaimed. He looked up at her, squinting a little as the rain fell in his eyes. He smiled, as their eyes met the thunderbolt hit, harder this time, like a truck. She struggled for breath. She looked down at him and the rest of the world fell away. Dex Rose was standing in the rain on her front lawn! It was like a scene from a movie. She was dying to speak but didn't want to interrupt him and ruin the moment. She felt scared, yet brave, a bravery that made her feel powerful. They were just strangers but the passion Millie felt rivalled nothing she had ever felt before.

He stood there looking up at her, overcome with emotion he couldn't sing anymore.

"Hi," he said shyly, feeling a bit silly. He felt as though his chest had been cracked open, his heart, his soul and all his emotion spilled over the floor for all to see.

"What are you doing here?!" she asked.

"Uh… well I was out on the town, so I came to your window, ya know, just to say hi," he joked. Millie laughed. His smile faded, replaced with a look of seriousness. "I had to see you," he said.

"You've flown all the way from America just to see me?" she asked, her heart almost bursting for him. "Uh… yeah, I have to fly home tomorrow," he replied. He knew he had to make tonight incredible! "You're crazy!" she said, a huge smile across her face.

"No… I'm In love." He'd never felt so compelled to say those words before. "Everything Lucie told you is lies. It's over. I ended it after seeing you on Friday," he added. His entire body ached for her, being so close to her but not touching her was torture, but without even touching her the passion he felt was intense, beyond any feeling he could have imagined. She was the one! He'd never been more sure of anything in his life.

"You're soaking! Come inside!" said Millie.

"No, you come out here," he said, remembering what Ricco had said about her loving the rain.

The idea sounded crazy to Millie for a split second, but she turned and ran down the stairs as quickly as she could, swung open the front door and ran to him, not even sparing a thought for the fact that she was wearing her pyjama shorts and a vest top. She ran to him, throwing her arms around his neck she jumped, wrapping her legs around his waist. She kissed him, nearly knocking him over with the force in which her body hit his. The kiss was fast and messy, neither stopping to catch a breath, hands were everywhere all at once and then gone again.

"I..." still kissing him she didn't have enough breath to speak. "I..." she tried again. "I love you too," she said quickly in between kissing and trying to breathe. He melted; they were the most intense words he had ever heard at exactly the right moment. The passion was so strong Dex tried to calm down a little, remembering that they were out on her front lawn!

Millie felt hot and exhausted, the cold rain pouring down on her felt amazingly cool on her skin, her hair hung drenched down the sides of her face and her clothes were completely stuck to her body, his warm hands wrapped around her back. His warm breath brushing her lips as he caught his breath intermittently.

He pulled back from her for a second to look at her face, he smiled, soaked to the bone with no makeup on she had never looked so beautiful. Dex ran his finger along her bottom lip, looking deep into her eyes. She looked right back, as if she could see inside his soul.

"So, where do we go from here?" asked Dex, feeling a little scared.

Millie knew what he meant but that wasn't a conversation for right now. "We go inside," said Millie, her face serious.

He could see the hunger in her eyes. He gently put her down on the floor, tilting her chin up to him he leaned down for one more kiss, slowly he touched her lips, lingering for a second before pulling away. He looked into her eyes. There was something about her that made him feel alive. He couldn't wait any longer, he scooped her up in his arms and headed towards the door, kicking it shut with his foot behind him.

He carried Millie up the stairs and into her bedroom, laying her down on the bed he looked at her for a moment. *This is the most incredible moment of my life so far*, he thought. This was the girl he wanted to spend his life with. He just knew, it was the strangest feeling. Crawling up the bed he knelt over her, the cool night breeze blew through the open window; he shivered, staring into her eyes. He knew this was the beginning of something incredible, the one thing that had been missing from his life. He felt complete.

Millie's phone beeped in Dex's pocket. He pulled it out and handed it to her, she quickly glanced at the screen.

How does it feel when you realise all of your dreams have come true? Own the night baby!

About M.Venn

Twitter - @AuthorMVenn

M. Venn is a 30-year-old mum of three little girls, living just outside the beautiful city of Bath in Somerset with her husband and young family. She's been a graphic designer and digital artist for nine years. Her life is one big juggling act between taking care of her three children during the day and running her design business in the evenings . . . and she even found time to write a book!

Thank You

Firstly and most importantly – A huge thank you to my family, friends and everyone who supported me and helped to make this possible.

Special thanks to
Rachel

Thank you for all your help and support, particularly in the very early stages of this book.

Without you, I don't think I'd have got to here.

P.S. It's not!

My R B Ladies

It had to be in here, right?

You all know who you are. Thank you for being some of the best, most supportive friends I've ever had. Thank you for all the help and advice and for putting up with me talking about my book 24/7!

Adam

My biggest critic, I did it! (Y) x

Thank you to Kasey at Wise Words Editorial who had the task of fixing 31,511 issues in my manuscript! – I'm sure that's some kind of record?!

And thank you to every musician that's ever stood on a stage in front of me, inspiring me to write this book!

ENJOYED THIS BOOK? WE'VE GOT LOTS MORE!

Britain's Next BESTSELLER

DISCOVER NEW INDEPENDENT BOOKS & HELP AUTHORS GET A PUBLISHING DEAL.

DECIDE WHAT BOOKS WE PUBLISH NEXT & MAKE AN AUTHOR'S DREAM COME TRUE.

Visit **www.britainsnextbestseller.co.uk** to view book trailers, read book extracts, pre-order new titles and get exclusive Britain's Next Bestseller Supporter perks.

FOLLOW US:

BNBSbooks   @bnbsbooks   bnbsbooks

BRITAINSNEXTBESTSELLER.CO.UK